SAFFRON ALLEY

Sword Dance Book 2

A.J. DEMAS

Saffron Alley

A.J. Demas

Cover art by Vic Grey
Cover design by Alice Degan

CHAPTER 1

THE SHEETS WERE SOAKED, the vase lay in pieces on the floor, and flowers spilled down off the bed onto the tiles. Telltale footprints led away from the puddle. Varazda looked at it and groaned.

"I told them not to let that creature in here!" he announced to the empty room.

He knelt to gather up the scattered flowers. There were spikes of dusty purple with a pleasantly astringent smell, a couple of sprays of bright blue cornflowers, a branch with clusters of jewel-like berries, and tall stalks of ornamental grass like small sheaves of wheat. It had been a nicely masculine arrangement—the purple flowers and the stalks of grass even looked a little like spears, which amused him—and he'd been quite proud of it. He and Remi had picked it all in the vacant lot at the end of the street.

He went through the kitchen with his armload of battered foliage, dumped it on the table, and hunted for the broom to sweep up the remains of the vase. Remi came down the stairs from Yazata's side of the house on her hands and knees, and began doing a circuit of the kitchen making snorting noises.

"Papa, I am something. Ask me what am I."

"Are you a horse?" He couldn't find the broom. It wasn't where it was supposed to be. Actually, he didn't know where it was supposed to be.

"No, *what* am I!"

"Oh. What are you?"

"A cent—a centimaur!"

"So you are! What a lovely centaur you are."

He found the broom leaning up against the wall outside the back door. Selene waddled in from the yard, looking dignified, and began following Remi around the kitchen with soft honks.

"Papa, what are you doing with our lovely flowers?"

"Tidying them up."

"Oh, did they have an accident?"

"Yes. Darling, can you take Selene outside?"

"She won't do a mess on the floor."

Of course she had already 'done a mess' on the floor, though not the kind Remi meant. Varazda sighed. He heard Yazata's steps on the stairs at his side of the house, and in a moment Yazata himself emerged, dressed to go out. He bent to scoop Remi up, and propped her on his hip.

"You're sweeping something?" Yazata blinked at Varazda in surprise.

"Oh, is that what this is for?"

Yazata gave his chortling laugh.

"Now you say, 'Don't hurt yourself,'" Varazda prompted.

"I wouldn't say that!" Yazata protested. It was true; it had already been a little daring of him to be arch about the broom.

Varazda kissed him on the cheek. "Going out?"

"Kiss me too!" Remi demanded. They both kissed her, one on each cheek.

"To visit Maraz," said Yazata. "Chares tells me she's almost recovered, though she's not well enough to go out yet.

I'm bringing her some cakes and a few of today's eggs." He picked up a covered basket from the kitchen workbench.

"Can I have one?" Remi asked, wriggling.

"An egg? You can fetch one yourself."

"No, a cake! Can I have a cake?"

"I saved one just for you." Yazata set his basket down again so that he had a free hand, lifted the cover of another dish on the workbench, and handed Remi the small golden cake inside. She gave a squeal of triumph and took a large bite.

"Give Maraz my love," said Varazda. "If there's anything we can do … "

"Of course. Oh, and um." Yazata rearranged the cloth over his basket, not meeting Varazda's gaze. His voice dropped almost to a whisper. "I may have forgotten to tell you about Pelike."

"Mm? I know about Pelike. She's coming to clean the house and watch Remi. She should be here any minute."

"I like Pelike," said Remi.

"I—I—I'm afraid Pelike's not coming," Yazata said in a rush. "She's at her mother's in Thuia, pickling."

"Pickling," Varazda repeated tonelessly.

"Yes, she had to go help pickle—something." Yazata's face twisted apologetically. "Oh dear, I should have told you."

"Well—it's all right, you forgot." Nevertheless, Varazda couldn't help giving a small, frustrated growl. "She can pickle her own head if she wants, just not today. The house is … it's … "

"It's what?"

"You can't pickle your *head*, Papa!"

"It's fine," Varazda forced himself to say soothingly. "If I had thought Pelike was not coming … " He'd have hired someone else, is what he'd have done. But he was careful not to mention that to Yazata, who was sensitive on the subject of hiring help.

"I don't have to visit Maraz today, it's just that Maia said —" He closed his mouth abruptly, as if swallowing something he didn't mean, or didn't dare, to say.

"Does Maia know Maraz?" Varazda asked, distracted.

"Oh. No."

Varazda didn't pursue it. "Well, you know it's the day that I'm meeting the ship." This was the euphemism that he had been employing around his family—*meeting the ship*—as if it was the ship that he had invited to stay with them.

"Yes," said Yazata in a small voice. "Do you want me to stay home?"

"No, of course not. You should visit Maraz. I'll take Remi with me to the harbour."

"Yay!" said Remi.

Yazata nodded. He set Remi down and picked up his basket again. "It might be for the best. Perhaps … " His voice dropped to a whisper. "Perhaps he ought to know sooner rather than later that you have a daughter."

Varazda remembered that night in the little bedroom of the slave quarters, showing Damiskos the miniature portrait of Remi, and the way he had looked at it, so carefully, as if he felt privileged to be shown this piece of Varazda's heart.

"Yazata, he knows already."

"Oh." Yazata looked genuinely surprised, and then suddenly apprehensive. "Was he not surprised? Does he not know you're a eunuch?"

That was a genuine question, asked with genuine worry. He thought—*what* did he think? Varazda found it too embarrassing to contemplate. He had no idea how much Yazata understood about the mechanics and varieties of sex, and he did not want to know.

"Go see Maraz, Yaza. Stay as long as you want."

When he looked around after Yazata's departure, Remi and Selene had disappeared from the kitchen but were not in the yard. He found them in the room Yazata and Tash

4

insisted on calling "the guest suite." Selene was eating the spilt flowers while Remi squatted on the floor, carefully picking up sharp fragments of vase.

"Let me take those, my sweet," Varazda said, dropping the broom and swooping down with visions of bleeding fingers and howling. He heard the front door shut behind Yazata.

They rescued the flowers from Selene and evicted her to the yard, cleaned up the vase, dried the water on the floor, stripped the bed, and hung the sheets and pillowcases on the line outside. Then Remi wanted to find a new vase and recreate the bouquet, so they spent some time doing that. Once it was back on the windowsill, not too much worse for wear, Varazda made a desultory sweep of the downstairs rooms on his side of the house, picking up things that were out of place, took them all upstairs, and dumped them on his bed.

Tash and Yazata's front door banged open while Varazda was upstairs, and he heard Tash running up the stairs on their side of the house. When Varazda was back in the kitchen, Tash came clattering down the stairs again, his hair and tunic white with marble dust as usual, with a bundle of evening clothes under one arm and a pair of elaborate sandals dangling from one hand.

"I'm going to be out late tonight!" he called, plunging into the sitting room on his side of the house. "Not—where did those sketches go—not back for dinner!"

He emerged after a moment juggling a set of wax tablets and a bundle of papers along with the rest of his burdens, with a stylus clamped between his teeth.

"Wook et—" he began before removing the stylus and tucking it behind his ear. "Look at this." He spread the tablets open awkwardly, showing a beautifully detailed sketch of a pair of feet.

"They're feet," Remi announced.

"Oh, uh, not those … " He flipped through the leaves. "That's a bum!"

"What?" said Tash indignantly. "That's heavenly perfection, is what that is!"

"Tash!" Varazda yelped.

"It's a *bum*," said Remi firmly.

"Here it is, look."

He produced one of the scraps of paper and held it up. It contained an elaborate drawing with several figures in complex poses, surrounded by bits of scenery. Varazda could tell that it was a good thing, of its kind, but he had no idea what it was.

"This is my design for the whole relief," Tash explained. "You see how the lines of Orante's arm draw the eye up to the flying dove at the top, and the clouds—well, you probably can't tell, but they'll look actually fluffy, not like these floating lumps you usually see. Themistokles said it's really good, and he wants me to show it to the committee."

"Oh, fantastic," said Varazda, because Tash was obviously happy about this, whatever it was.

"We're having dinner with some of them tonight, that's why I won't be in. And I might go out for a drink afterward, depending on how it goes."

"You're, uh, going to bathe before dinner, right?" said Varazda.

Tash tsked and rolled his eyes. "I am going to bathe, I'm not an idiot."

"You can see her bum too." Remi pointed at the sketch.

"Yeah, but *through the fabric of her gown*, look—it's a really good effect, when you can pull it off."

Remi wrinkled her nose sceptically.

"I'm surrounded by such lowbrows," Tash groaned.

"It's great," said Varazda. "I mean that. They're considering it for the Palace of Letters?"

"No, no, we're all finished the work on that—the dedication's going to be in a couple of days. This is for a different project. Shi—oh, poop, I'm going to be late. Got to go!"

Tash gathered his armload of clothes and sketches and pelted out of the kitchen.

"Good luck!" Varazda called after him.

A moment later he heard Tash nearly collide with someone on the doorstep, and an irritated exchange.

"Haven't you ever heard of knocking? What? Yes, it's his house, but I'm not him—get out of my way!"

Varazda looked out into the hallway to see a sleek-haired messenger boy boldly marching in the door and looking critically around the interior of the house.

"Hello," said Varazda, "yes?"

"Pharastes the dancer?"

"Yes."

"I've a message for you. My master, Lykanos Lykandros, desires you to dance at his house on Market Day evening. What answer shall I return?"

Lykanos Lykandros can go fuck himself, was the answer Varazda would have liked to return, or at least, *I deeply regret I am not available that evening.* But Lykanos Lykandros, a spice merchant who owned a monstrous pink marble house near the agora, wasn't just a client; he was an assignment.

"Of course I'll be honoured," he told the boy, without even a token attempt at sincerity, and mentally crossed Market Day off his list of free evenings.

The boy had been gone only a few minutes when someone else knocked at the door. Varazda ran down the hall hoping it was Maia from across the street and that he could foist Remi on her for the rest of the afternoon.

It wasn't Maia; it was a potter's apprentice bringing a wheelbarrow full of clay and wanting to be paid for it. The wheelbarrow left muddy tracks through the house, and the potter's apprentice was very pedantic on the subject of proper storage of clay, and wouldn't listen to Varazda's instructions to just dump it in the middle of the yard. Selene made matters worse by hissing at him. Once the clay had been safely deposited, money had been found to pay the apprentice, and he had been sent on his way, Remi was beginning to complain that she was hungry. That was when Varazda discovered there was nothing to eat in the house.

There was food: flour, oil, a couple of chicken eggs, some salt fish, spices. Nothing you could just *eat* without cooking it first, and cooking was an absolute mystery to Varazda. He didn't even know how to build a proper fire on the stove.

Yazata knew this very well. He was the one who kept the house stocked with food, who took care of all the meals and worried that the others weren't eating enough. Yet he had gone off to visit his friend, on a day when they were expecting a guest, without leaving so much as a half-loaf of bread or an apricot in the house. It was unlike him.

"Right," Varazda said aloud, impressed by his own calm. "Put your shoes on, Remi. We're going to the market."

Maia across the street was out, of course—probably pickling things in the countryside with Pelike's mother—so there was no leaving Remi with her or asking to borrow anything from her kitchen. They had to shut Selene in the yard, which neither she nor Remi liked. Then they had to walk all the way to the market, negotiate Remi's fickle preferences to find her something to eat, visit six different stalls to buy everything Varazda could think of, walk home, dump their purchases in the kitchen, and by then it was well and truly time to leave to meet the ship—if they were lucky.

They were halfway down Fountain Street when Varazda realized he had left without changing his clothes, painting his eyes, or even combing his hair. It was too late to do anything about it.

8

Three quarters of an hour later, as the late afternoon sun of the warm autumn day slanted golden out of the sky, they were at the harbour.

Varazda was by now hot and sweaty from carrying Remi at a brisk walk most of the way. He set her on top of a stone pylon on the pier by the customs house, where she could see over the crowd, and scanned the busy quay himself, keeping an arm around her little waist. They were in time: the *Swift* from Pheme had just docked, and its passengers were disembarking. Remi leaned against him.

"Is that him?" She pointed with a tiny finger.

Varazda followed the gesture. "No, that's a little boy. My friend is a grown-up man."

Maybe they should get closer to the ship. But they had a good vantage here, and it was easier for Remi not to get lost in the crowd. Varazda rubbed his upper arm, which was hurting where it had been injured a month earlier.

A month was also how long he had been looking forward to this meeting, and yet it was coming about in a shambles of last-minute bumbling, and that irritated him.

"A grown-up man," Remi repeated. "Is he big?"

Varazda smiled. "Tall, yes, he's tall."

And broad-shouldered, with delightful muscles—and then other parts of him were big too …

"Taller than me?"

"Taller than *me*, even."

Remi digested that, looking up at Varazda.

"That's tall."

"He's nice," Varazda said. "You will like him."

That was a safe bet—a given, almost. Remi liked anyone who liked her, and she was easy to like: always smiling, always laughing and talking, and so pretty, with her big dark eyes and dimples and wispy-soft black hair.

"Is that him?"

"No, that's a woman."

Remi wrinkled her nose at him and pointed again. "Is that him?"

"That's a goat!"

They giggled over that for a bit. And then, while Remi was looking for something else ridiculous to point to, there he was, emerging from the press of people on the pier by the *Swift*.

"Look, there." Varazda pointed. "Do you see the man with the ... "

With the what? With the beautiful hazel eyes, the clipped dark curls threaded with silver? With the look of settled sadness that sometimes melts into an adorable smile?

"That tall man there, with the nice face."

He would *not* say, "The man with the cane."

Remi considered Damiskos for a moment. "He has a sword. Does he dance with it?"

"Uh, well, no. He uses it for other things."

"What?"

"Protecting people."

"Oh."

The cane was a surprise, though not a big one. Dami hadn't used a cane at Laothalia a month ago, but Varazda didn't know what its appearance now meant. Had he aggravated his injury? Done too much walking? Or maybe he only used the cane under certain circumstances. Observation would answer the question without Varazda having to pose it, which he would never do.

Damiskos looked well, though, fit and fresh after the short voyage from the city of Pheme. He wore his usual not-quite-beard, a plain tunic, and a short travelling cloak tossed back from the shoulder where he carried his bag. His sword hung sheathed from his belt.

He had stopped and was looking around the quayside. He looked sternly nervous, a brave man facing down a situation that made him irrationally anxious. His gaze passed over

Varazda and Remi without pausing, roamed over the other people on the quay, and did not return.

"Let's go meet him," said Varazda, lifting Remi down from the pylon and setting her on her feet on the dock. She clamped her arms around his knee and buried her face in the folds of his tunic and refused to move.

"Come, Remi, let's meet my friend."

It took him a few moments to get her moving; he could have picked her up, but he really rather wanted at least one hand free. By this time, Damiskos had started to walk down the pier.

It was like him to think that Varazda might not be waiting for him on the pier. Damiskos walked faster and more easily with the cane than he had without, but it gave him an unmistakable look of an *ex*-soldier, someone whose disability was permanent. Varazda thought that might have been the whole reason he hadn't used it at Laothalia.

"First Spear!" Varazda called.

Damiskos turned, and his eyes widened in surprise.

"First Spear!" Remi squeaked, then hid her face in Varazda's tunic, clinging to his leg again and vibrating with nervous excitement.

That meant Varazda couldn't move again, so it was Damiskos who came back up the pier to meet them.

"Hello," he said. He smiled, tentatively but beautifully, down at Remi. "Were you waiting by the ship?"

"We were," said Varazda.

"I'm sorry. I didn't—couldn't pick you out from the crowd." He looked mortified. "I didn't recognize you."

That was such a very Damiskos thing to say—to admit, when it was absolutely unnecessary, that he had not recognized his beloved after a month apart—that Varazda almost laughed aloud. He picked up Remi and propped her on one hip, giving up the idea of an embrace which Damiskos was obviously much too embarrassed for anyway.

"You've never seen me in Pseuchaian clothes before," he pointed out.

"No. I didn't know you ever wore them."

Varazda nodded. "Most of the time, actually. When I'm not working."

He could hear his tone growing slightly cold, his pride snapping to attention at the possibility—completely hypothetical—that Damiskos might not like him in this style of dress.

He was wearing a short, wine-red tunic with simple sandals and almost no jewelry. He had put his hair up in a slapdash knot earlier in the day and hadn't had a chance to do anything else with it.

"You look amazing," said Damiskos, looking both enchanted and desperately tense.

At that Varazda did laugh out loud. Remi laughed too, because she always laughed when anyone else did.

"If we were in a romantic novel," Damiskos said, relaxing a little, "I would have to—I don't know—perform a feat or, or go on a quest to prove my devotion after not recognizing you."

The way he was looking at Varazda, no one with a heart could have doubted his devotion.

"There's a good one in the prologue to the *Tales of Suna* that you might try," said Varazda, deadpan. "I'll tell you about it some time."

They stood an agonizing moment longer, then Varazda leaned forward and gave Damiskos a kiss on the cheek.

"It's good to see you," Varazda said simply.

"Yes. It is very good. I'm sorry it's been so long."

"No, I understand. You had things to do in Pheme. This is Remi."

"Hello, Remi."

"Remi, this is my friend Damiskos."

"I saw a picture of you," said Damiskos. "You are even prettier in person."

"What do you say, Remi?"

"Thank you." She clung to Varazda and kicked her feet excitedly.

"Do you have to go through customs?" Varazda asked Damiskos. "Because of the sword?"

"No, I get a pass for being an ex-officer." He lifted his wrist with the bronze bracelet.

"Ah, that's good. I remember when we first came, they were very strict. I had to convince them that my swords were just for dancing."

"Are we going to have fritters?" Remi asked suddenly.

"Right. I did say we would. I'm sorry—I had to promise her fritters in order to get her out of the house, and I had to bring her because … well, it's a long story."

"We'd better get fritters," said Damiskos. To Remi, he added, "Do you like the sesame ones or the fruit ones?"

He wasn't exactly a natural with children, Varazda thought, but he was making an effort, in his serious, work-manlike way, and—as one would expect—he was doing a good job.

"It's this way," Varazda said, after Remi had finished explaining her fritter preferences, which were complex and probably pretty unintelligible to Damiskos. "Our favourite shop is just inside the city gates."

"Good," said Damiskos. He gave one of the curt, military nods that he probably didn't realize were unspeakably cute. "Lead the way."

They set off up the long ramp that led from the harbour to the city. It was well maintained, the paving stones fitted neatly together, but it was steep. Varazda had never noticed these details before. He set Remi down so she could walk again, giving his arms and back a rest which they badly needed. She was too heavy these days to be comfortably carried long distances.

"Is your stick for protecting people too?" she asked, tipping her head sideways to get a good look at Damiskos's cane.

"It could be," said Damiskos seriously. "But mostly I use it to help me walk. You see? One of my knees doesn't bend all the way."

"Why?" Remi asked, inevitably. Varazda gave fleeting thought to stepping in to nip this in the bud, but decided Damiskos could handle it.

"Well," Damiskos said, "it got hurt."

A pause, then: "Why?"

"It broke."

"*Broke?*" Remi repeated sceptically, as if she thought he might have used the wrong word. "Why did it broke?"

"It, well, it got hit with something."

An iron rod, specifically. While he was tied down and held in place. Varazda had seen it done—not to Damiskos, but to other men.

"Why?"

"Because I made somebody angry." He was surprisingly quick with that one. He was getting the hang of this.

"Why?"

"Because I was doing my job. I used to be a soldier."

"Why?"

"Because the Republic needs to be defended sometimes." He didn't miss a beat there.

"Why?"

"Because the gods have so ordered the affairs of mortal men that wars arise between nations."

"Ah yah," Varazda murmured. "Well done."

"Thanks."

Remi frowned at Damiskos for a moment. "I like the gods," she said finally. "Do you like them?"

"I do. One that I like a lot is called Terza. Have you heard of him?"

She nodded uncertainly.

"You have heard of him, Remi, remember?" Varazda put in. "Sorgana talks about him. The one with the bull and the, uh—"

Dami gave him a humorous, expectant look.

"Well, there's a bull, I know that much. And he wears a hat."

"The bull doesn't wear a hat!" Remi scoffed.

"She's right," said Damiskos.

"No, I … I got confused. I meant Terza wears a hat."

"A floppity hat," Remi added authoritatively.

"A floppity hat," Damiskos agreed.

"Her friend Sorgana is very keen on the, uh, what do you call it, the pantheon? He's seven."

Too late Varazda realized how condescending this must sound. As if he considered Damiskos's religion basically a child's game.

"I hope I get a chance to meet him," said Damiskos neutrally.

They reached Chereia's in the street by the sea wall, and Remi picked out a sticky fig fritter. The shop was busy, the girl behind the counter unfamiliar—a new hire, probably because the previous girl had had her baby—and there was no sign of Remi's friends Sorgana and Lysandros, though of course she had to look for them and ask where they were.

"Sorgana is at school, and I expect Sandy is shopping with his mother," Varazda said, herding her out of the shop. Only then did he realize Damiskos had not followed them out but was still inside at the counter, buying a fritter of his own.

"Sorry," Damiskos said when he emerged, his cane tucked under his arm so that he had one hand free to steady the strap of his bag and the other to hold his fritter.

"No, I'm sorry. I didn't realize you wanted one." He would have paid for it if he had. He was annoyed to have already failed in his duty as a host.

"They looked so good." After a moment, a little uncertainly, "Would you like a bite?"

Varazda leaned over and took an elegantly tidy bite of the fritter, catching a drip of honey with the pad of his thumb and licking it delicately off. It was a provocative display, and he knew it. He could have done it in front of another man, or even a certain type of woman, if it suited his purposes, and felt nothing about it. With Damiskos there was a thrill, and a promise, and somehow at the same time a *safety* in such a gesture that was unlike anything in Varazda's experience. And all Damiskos did was give him a friendly, appreciative grin in response.

"I enjoyed your letters," Varazda said.

"Did you?" Damiskos looked surprised.

"Yes, they were … very like you."

Damiskos nodded with a wry smile. "Terse and awkward, you mean."

"Easy to read," Varazda amended.

Dami snorted.

There had been three letters, all short and written in a clear, educated hand. The first had arrived a week after Varazda's return to Boukos, along with a parcel containing the clothes he had left behind and his favourite pair of earrings, the ones Aristokles had talked him into giving away to Nione. In the letter, Damiskos had explained that Nione wanted to return them when she realized they were Varazda's.

The rest of the letter had said: *I have returned to Pheme and will shortly tender my resignation from the Quartermaster's Office. Owing to the demands of work and duty to my family, I will not be able to leave until the end of Euthalion Month. I wish it could be sooner.*

Come to think of it, it was a pretty terse letter.

The other two had been a little less dispatch-like, basically conveying the information that Damiskos missed him and looked forward to seeing him again, and finally specifying which ship would bring him to Boukos.

They had been like rays of light piercing the cloud that Varazda had passed under in the weeks after returning from Laothalia with his arm in a sling and his nerves in shreds. But that was not something he was prepared to explain to Damiskos. There was no need for Dami to know it; he would only feel guilty for not being there to help.

"Is it far to your house?" Damiskos asked, licking honey off his own fingers without any seductive flair. He didn't wait for an answer. "I remember from when I visited Boukos a few years back that there were lots of places to hire chairs. I wouldn't mind that. And Remi can ride with me, if she likes, so you don't have to carry her all the way back."

Varazda smiled warmly at him, glad that he had raised the subject—proud of him for it, in a certain way.

"I wouldn't mind that either."

They hired a chair, and Varazda walked beside it—they told the bearers to go slowly. At first Remi wanted to walk too, but she quickly tired of that and agreed cautiously to climb up into Damiskos's lap. He brought out a present for her from his bag, a little painted wooden horse, and she swooped it around and made neighing sounds.

The light was beginning to fail as they reached the sleepy suburb where Varazda and his family lived. They stopped outside a cookshop, because Varazda wasn't at all sure that Yazata planned to cook dinner, and bought grilled lamb and cheese pies. They paid the bearers and walked the rest of the way, Varazda carrying Remi again. They were not talking much, but it felt comfortable rather than awkward. Damiskos looked around, taking in the details of the neighbourhood.

The streets here were narrow, unevenly cobbled, overhung with flowering vines carefully tended by elderly people leaning out their upstairs windows with water pots. There were no columns or marble cornices, but the whitewash was fresh on all the walls, and the streets were always swept, the gutters almost pristine.

"It's a nice neighbourhood," Damiskos remarked.

"I like it. It's a little out of the way, but it's quiet, and there are lots of other children for Remi to play with. Here's our street."

They had turned from Fountain Street into their cul-de-sac, the entrance to which was narrow enough that you could miss it if you weren't looking for it. Damiskos gave an audible gasp.

"Gorgeous," he said.

"I like it," Varazda said again, trying to look only moderately pleased, failing, and not caring. He set Remi down, and she ran off to pick up Hermia and Doros's cat, which was stalking across the pavement.

From the narrow entrance, the street widened into a tiny plaza, paved in pale stone, with a worn wooden fence along the far end, beyond which was the vacant lot and a surprising glimpse of blue-green countryside in the distance. Three whitewashed houses, doors and windowsills and shutters painted in different colours, occupied each side of the street.

"We call it Saffron Alley," said Varazda. "Yazata named it."

Damiskos laughed. "After the Saffron Valley, near Rataxa?"

"Exactly." Varazda beamed. "That's where Yaza's from." He gestured to the three connected houses on the right-hand side. "These are mine."

"*These?*" Damiskos repeated.

"Yes, I own everything on this side of the street. The one on the corner is let out as a shop, and there's a dance school on the upper floor that I have a share in. The house at the

other end is Yazata and Tash's, and I have the middle one."
He pointed to the rose-coloured door and yellow shutters of
his house. "Though as you'll see, we've taken out some of the
walls so they're more like one house at the back. Come, let's
go in."

He stepped toward the door and held out a hand,
looking back at Damiskos with a smile. He had been looking
forward to doing this for a month.

CHAPTER 2

THE HOUSE WAS shadowy and empty when they entered, with Remi darting around their legs, trying to keep hold of the cat, who didn't want to be held. Damiskos propped his cane by the door and divested himself of cloak, bag, and sword. Varazda hung them all up on the pegs in the hallway.

"I'll show you around. This is the dining room." He gestured through the arch on the right to the dark room beyond with its draped Pseuchaian-style couches. "We don't use it much, only when I entertain. Remi, love, please let that cat go. He belongs outside. And this is my practice room, which I use every day."

He opened the door on the other side of the hall and walked across to push open the shutters, so that Damiskos could see the room, with its wood floor, perfect for dancing, its walls frescoed with flowers in sunset shades, Varazda's bronze swords hanging on the wall opposite the door.

Of course when the light entered from the window, Varazda noticed that there were some scarves and an apple core on the window sill, a coat crumpled up on a chair, and a hopscotch board chalked prominently in the middle of floor.

He couldn't remember whether he had even come into this room in his whirlwind tidying effort earlier in the afternoon.

He smiled wryly. This was a side of him that Damiskos had already seen.

"The kitchen is through here," he said, stepping over the cat, which Remi had released in the hallway. There was still mud from the cartful of clay on the hallway floor, dried and crumbly now.

"I'm hungry," said Remi, eyeing the parcel of cookshop food which Varazda carried.

"We'll eat soon, my sweet."

He led the way into the kitchen, where he put the food down on the table with the shopping from the market, which lay untouched, evidence that Yazata had not been back. There was no sign that Tash had been either.

"It's a lovely house," Damiskos remarked, looking around while Varazda lit a lamp. "This is where you took out the wall, I see."

"That's right." He brought out one of the cheese pies and cut it in half for Remi. "Here you go, love."

The two kitchens had been joined by a large archway through the middle of the connecting wall, making an airy room with two sections: a table and benches for family meals on Varazda's side; pantry, shelves, stove, and workbenches on Yazata and Tash's side. Louvered doors opened onto the terrace at the back of the house and the weedy, neglected garden with its blocks of marble and half-finished sculptures.

"The upper storeys aren't connected," Varazda explained, "so there are two sets of stairs, mine and theirs. This is my sitting room, but we all use it really."

He gestured Damiskos through the arch on the other side of the stairs, and the light from his lamp fell on the room with its divans and patterned carpets.

"It's sort of a hybrid of a Zashian and a Pseuchaian

room," Damiskos remarked, smiling as he looked around at it.

This was exactly what Varazda had wanted the effect of the room to be. The walls were painted in a bright, local style, the divans covered with a mixture of Pseuchaian stripes and Zashian embroidery, and the rugs lay over a simple black and white pebble mosaic. The lamps and braziers were Boukossian-made; the tables were Boukossian tables with the legs cut down to the level of the divans. Some people found the mixture of styles odd, but it was clear Damiskos liked it. Varazda was pleased. He hadn't necessarily expected Dami to notice or care about the details of his house. But maybe it was obvious that Varazda took pride in them, so of course the considerate Dami would take time to sincerely admire them.

Varazda walked across the room to a narrow door on the far side, in a gap between two of the divans.

"This," he said, opening it, "is your room."

Damiskos gave him a slightly puzzled look, which Varazda could not interpret. Varazda led the way into the room.

"Oh," said Dami, "now this is pure Zash."

There was rich colour and pattern everywhere, and a scent of incense in the air. The restored bouquet stood on the windowsill at the far end, framed by pierced shutters of dark wood, above the stripped bed, which was a Zashian-style pallet raised up on a platform.

"It's beautiful," said Damiskos. "I feel as if I'm back in Suna. This is your bedroom?"

"No, no—my room is upstairs." And it looked nothing like this.

"Ah."

Varazda glanced back out into the sitting room to see what Remi was doing. She was sitting on a divan munching her cheese pie and swinging her feet.

When he looked back, Dami was staring at the south-west wall of the room, at a small niche beside the door.

"That's in just the right place for a shrine to Terza," he said, sounding surprised.

"I know," said Varazda proudly. "I asked around."

Dami looked at him, then turned to survey the rest of the room again, his expression almost alarmed. "The bed? It's a Zashian bed, but you've got it raised up, so … so I can get in and out more easily?"

Varazda nodded. "I had the box built to match that table —" He pointed. "—which was in the sitting room before. The shutters too—I mean, they weren't in the sitting room, but I had the same carpenter do them. The other furniture in here I had already. The room wasn't being used for much—it was a storeroom at the back of the music shop. If you look behind those hangings, you can see where I had the door walled up, and then I had this one knocked through. I'd been meaning to do it for years, and I thought … " He smiled. "I thought the time had come."

"I see. That … sounds like a lot of work."

"Oh, not too much, really. So," he asked casually, "how long do you think of staying?"

"Right." Damiskos looked uncomfortable. "I've—I have a week."

"Ah."

"I was hoping it could be longer."

"Yes."

Varazda had assumed it would be quite a bit longer. He felt his defenses rising. He had shown himself far too eager. He should have made it sound as if he'd put the bed on some old boxes he'd had lying around, and the niche was a coinci-dence, and he shouldn't have said anything about walling up and knocking through doors.

Damiskos went on: "I wasn't … able to resign, entirely. It turned out my superior officer was implicated in the

Laothalia affair—he was part of the conspiracy to buy the documents that Helenos had stolen—and when he was found out, he fled Pheme and left behind a disastrous mess. Records burnt or just missing, funds unaccounted-for, a major shipment of grain dropped at the wrong location and left to rot—it was pretty bad. I couldn't leave in the middle of that, and I … in point of fact, I was promoted, I have his job now, and a week was the most time I could get away."

Varazda laughed rather sharply. "So when you say you couldn't resign 'entirely,' you mean you didn't resign at all."

"I did resign," Damiskos said patiently. "I'm Acting Quartermaster until someone suitable is found to replace me."

"I see. I'm sorry."

"No, I understand—I should have explained that it would only be a short visit, but I … I didn't want to presume."

Suddenly Varazda could picture it: Damiskos back in his miserable life in Pheme, with his ridiculous job, his cramped living quarters, his horrible family, stewing in uncertainty about whether Varazda even wanted him any more, let alone how long he might be welcome to stay.

It couldn't have helped that Varazda had never answered any of his letters.

"I'm sorry," Varazda said. "I did not mean to leave you uncertain. Of course you are welcome to stay as long as you can. A week will be lovely."

Damiskos smiled gratefully. After a moment he said, "Can I kiss you?"

"Oh, yes, please."

He drew Varazda to him, and it was all Varazda could do not to whimper abjectly. It felt so good to have those strong arms around him again. He wrapped his own arms around Damiskos's neck, and they kissed in sweet absorption, bodies pressed together. Varazda had craved this all the while they had been apart: the hard contours of Dami's body, the gentle heat of his lips. He had dreamt of this, in fact, and woken feeling oddly guilty.

After a moment, Damiskos's hand slid up Varazda's thigh, under the skirt of Varazda's tunic, just far enough to be tantalizing, just slowly enough that Varazda could have pushed it away if he had wanted to, which he didn't.

"I've been wanting to do that since I first saw you at the harbour," Damiskos murmured into Varazda's neck.

"Since you first *recognized* me, you mean."

Damiskos groaned.

Varazda reached up to untie his hair and shook it out, while they still stood clasped body to body. Damiskos drew a handful to his lips and kissed it, a surprisingly heated gesture. Varazda could feel Dami's arousal through the thin layers of their clothes. He had to remind himself that it was no reason to tense up and pull away.

In the distance, Varazda heard a door open, and Remi called out, "Yaza! Papa, it's Yaza!"

Yazata was coming through from the front of his house into the kitchen when Varazda and Damiskos emerged from the sitting room. He stopped, hands tightly gripping the handle of the basket he carried, face frozen.

Remi was dancing around in front of him with her half-eaten pie, telling him all about Damiskos: "He has a sword *and* a stick, Yaza!"

"You bought dinner from a cookshop?" were the first words out of Yazata's mouth, in a tone of anguish such as one might have used to say, "You were forced to eat your shipmates?"

"We weren't sure when you would get in, that's all,"

Varazda said soothingly. "Yazata, this is Damiskos. Damiskos, Yazata."

"But he doesn't *dance* with his sword, he—um, um— collects people," Remi explained.

"It is a great pleasure to meet you," said Damiskos, stepping forward after Yazata had set down his basket and holding out his hands for the Zashian-style greeting.

Yazata looked at them for a moment as if he had never seen such a thing before, then he clasped them gingerly and let go almost as if he were dropping something hot. Damiskos showed no sign of offence.

"And his knee got breaked because there was a war," Remi was saying, "and Yaza, Yaza, do you know about Terza? He has a hat!"

Yazata reached down to stroke Remi's hair, and slightly, subtly, gathered her against himself, as if he thought she might want protection. She wriggled away.

Yazata was bigger than Damiskos: fully as tall, broader in the shoulders, and fat. He was strikingly handsome, with a strong nose and wide-set eyes, his skin a few shades lighter than Remi's, his long, thick black hair always pulled back into a tight single braid. He moved majestically, like a big ship on a smooth sea.

Yet it was hard to imagine anyone less physically threatening. And Damiskos—well, he was rather the opposite. It was not surprising if Yazata was a little scared of him.

"I am going upstairs to change my clothes," Yazata murmured in Zashian, not meeting Varazda's eyes, "and then I will cook. But of course if you'd rather eat your cookshop food … "

"A floppity hat! Yaza, did you know that?"

"Remi's eating now because she was hungry," said Varazda, trying not to make it sound like a criticism. "Damiskos and I can wait." He glanced at Damiskos.

"Of course," Damiskos agreed eagerly.

"What are you going to cook?" Remi asked, Terza forgotten, following Yazata to the foot of the stairs. "Can I help?"

"Not tonight I'm afraid, Umit. Perhaps tomorrow." He made his majestic way up the stairs.

"I'm not an Umit," Remi called after him earnestly. "I'm just a Remi!"

Varazda realized his was grinding his teeth and tried to stop. "Come sit at the table and finish your pie, Remiza."

She scrambled up onto the bench on the right side of the table and scooted down to her usual spot in the middle.

"Are you going to sit with me?" she asked, looking up at Damiskos.

"May I?"

"Please," said Varazda. "Sit—and eat, if you like."

"Wouldn't dream of it," said Damiskos, lowering himself onto the bench. He had a neat, efficient manoeuvre to do it without bending his bad leg more than was comfortable. He made it look easy; it probably wasn't.

Varazda began moving food off the table onto the workbench on the other side of the kitchen. Remi reminded Damiskos that she was a Remi, not an Umit, and Dami nodded seriously.

He began explaining to Remi that he had a brother named Timiskos, and people confused their names. "It would be like if you had a sister called Nemi," he suggested.

"I have a sister," said Remi. "Amistron is my sister."

"Oh," said Damiskos, looking to Varazda for help.

"Imaginary sister," Varazda supplied. He didn't need Dami wondering if there were more children in his family than he'd admitted to.

"Papa, you maked a joke!" Remi observed hilariously. "Amistron's not *imaginary*!"

"Silly me," said Varazda. He caught Dami's eye and shook his head reassuringly.

Yazata came downstairs again, his trousers and coat

replaced by his more usual shapeless robe and slippers, and began cooking. Varazda went to stand beside him, his hip propped against the workbench, while Remi and Damiskos were still talking.

"How's Maraz?" he asked.

"Much better!" Yazata's face lit up. "She is starting to look like her old self again, and to make jokes as usual. Her mistress has been treating her very well." He scooped lentils out of a jar and began picking through them. "Oh, that reminds me. Did you see Maia today?"

"No. I went over there, but she was out."

Yazata nodded. "I should check on her. She has seemed worried recently. I'm afraid it's because Stamos's ship is due back soon."

Varazda groaned. "I keep hoping for a shipwreck."

"Oh dear, don't say that. Think of the other men on the ship!"

"I just said I hope for it, Yaza," Varazda said, patting Yazata's arm, "not that I'm out there rearranging rocks. I hope that the other men make it safely to shore—how's that?" He caught Dami's eye from across the room, and Dami smiled.

"Perhaps she's worried about something else, though," Yazata went on, "with one of the children. There are so many things for a parent to worry about. I must think of some way to find out what it is."

"You could ask her."

"I couldn't," said Yazata, as if this should have been self-evident. "She would be embarrassed to know that I've noticed. I know what I'll do. I'll take over a basket of eggs and ask how many she wants. Then perhaps she'll say, 'I should take an extra one for Stamos,' if she is expecting him."

"Stamos doesn't deserve our eggs."

Yazata ignored that. "If he is due back, we'll have the children over here to play, or I'll take them on a picnic—how would that be?"

"That's an excellent idea. I wish we had a house in the country for occasions like this." Yazata shot him a worried look, and Varazda added, "I'm not thinking of buying a house in the country. I'm aware I can't afford that."

Yazata allowed himself a slight chuckle. "I never know," he said mildly.

"I should go unpack some of my things," said Dami, moving to rise from the table. "Could—er, would that be all right?"

It wasn't the most subtle way of leaving Varazda and Yazata alone to talk, but subtlety wasn't really required here. Varazda gave Dami a wry smile.

"Sure, go ahead. Remi, you stay here and finish eating, please."

Yazata concentrated studiously on the lentils as Dami left the kitchen. Varazda waited a moment to see whether he would speak, but he did not.

"Yazata, my dear, I'm worried that perhaps you stayed away so long today because you were afraid of meeting Damiskos. You could tell me if that were true, right?"

Yazata looked up. "I'm always a little afraid of meeting anyone, Varazda. But no—no, I'm all right." He leaned over to give Varazda a kiss on the cheek. "I'll be all right."

It wasn't as reassuring as Varazda had hoped.

Dami didn't have much to unpack, and he came wandering tentatively back into the kitchen after a short time. Varazda was sitting at the table with Remi. Yazata looked over his shoulder.

"I make a famous dish from my homeland," he explained rather loudly, his Pseuchaian more laboured than usual. "I hope you will like."

"I am sure I will," Damiskos replied. He slid onto the bench on the other side of Remi. "Varazda tells me you are an excellent cook."

Yazata looked surprised, caught slightly off balance.

Varazda was honestly a little impressed by the lie, and the smooth manner in which Damiskos carried it off.

Obviously he must have social skills of some sort, to have risen as far as he had in the army. And Varazda had already seen that he was very good in a crisis.

Remi finished her pie and tried to entice Damiskos to come out and be a centimaur with her in the dark yard. Dami plainly could not figure out what that was, and looked rather panicked. Varazda vetoed the whole thing and was met with howls of protest.

"Perhaps Umit could go out for a little while," Yazata suggested.

"Pleeease?" said Remi hopefully.

"No," said Varazda. If there was any rule to be enforced in their household, he generally had to been the one to do it. Yazata's instinct to pacify was so strong that he would give in to almost any plea.

Varazda's stomach growled embarrassingly. He pulled the parcel of grilled meat across the table toward himself and selected a skewer.

Damiskos was looking at him now over Remi's head, with a humorously wide-eyed expression, as if to say, "Are you sure you know what you're doing?"

Varazda sank his teeth into a piece of meat and pulled it off the skewer with a flourish. Damiskos fanned himself with one hand, and Varazda grinned. Remi half-scrambled up onto the table to reach for a skewer of her own. Varazda pulled a chunk off his skewer and offered it to her. She took it with her teeth instead of her hand, to her own great amusement. On impulse, Varazda slid another piece of meat from his skewer and held it out to Damiskos.

Damiskos looked into his eyes for a moment and leaned forward to take the food from his hand. Remi, between them, shrieked with laughter. Yazata looked over his shoulder, saw what was going on, and looked away with a strange expression: not anger or disappointment that they were eating the cookshop meat, or disgust at the show they were making of it, but something like determination. Almost as if he were nerving himself up for something. Varazda did not know what to make of that. But he did not spend much time on it. Dami was here, eating at his table, and Varazda was going to enjoy this week.

Yazata made labash for dinner. He began explaining it to Damiskos as he sat down at the table and dished it out.

"This is very popular dish of Zash," he said, slopping a green mass into one of their largest bowls, "made from lentils and seeds of pomegranate and many different grasses."

"Herbs," Varazda supplied in an undertone.

"I don't like blablash," said Remi glumly.

"It's all right, love," said Varazda, "you've had your cheese pie and meat."

In fact, Varazda was no longer very hungry himself. In the time it had taken Yazata to cook the labash—easily three quarters of an hour, it had been a terrible choice in more than one way—he and Damiskos and Remi had finished most of the grilled lamb.

"Well, I like it," said Damiskos, pulling the bowl toward himself. "Thank you. Ah, you've made it spicy!"

He tore off a piece of bread for himself, balanced it on the edge of his bowl, and looked up smiling. Yazata froze like a startled hare. Damiskos had spoken in Zashian.

He spoke Zashian with a strong accent, without the musical inflection that the language had in the mouth of a native speaker. But he spoke it fluently and clearly.

"Damiskos served in Zash for several years," said Varazda mildly, accepting his own bowl of labash. "You remember, I mentioned it."

"I want to get down," said Remi. "Can I get down?"

That offered Varazda the perfect opportunity to say, "Wait until Yazata has said the blessing," which would have warned Damiskos to wait too. But Varazda could see that Damiskos needed no warning. He was waiting already. Varazda made a shushing gesture to Remi and said nothing.

Yazata stood an unnecessary moment over his bowl of labash, eyes on Damiskos. Finally he folded his hands and said a long and flowery version of the blessing of the food. Remi began kicking her feet under the table.

Yazata sat at last, but went on watching Damiskos, who knew he was being watched and put on a nonchalant display of competence, ladling sour cream into his dish and scooping up lentils with his bread as if it would never have occurred to him to ask for a spoon.

Remi got down from the table and went out into the yard. If Varazda had been paying attention, it would have occurred to him what would happen next. She reappeared in the kitchen door in a moment, carrying Selene.

"Damikos, look! This is my—"

Selene surged out of Remi's grip with a flapping of wings and an indignant hissing, and made straight for Damiskos, neck stretched, beak wide and ready to bite. Damiskos, taken completely by surprise, half-started out of his seat with a cry of alarm, nearly upsetting his bowl of labash.

"Terza's co—ghh—" He swallowed the oath awkwardly.

"Goose," Remi finished.

"Yes," said Damiskos manfully, still standing with one hand braced on the table, while Selene made hissing, flapping lunges at him from the floor.

"Remi—" Varazda began, aware that Yazata was giggling behind his hand.

"Are you scared of gooses?" Remi asked solicitously.

"You know," said Damiskos, "I think I may be, a little. But it's—very pretty. What's its name?"

"Selene. She will be your friend."

"Can you take her outside now, love?" Varazda suggested. "I don't think she's ready to be Dami's friend yet."

"Come, Selene." Remi managed to gather up the enraged goose, who was deeply attached to her and would never have bitten her, and carry her back out into the yard.

"Well," said Damiskos, sitting down again. "That was exciting."

The labash was absurdly spicy. Varazda added huge scoops of sour cream to his bowl. Yazata began talking about religion.

Varazda couldn't sleep. He lay looking up at the moonlit ceiling of his room and listening to the soft sounds of the night and wondering whether this had all been a mistake.

After his initial blunder, Varazda had been so careful to tread lightly as the day of Dami's arrival had neared. He knew Yazata feared any change in their routine, or even the slightest suggestion that his own security might be at stake, that he might be displaced by someone new. Varazda had deliberately avoided talking too much about his lover, keeping his own excitement on a short rein, lest it alarm Yazata further. He was grateful for how well Yazata seemed to have adapted to the idea of a man in the house, given how Yazata felt about men in general. Yazata's early years had been spent in a household headed by a violent tyrant, and he'd been left with a deep distrust of men. Varazda had known that.

So he'd made sure that Damiskos could be accommodated with the minimum of disruption; the new room was out of everyone's way, no one was being displaced even a little bit, and it was quite true that he had always intended to renovate that room one day anyway.

And now here they were, and Dami was so obviously *trying*. He wasn't getting anything wrong, either. He didn't try to speak Zashian when Yazata spoke Pseuchaian to him—at the dinner table, he'd dipped into the language only because Remi and Varazda had already been speaking it—and he'd been incredibly polite about the spicy labash, allowing Yazata to explain its ingredients and history to him even though it was clear he was already familiar with it.

Even the discussion of religion had gone remarkably well. Damiskos had listened politely, hadn't got offended, hadn't asked stupid questions or tried to change the subject. It was really the best that could have been hoped for. Still Varazda had felt his anger mounting through the whole thing. He couldn't vent it on Yazata, but that felt increasingly unfair. It had been so obvious that Yazata was trying, as much as his gentle nature would let him, to make Dami uncomfortable.

I don't want him to be uncomfortable here. I want my home to be a haven for him, the way it is for the rest of us. I want him to escape his unhappiness here; I want to take care of him.

And that was something of a revelation. When had this become so important to him? It hadn't started out this way. He wasn't even sure if he had felt this way when he left Laothalia. Maybe it was a desire that had grown in his heart since then.

Maybe he had fastened on this as a hedge against his doubt that he would ever be an adequate lover.

Dinner had ended in profound awkwardness. Remi had got to the stage of tiredness where she began banging spoons on the kitchen floor, and Yazata had shown no sign of intending to put her to bed, instead getting up and ostentatiously beginning to wash dishes. Varazda, finally out of patience, had stalked out to the yard to retrieve the sheets for Dami's bed. Remi had "helped" as he remade the bed, and when they were finally done, Damiskos had taken the hint

34

and retired meekly for the night, leaving Varazda free to scoop Remi up and take her upstairs.

Of course, he didn't want Yazata to be uncomfortable either. This was Yazata's home, *his* haven, and Varazda loved him. He couldn't hurt Yazata on purpose—hadn't thought that this was going to hurt him. Maybe he was asking too much, of everyone.

He tossed aside the covers and swung his legs out of bed. He was wearing pyjama trousers with no shirt because the night was warm, and also because the room was such a mess that he had not been able to locate a shirt. He raked his hands through his hair and got up.

Lighting a lamp, he made his way downstairs to the kitchen. He got down a wine cup and found an open bottle in the pantry. In the sitting room he hung his lamp on a stand and pushed open the doors to the terrace to stand leaning against the doorpost with his cup of wine, looking up at the night sky visible above the roofs of his neighbours' houses.

At a soft sound, he looked back over his shoulder toward the door to Dami's room. Dami stood on the threshold, looking out.

He looked like he had been asleep; his curls were a little tousled, and he squinted in the lamplight. He was wearing the trousers of the pyjamas Varazda had left for him in the room—blue cotton, with a simple woven pattern—also without a shirt.

At any time Damiskos was a good-looking man, with an easy, rough-edged beauty that scars and greying hair complicated but couldn't mar. Standing in Varazda's house bare-chested and wearing trousers, low-slung on his trim hips, he was a sight Varazda could happily have looked at all night. Those shoulders and arms, that chest—he wasn't overbuilt, his muscles compact and functional, but there was still somehow a *lot* of him. And that dark hair, spreading in a

35

light fuzz over his chest, thickening to a trail over his belly that vanished inside the pyjama trousers. Varazda raised his eyes to Dami's face again and got one of those wry, adorable smiles.

"I hope the light didn't wake you." He looked coyly up through his lashes.

"No," said Damiskos gravely. "I—er, can't sleep." He put his fist to his breastbone. "Indigestion."

CHAPTER 3

"Oh, God," Varazda groaned. "You ate that entire bowl of labash. I'm so sorry."

"I'm fairly sure you didn't put him up to it," said Damiskos.

"God, no."

"And it was very good—I'd've enjoyed it if I hadn't already eaten all that greasy ... You know what, I don't want to talk about it."

Varazda waved a hand. "Right, no. What's good for indigestion?" He recalled Yazata making some sort of tea for Tash once. "Ginger, isn't it? We have some of that." He'd found a big, useless lump of it when he was looking for something to feed Remi that afternoon.

"Yes, that would help."

What did you do with it, though? Boiled it in a pot of water? Surely he could manage that without having to wake Yazata.

They stood there a moment longer, each in his own doorway.

"I don't think wine helps," said Damiskos into the silence.

"Hm?" Varazda glanced down at the cup he had forgotten he was holding.

"With indigestion."

"Oh. No, I'm not—it's not that. I just couldn't sleep."

"Right. Well, it does help with that."

"It does."

They stood a moment longer. Several moments, really.

"There's no chance that ferocious goose is going to come in, is there?" Dami gestured to the open door.

"No, she sleeps outside with the chickens. There's a gate." Which he hoped Remi had closed for the night.

Finally Damiskos said, "It's hard, isn't it? Picking up where we left off."

"I don't know if I remember exactly where we left off," Varazda admitted.

He moved finally toward the kitchen, taking the lamp from its stand. Damiskos followed him. The kitchen tiles were cool underfoot. Varazda set his wine cup on the workbench and lit another lamp. He rooted in the pantry for the ginger he had seen earlier.

He felt hyperaware of every movement—where he put his hands, how he knelt and stood, how his hair slithered over his bare back. He had been used to moving with deliberate grace, for almost as long as he could remember. He had been pretty as a child, and as an adult was striking—to some eyes more than that—and knew how to make the most of it. This was different. This was Dami, who had conceived that Varazda might have desires and thought that mattered, who had told Varazda he was beautiful and then said, "You don't owe me anything for thinking that."

Damiskos, he saw to his surprise when he turned around with the ginger in hand, was building a fire on the stove.

"You know how to cook?"

Dami shot him a look. "Sure. Over a campfire—but the basics are the same."

"Are they."

So Varazda stood in his own kitchen, one hip propped against the table, and watched Damiskos make ginger tea for himself.

"I think I know what you mean," Damiskos said. He stood with his arms folded over his chest, watching the slices of ginger bob around in the boiling water. "About not knowing where we left off. It all happened very fast—it's hard to know … why things went the way they did."

"I'm sure there is some lyric poet who could fill us in."

Damiskos laughed—he had a low, gorgeous chuckle that always seemed to hit Varazda right in the pit of his stomach.

"I meant," Varazda admitted, "not knowing where we were in terms of, well, how these things usually go."

"Oh. Right." Dami seemed not to find this disconcerting or ridiculous—rather the opposite. "Well, we had what you might call a fling at Laothalia, in that we went to bed together without knowing each other particularly well." He stirred the pot of tea unnecessarily. "And without the expectation that we'd have much time to spend together. But I think you know I'd already fallen hard for you before that first night in your room." He looked up at Varazda, sidelong.

"I've had men tell me that before," Varazda said slowly. His throat felt constricted. "That they were in love with me. 'Your beauty has pierced my heart, I have caught my death from your eyes,' and … so on. And I have felt nothing. Just —nothing." He hurried on because he saw Damiskos beginning to wince apologetically. "But when you say that—and I like the way you put it much better, by the way—I feel as if I finally understand how it works. As if when they said it, it was just noises, but yours—yours has a tune."

He had to stop speaking then and swallow down the lump in his throat. For him to start crying at this point would be not only wildly out of character but apt to send Dami into a spiral of guilt and apology. He was so sensitive.

He was watching Varazda carefully, but after a moment he said lightly, "I would never say, 'You stabbed me with your eyes' or whatever."

Varazda snorted. "No, you wouldn't. I know. You made such a point of telling me I'd made you happy."

It wasn't really something to be spoken of lightly; it had meant the world to Varazda, had maybe changed something in his heart for the better. But Dami was trying to help him keep from crying by making a joke, and Varazda didn't want his effort to be in vain.

"Do you want honey?" Varazda pushed himself away from the counter. "I know we have some honey. I was looking desperately for something to feed Remi after Yazata went out unexpectedly ... Here it is. Yes, well, anyway, I know exactly what we have in the kitchen as a result—it wasn't much, at the time, so we had to do some shopping, which I *also* wasn't expecting ... "

Now he was babbling, which was foolish and needless. Damiskos was supposed to be the anxious, inarticulate one.

"I'm sorry about Yazata," Varazda said, as Dami drizzled honey into his cup.

Dami made a noncommittal sound. "He doesn't seem to have warmed to me," he said diplomatically. "But I'm not offended."

"He doesn't like change," said Varazda. "And he doesn't like, well, talking about things directly."

"That's ... not uncommon," said Damiskos, and Varazda had the impression it wasn't what he had been about to say. Dami picked up his cup and blew on the surface of the tea. "I hope he and I can get to know one another better."

"Let's go sit down." Varazda gestured toward the sitting room.

They settled side-by-side on a divan, Varazda with his wine cup, Damiskos cradling his ginger tea. Varazda was pleased to see Dami take the corner seat where he could stretch out his legs; he had rearranged the divans with exactly this in mind.

"For what it's worth," Varazda said, "I doubt it's you personally that Yazata objects to. I think it's partly that he's upset with me. He's been on edge ever since he realized … Well. I wasn't especially direct myself, when I told Yazata about you. But I have no experience in this area."

"Mm. What did you say?"

Varazda sighed. "I told them both the whole story—well. I told Yazata the whole story. Tash doesn't know the truth about my work, and didn't know quite what I was doing at Nione's villa. So I told two versions of the story: one for both of them when I first came home, and another for Yazata later, with more accurate details. Of course I talked about you in both versions. I just didn't, in my first account, mention that we'd slept together."

"As one doesn't."

"Oh." That brought him up short. "One doesn't?"

"I mean … " Damiskos sipped his tea and shrugged. "One *can*. It depends on your audience. I suppose with your family, you shouldn't keep secrets. But, you know, it's not always everyone's business. If I were giving an account of a campaign, for instance, I wouldn't stop to mention that my standard-bearer gave me a blow-job on the night before an engagement. It wouldn't seem relevant. Not to mention that it would be no one's business but mine and the standard-bearer's."

"I see." He couldn't help asking, "Was that a hypothetical example, or was there an actual standard-bearer?"

Damiskos looked thoughtful for a moment, as if he had to consider the question. "There was an actual standard-bearer, but there was no actual blow-job. It was … something else."

"Ah." Varazda was half-intrigued, half-fearful. He both

wanted and didn't want to know more about what Damiskos liked in bed.

"It wasn't within the last month," Damiskos added quickly.

"What? Oh! Goodness. No, of course not. I know that. I mean … "

What, by all the angels of the Almighty, did he mean? That the thought of Damiskos sleeping with other people had never even occurred to him? Because that was true. But it was, he realized belatedly, probably not flattering to Damiskos.

Also, now that it had occurred to him, it brought with it a whole flood of unanswerable questions. Did he want to? Would he want to, eventually? Did Varazda want him to? Actually, that one wasn't unanswerable.

"Anyway," said Damiskos, after taking a rather large swallow of tea, "you were saying?"

"Was I? Oh. Yes. So I'd told them about you, to an extent. And I thought, honestly, that they realized we were lovers. You know how Zashians are—we say a lot of things without really *saying* them, and I thought I'd 'said' that there was something between you and me. But apparently the idea was so far-fetched that it never crossed their minds."

Dami gave a huff of disbelief that Varazda found absurdly flattering.

"Well, Yazata was upset, and, you know, I understand that. It was a blunder on my part. I should have known I wasn't preparing him well enough. I tried to make up for it— I tried not to alarm him further, but I can see I didn't do a good enough job of it." He shook himself. "Ah, well. My fault."

"What about Tash?" Dami asked.

"Tash… well, Tash is very young. And not very Zashian. He has no trouble being direct. I didn't know this, but apparently for two men in their thirties—not that we're both men,

42

but that's a whole other subject—but for two men our age to be lovers is … not fashionable? I don't know. Tash described it as 'social suicide.' What that means, exactly, or why he thinks it's something I'd care about, is quite beyond me."

"Indeed."

"Nevertheless. Somehow it affected me. And I … " He covered his face in his hands and drew a deep breath and said, "I was already feeling pretty unloveable." He looked over his fingers. "Don't say anything. That wasn't a plea for reassurance, or for compliments. It's just the truth. It's not very easy for me to say things like that—I'm about nine-tenths pride, and the rest is nerves. It's not a very loveable combination."

Damiskos sipped his tea and shrugged expressively.

"What?"

"You told me not to say anything."

Varazda made a noise of exasperation. "What would you have said?"

"'I don't know about that.'" He sipped his tea again. "It works for me."

Varazda dissolved into laughter. He felt as if he might slide off the divan onto the floor like a silk coat.

"Look," said Damiskos, leaning forward to put his empty cup on the table, "obviously I don't agree—I find you very loveable. But I understand why … no, I mean I'm not surprised … no, that sounds insulting, and it's not really true either. Terza's head. What I'm trying to say is, you ought not to feel unloveable, *but*, if you do, there's no shame in it. And if you do want to be reassured every so often, you know, that is something that people who love one another do. You've done it for me. If we were keeping score, you'd have a substantial lead in that contest." After a moment, with a mock-serious expression, he added, "We're not. It doesn't work like that. Just to be clear."

"Thank you. Are you feeling better?"

Damiskos rubbed his chest with the heel of his hand. "Much better. The ginger helped. I think I should sit up a while longer, though."

"Good idea."

Varazda tossed back the remainder of his wine and set the cup on the table. He drew up his legs and moved along the divan to rest lightly against Damiskos's side. Damiskos brought his arm around Varazda's bare shoulders; Varazda reached over and laid his arm across Damiskos's waist. He breathed in Dami's scent, clean and straightforward, felt the rasp of Dami's stubble against his cheek.

"I missed you," Dami said, gathering Varazda a little closer. "And at the same time, I was happier than I've been in years, this last month, looking forward to this."

"I looked forward to this too," said Varazda.

There was much more that he wanted to say but could not—he was not experienced in speaking directly himself, and he had already made one exhausting confession.

He wondered whether Dami wanted to know what had happened to the prisoners Varazda had brought back to Boukos, the details of the trial and its aftermath. He might, but probably not right now, which was fine, because Varazda strongly did not want to talk about that now.

"This healed up well," said Damiskos, drawing a finger very lightly along the fresh pink scar on Varazda's upper arm. Varazda made an assenting noise.

Damiskos had scars on both arms in roughly the same place, one on his forearm, the mark of a puncture-wound just under his left shoulder, and a long sword-cut across his ribs on the right. There was a straight, precise scar on his lame leg—hidden now by the pyjama trousers—that looked like it might have been from surgery to try to fix his knee.

The fingers of Dami's left hand carded slowly through Varazda's hair. "Your family took good care of you?"

"Yes." His head was fully resting on Dami's shoulder now. It was like warm stone. "They're very sweet, really."

"Good."

Dami's fingers burrowing in a little further now, touching the back of Varazda's neck. "Talking of being direct ... "

"Yes?" Varazda smiled. Direct was one thing Dami never had any difficulty being.

"Just to be clear." Dami coughed slightly, covering his mouth with his fist. "I'm still not feeling wonderful, so I'm entirely content just to cuddle right now. But if you want anything, just say the word. Or, you know, allude to some sort of flower and I'll try to work out what you want."

Varazda snorted. "What I want is exactly this." He pressed closer to Damiskos's stroking fingers, cinched his arm tighter around Damiskos's waist. *Please let this be enough.*

"Is there a section in *The Three Gardens* on cuddling?"

"There is. It's the Lilac Bower in the Garden of Jasmine. Less of a practical guide, more of a lyrical appreciation." He shifted comfortably against Damiskos. "One of the better pieces of poetry in the book."

"You've read it?"

"Heard it read at a party. I ... don't read Zashian."

"Right. No."

After a long moment: "I *barely* read Pseuchaian. I'm sorry I didn't reply to any of your letters. I tried—I made a start—but I've never written a whole letter before, and it didn't go well."

Dami kissed softly into Varazda's hair.

"I didn't expect you to write back." After another pause he added, tentatively, "It's something to be proud of, being able to read a foreign language—any language."

"You can read Zashian, I suppose."

"Ye-es. A little."

"I only know how to spell my own name because a friend at the embassy taught me. I don't even know the rest of the

45

letters. But everyone in the Basileon's service is always sending confidential Pseuchaian notes to one another, and I couldn't very well get my friends to read them for me, so I set myself to learn. I didn't find it very easy—I suppose I am proud of it. I still sometimes have to get help with difficult words. There weren't any of those in your letters," he added hastily.

"I'm not a difficult sort of fellow."

Varazda smiled up at him. "No. You're not."

Damiskos's left hand was fully immersed in Varazda's hair. With his right, he cupped Varazda's cheek, thumb touching the stud in Varazda's nose. He trailed his little finger along the smooth line of Varazda's jaw. There was a band of lighter skin on his strong, sun-browned wrist, where he usually wore the bronze bracelet of the Second Koryphos. Varazda tipped his head back, and Damiskos's hand slid warm down over his throat, thumbed the dip of his clavicle, paused on his chest.

"Does this still count as part of the lilac whatever," Dami whispered, "or are we heading to a different part of the garden?"

Of all the adorable things about Damiskos, this—stopping to find out what Varazda wanted, asking permission, giving him time to react—might have been the most adorable.

The other men Varazda had gone to bed with, almost without exception, had made a big show of being unable to restrain themselves. They tore off clothes or bit to leave a mark, they used words—when they used words at all—like *conquer* and *devour*. Varazda had no doubt that Damiskos could have done all that with a partner who asked for it, but even then he thought Dami's heart wouldn't have been in it.

He hoped so. He hated the thought of reaching the point where he would no longer be able to satisfy Dami with the limited range of things that he enjoyed.

He gave Damiskos a soft, light kiss, a teasing non-answer to the question. That won him another low, delicious chuckle. Dami's mouth tasted like ginger and honey.

The door from the terrace into the kitchen rattled open and banged shut.

Damiskos stiffened and drew back, but did not let go of Varazda, his grip becoming instantly, instinctively protective. From the dark kitchen they heard the sound of a heavy object dropping and rolling, and Tash's voice wailing, "Anaxe's tits!" In another moment Tash himself appeared in the archway, hopping on one foot and rubbing his shin.

It was late, and Varazda was tired. Also, he didn't care what Tash thought. He remained sitting on the divan, with Dami's arm lying along the cushions behind him.

"You're back late," he remarked. "This is Damiskos. Damiskos, this is Tash."

"*Ariston*," Tash corrected him, fiery-eyed. He gave Damiskos a bleak look. "My name is Ariston."

This was quite new, and Varazda had honestly forgotten about it. "Sorry," he said, rather sourly.

"It's a pleasure to meet you, Ariston." Damiskos swung his legs down from the divan and got up, extending a hand Pseuchaian-style.

Tash remained where he was, on the other side of the sitting-room. Varazda could feel all his tension returning, amplifying, a headache clenching like a vise at his temples.

Tash was dressed for the dinner party where he had been headed earlier, in a flashy blue tunic and a white mantle that now looked creased and shopworn. He had taken off one elaborately laced sandal but not the other—probably what had caused him to bark his shin in the kitchen.

He was a tall young man, with the gangly look of a boy in the middle of a growth spurt. With his unbroken voice, he could pass for a large fifteen-year-old. In fact, he was twenty-one and was beginning to want people to know it. He wore

47

his dark brown hair cut short and straight across his forehead in a style that made it look oddly like a hat; it was apparently the height of fashion.

To Varazda's surprise, after a moment more of standing rudely in the archway ignoring Damiskos's outstretched hand, Tash finally moved, reached across the table, and shook it limply. He did it with the worst grace in the world, but he did it, which was more than Varazda had expected. Looking up at Damiskos's face, Varazda saw why. He'd seen that expression before; it was pure First Spear of the Second Koryphos. Tash was no match for it.

Damiskos gave one of his curt nods and resumed his seat, all ease and friendliness again, draping his arm back across the pillows where it had been before.

Tash flopped down onto one of the other divans and gave his attention to his elaborate sandal, which he tossed under the table when he had got it off. He sat with his elbows on his knees, looking into the lamp flame. Damiskos shot Varazda a questioning look and tilted his head subtly toward the door of his room. Varazda shook his head minutely.

He would have liked to go in to bed with Damiskos, if only to spend some more time in the Lilac Bower, but he knew Tash well enough to know that he had something he wanted to say.

Tash was looking at them now, his expression sullenly pained. Then he leaned his head back and looked at the ceiling. Then he looked down at the lamp flame again.

Then he said, "I've killed a man."

CHAPTER 4

VARAZDA'S first impulse was to say, "No, you haven't."

He bit his lip to keep from saying that. He had realized that never being taken seriously wasn't helping Tash learn to be a person who deserved to be taken seriously.

"In a fair fight?" said Damiskos into the silence. "Or by accident."

Tash looked up at him as if he had spoken gibberish.

Damiskos sat forward, taking Tash quite seriously. "How can we help?"

"No one can help me!" Tash flung himself to his feet and tottered a bit as he stepped on the hem of his mantle. "I *killed* a man. And I'm—I'm not sorry." He did not sound very convinced.

"Whom did you kill?" said Varazda, mostly to come to Damiskos's aid.

"Themistokles," said Tash miserably.

This was more concerning. Themistokles was Tash's sculpting master.

"It was an accident, then," Varazda prompted. "You and Themistokles are good friends."

"No! Yes. I don't know!"

"You were defending yourself?" Damiskos suggested. "That would excuse you in the eyes of the law, but it's still hard to bear, I know—I remember the first time I killed a man."

Tash gave him a wild look.

"He was a soldier," said Varazda patiently. "Not whatever you're imagining."

Tash relaxed a little. "I killed him … because … I was jealous. He said … he said he was going to let me work on the new commission for the Hall of Justice, and then, uh, he changed his mind. He said he would do it himself after all. So I was jealous."

That might sound like a convincing story the second time he told it, but this time it was clear he was making it up as he went along.

Damiskos shot Varazda a wide-eyed, alarmed look. Then he turned back to Tash.

"Ariston," he said seriously. "What do you need us to do?"

Tash looked at him for a moment as though the question confused him. Damiskos looked as though he was prepared for the answer to be, "Help me hide the body."

Was it possible that this was Tash's version of Yazata's gambit with the sick friend and the labash? It was possible, Varazda decided, that Tash would do something like that, but it would have looked different. His story would have been better rehearsed, and he would have given himself away halfway through by snickering or smirking. This was something else. He was lying, but something about his distress was genuine.

The silence was broken by the sound of Remi's little voice from the top of the stairs: "Papa?"

Remi wanted a drink of water. Then she wanted the shutters by her bed opened. Then she wanted a song to help her fall asleep again, but before Varazda had got through the first verse there was shouting from downstairs. And a crash.

"Let me go!" That was Tash's voice. Dami's response, lower and quieter, was impossible to make out.

Varazda started for the door, but Remi bolted from her bed and clung to him with a howl. He had to pick her up and sling her onto his hip as he ran for the stairs. She started to cry.

"It's all right, my love—it's just Tash being silly."

"Let me go, I tell you, let me go!"

Tash was making a truly impressive amount of noise, and Varazda guessed what he hoped to accomplish—waking Yazata. It worked. By the time Varazda reached the top of his flight of stairs, Yazata was already thundering down the stairs on his side, hair flying, unbuttoned pyjama top flapping.

"You let him go!" he shrieked in Zashian. Varazda had never seen him so agitated.

Tash and Damiskos were in the kitchen. The light from the sitting room showed a dim silhouette of their forms: Tash squashed face-first against the wall, Damiskos pinning his shoulders with a forearm and twisting Tash's left arm behind his back.

Time slowed to the consistency of syrup. Varazda had time for a series of panicked thoughts—he'd somehow been wrong about Damiskos all along, what had he done, this would spell the end of his family and he should have known, Damiskos had clearly been too good to be true—in the split-second before he whirled to deposit Remi at the head of stairs, realized he physically could not get her to let go of him, and instead plunged down toward the kitchen still holding her.

Yazata arrived first. He seized a frying pan from the stove and swung, aiming for Damiskos's head. Damiskos ducked sideways, dragging Tash with him, but his weight landed on his bad leg, and he had to release his hold on Tash to grab the edge of the table. Tash fell in a tangle of grubby white mantle, writhing half-under the table. Yazata raised the frying pan again.

Remi was howling and gripping Varazda around the neck with trembling ferocity. Varazda was shouting too, he wasn't sure to what end. He grabbed a fistful of Yazata's shirt with his free hand and tried to haul him away, but the cloth tore and slipped out of his grasp.

Yazata swung the frying pan a second time. Damiskos, still braced against the table, caught Yazata's arm mid-swing with one hand and held off the blow as if Yazata were a child. Yazata screamed.

"Drop it," Damiskos instructed. Then as Yazata strained forward in an effort to drop the frying pan on Damiskos's head: "Drop it *over there*."

Yazata flung the frying pan backward and then, while Damiskos was pulled fractionally off-balance by this manoeuvre, lunged forward and smashed his forehead against Damiskos's.

Damiskos staggered back, cracked his hip against the table, and was let down again by his injured leg, which couldn't take his weight and pitched him sideways. He landed well and had pushed himself up on one hand again in a moment, blinking to clear his vision.

Yazata, who had certainly never tried to knock anybody over with his face before, had crumpled to the floor with a whimper. Varazda managed to let go of Remi now only because she flung herself off him with a wail to wrap her arms around Yazata. Varazda strode forward to stand over Damiskos.

"What. Were. You. Doing."

He got a look of almost feral, pain-fuelled ferocity back, but Damiskos did not rise from the floor.

"Trying to prevent Ariston running out into the night to turn himself over to the public watch. Which—" He gestured toward the back door, open onto the dark yard, and Tash's white mantle straggling empty over the lintel. "—he has now done."

Varazda got Yazata a cold compress for his nose, and Yazata sat at the table, breathing heavily and looking darkly over the top of the cloth at Damiskos, who sat on the opposite bench with a stern, closed-off expression on his face. Varazda wouldn't have blamed him if he had walked out of the house.

He couldn't blame Yazata for the dark looks, either. Angels of the Almighty, but this was a mess.

Remi fell asleep on Varazda's lap.

There was no point chasing after Tash. They had checked the yard, but of course he was long gone, through a gate in the corner that opened onto a tiny slit of an alley next to the music shop. In the dark streets he would be nearly impossible to follow, and they had no idea where he might have gone in his effort to track down the watch.

They just had to hope that he wouldn't be successful.

"He must have said something to Tash," Yazata said thickly, glancing at Damiskos. "What did he say to him?"

"Nothing," Varazda insisted wearily. "He tried to be helpful. Tash came in here babbling about having done a murder, and Damiskos asked how he could help."

Yazata looked unconvinced.

"But … "

Dami cleared his throat. "I laid hands on a member of your family. I have trespassed against the laws of hospitality —I realize that. I would not have used force if I hadn't thought it necessary—and I regret that. I am not able to run. I was concerned I would not be able to catch Ariston if I let

53

him go. Unfortunately he resisted—more strenuously than I expected—and began to shout the house down. And so here we are. I'll leave if you want me to." This last was addressed, gravely, to Varazda, but it was obviously intended for Yazata.

"Why does he call Tash 'Ariston'?" Yazata whispered in Zashian.

"It's his new name, remember?"

"Oh. Oh, yes."

"Please don't go," Varazda added to Dami. "I'd tell you to sleep out here on the divan, but—under the circumstances …"

Damiskos looked confused for a moment and as if he was about to say, "Of course, whatever you want."

"That was an attempt at a joke," Varazda clarified. "There's really nothing to be done now except wait for morning and hope Tash turns up, having thought better of the whole thing. I am hopeful that he will. He clearly hadn't thought about it for very long when he told us his story. With any luck, it will take him long enough to find the watch that he'll have time to reconsider."

"Yes," said Damiskos. "I can see how he might."

"Yaza, how's your nose?"

"Better," Yazata admitted. "I don't think it's broken."

Varazda leaned across the table as best he could with Remi in his lap to look at it. "Oh, it's not remotely broken. Would you take Remi to bed, please?"

"I will take Umit to bed, yes." Yazata got up from the table and gathered Remi up gently without waking her.

"I really am sorry," said Damiskos doggedly when Yazata had disappeared up the stairs. "I'll sleep anywhere you want me to."

"No, please. You didn't do anything wrong."

Dami nodded, almost meekly. After a moment, he said, "You know, Ariston gave me a little speech about not breaking your heart before he tried to flee into the night."

"He *did?*"

"Well, not in so many words, but that was what it amounted to. He professed to be concerned about your 'reputation'—but I really think he was more worried about … about you. Your happiness." He paused for a moment, then said, in a voice strained with anxiety, "I know I will have some work to do to earn their trust, after this. I hope—I hope I still can."

Varazda sighed. He knew any reassurance he could offer now wouldn't come out sounding convincing, so he said nothing.

Yazata came back downstairs. He stood in the doorway looking in at the two of them, arms folded, expression resolute. A bruise was forming on his forehead where it had made impact against Damiskos's.

Varazda tried to think when he had last seen Yazata like this. He had, though it hadn't happened often, in the years that they had known one another. Yazata did not get angry easily, did not usually show it even when he was angry, because, as he had once told Varazda, strong emotion of any kind made him uncomfortable. He was an easy person to live with, ordinarily.

Varazda got up from the table. "I might sit up a while," he said, pointedly looking away from Yazata to Damiskos. "But you should get some sleep."

Damiskos nodded in that way that made you feel like his commanding officer, and levered himself up from the table. He was moving more stiffly than usual, and his lighter skin showed the bruising over his brow even more strikingly.

"Are you all right?" Varazda asked.

A look of startled guilt passed across Yazata's face, a much more Yazata-like expression than the stern glare.

"Mm?" said Damiskos. "Oh, I'll be fine. Not that I want to take you on again any time soon, sir," he added with a wry smile at Yazata.

Yazata, of course, did not smile back. After the briefest hesitation, Damiskos leaned across the table to kiss Varazda's cheek lightly. He straightened up, said good night in Zashian, and turned toward his bedroom.

"God guard your sleeping and your waking," said Varazda without thinking.

Dami looked back over his shoulder and flashed a smile.

When he was gone, Yazata took a couple of steps into the room, the sternness disappearing from his expression.

"What is it?" he hissed urgently.

"What?" Varazda demanded.

Yazata made a shushing gesture. "My dear, what is happening to you? What *has* happened to you? You can tell me."

Varazda gave him a mystified frown. These were questions that he thought, more properly, he should have been asking Yazata.

"Can I? It hasn't seemed that way. Which—" He unbent, with an effort. "—is fine. We're not alike, in this respect. If you thought we were … I am sorry." He hadn't thought that was the case; he had thought his friend understood him better than that.

Now Yazata looked confused. Finally he said, "I do have experience of … this type of thing. I can help."

"Are we talking about the same thing?" Varazda asked, after another confused moment. He wondered fleetingly whether he was half-asleep already.

"Yes." Yazata glanced pointedly toward the door of Dami's room.

At that moment the door opened, and Dami shooed the cat out. He gave the two of them a questioning look, then shut the door.

"Remember what I said," Yazata whispered earnestly, then turned and fled up the stairs on his side of the house.

On the edge of falling asleep where he sat, Varazda

remembered when he had last seen Yazata similarly angry. It had been a couple of years ago, when Maia moved in across the street and they first met her worthless husband, Stamos. Yazata hadn't tried to hit him with a frying pan, but then there hadn't been any frying pans handy; it was hard to say what might have happened if there had been.

CHAPTER 5

VARAZDA WOKE on a divan in the sitting room and for a moment couldn't remember what he was doing there. He pushed himself up and raked his hair out of his face. The events of the previous night came back to him. He groaned.

The room was bright with sun, the house quiet around him. When he looked through the door to the kitchen, there was evidence that at least one person had breakfasted, and a bowl covered with a cloth on the table. He went back into the sitting room and eased open the door to Damiskos's room, thinking he would like to look in at Dami sleeping.

Of course Damiskos was awake, sitting on the bed with his good knee drawn up, looking out the window.

"Good morning," said Varazda.

Damiskos smiled. "I like the flowers," he said, indicating the bouquet on the window sill.

"I'm glad. Remi and I picked them for you. Did you sleep … at all? 'Well' would be a stretch, I realize."

"Not too badly." He swung his legs over the edge of the bed. "No sign of Ariston?"

"Not yet."

Dami nodded. "I, uh, thought I'd wait for you to wake before I ventured out. That's probably cowardly … "

Varazda laughed wryly. "Not at all. It's probably very wise."

The bowl on the table contained warm saffron buns. Dami sat at the table and buttered one while Varazda jogged upstairs to see whether Remi was still in bed.

Her little alcove in his bedroom was empty, both her bed and his own neatly made. Varazda smiled to himself at this evidence of Yazata's thoughtfulness—his love, in fact, for both of them. He went back downstairs.

"These are good," Dami said, holding up his half-eaten bun.

"Have you not had saffron buns before?"

"Yes, I just meant … er, they're very good saffron buns."

This was clearly not what he had intended to say.

"You mean," Varazda guessed, "that you're surprised there are no goose turds or, I suppose, fish sauce in them?"

"I'm sure I deserve both, after last night," said Dami, looking at the table, "but I didn't mean to suggest that Yazata isn't forgiving."

"He is," said Varazda. *Usually.* "But it was brave of you to try the buns."

"I'm known for my courage. Is Remi still asleep?"

"No, I think she's gone out with Yaza." He glanced through the open door to Yazata's sitting room, which was empty. "I'm just going to check whether they're outside." He shrugged apologetically. "I like to know where she is."

He'd been some years older than Remi when he was abducted from his own family home, which had been a fortress far more secure than any of the houses in Saffron Alley. He never explained to anyone how this coloured the way he raised his own child.

"Of course," said Dami, getting up from the table

himself, a second saffron bun in hand. He followed Varazda down the hall to the door.

Varazda pulled open the front door just as the tall, bearded man on the doorstep was raising his hand to the knocker. It was hard to say which of them was more startled.

"Marzana!"

"Varazda, good morning." Marzana collected himself more quickly.

"Just the man I wanted to see."

"Yes, I daresay." Then Marzana's eyes widened as he caught sight of Damiskos over Varazda's shoulder. "I, uh … " He obviously forgot what he had been about to say.

"Damiskos, this is my friend Marzana," Varazda supplied quickly. "He's chief officer of the city's public watch. Marzana, this is Damiskos. He's—"

"Delighted to meet you," Marzana interrupted, too heartily.

He all but lunged to clasp Damiskos by the hand, and there were several false starts before they sorted out whether they were going to shake hands in the Pseuchaian fashion or the Zashian—rendered even more complicated by the fact that Dami was still holding a buttered saffron bun—and they both laughed a little too loudly about it.

From the street Varazda heard a familiar squeal, and looking past Marzana he saw Remi chasing one of Maia's daughters, Selene waddling after her, and Yazata sitting on the steps of Maia's house with Maia, shelling peas and talking earnestly. Varazda wondered if Yazata had come up with a sufficiently Zashian way of asking whether her husband was due home. He hadn't heard whether the gambit with the eggs had been successful or not.

Maia was a tiny, blonde woman who could not have been more of a contrast to Yazata in appearance, but in temperament they were extremely alike and had been close friends ever since her family moved to Saffron Alley. The two of them glanced up at Varazda at the same moment, waved, and then went on talking. About him, presumably. They weren't even trying to be subtle about it.

That part of his family accounted for, Varazda turned to beckon Marzana into the house. He left the door open behind him.

Marzana followed him down the hall, and Damiskos followed Marzana. No one said anything until they were in the kitchen, and then the best Varazda could do was, "Would you like a saffron bun?"

"Thank you, no," said Marzana.

There was a moment's awkward silence. Marzana glanced at Dami, who was looking a little warily at him. Marzana was about his size, and very Zashian-looking, though he had lived in Boukos for nine years and had a Boukossian wife and Boukossian sons. He still wore his hair long, his beard hennaed where it had gone grey, and dressed in trousers more often than not. He could probably tell that Damiskos was an ex-soldier, because he was one himself; he even walked with a limp, though it was very slight compared to Dami's.

"Yes," said Marzana, drawing himself up a little as if recalling himself to the matter at hand. "The reason I called this morning. Do you have any idea why Tash presented himself to my watchmen last night claiming to have killed a man who is not dead?"

They convinced Marzana to take a saffron bun after all and sit at the table with them while they explained what had happened the previous night. He in turn told them what he knew.

"Tash presented himself at the watch-house in the early hours of the morning. The night shift was about to go off duty, and I had not yet arrived. Apparently the first words out of his mouth were, 'If you're looking for the murderer of Themistokles Glyptikos, I am he.' He seemed nonplussed to learn that they were not looking for Themistokles's murderer. He refused to explain how or why he had done the murder—he didn't even seem sure it had been a murder rather than, say, an accident.

"My men did their duty and detained him while they sent some of their fellows to Themistokles's house to investigate. By this time the sun was up, and when they knocked at the door, Themistokles answered. He was up early, working in his studio. He said he had passed a peaceful night and had no altercations with anyone, nor seen any sign of a break-in or other foul play about his house.

"When my men described Tash, without revealing what he had told them, Themistokles readily identified his student and asked whether Tash was in some trouble as if it surprised him. As, indeed, it surprised me when I heard about it.

"When the men returned from Themistokles's to say that he seemed in good health for a murder victim, Tash had nothing at all to say for himself—refused to utter a word. They released him from the cells, not knowing what else to do, and left him in a courtyard room awaiting my arrival. By the time I got there, of course, he was gone. I take it he hasn't been back here?"

"Not to my knowledge," said Varazda. "So Themistokles is alive and well."

"The last I heard. I left a guard on his door for the sake of caution. And obviously I want to speak to Tash to find out what this is about."

"Perhaps he killed someone else thinking it was Themistokles," Damiskos suggested.

"That is what I suspect," said Marzana, nodding. "A fight in the dark or some such thing."

"He was clearly distraught about it," Dami went on. "He

62

didn't know whether he'd meant to do it or not. As one doesn't, sometimes, in the heat of the moment."

"Exactly. One strikes a killing blow knowing that it may kill, yet not *desiring* the other man's death. He feels confused."

"For some reason he thinks it was his master that he struck. Perhaps he was expecting to meet him in a certain place, and when someone else—a thief, say—showed up instead, he struck out in his own defence without realizing his mistake."

"I wonder if he had some reason to fear his master. I have never heard anything credible against Themistokles."

"I think Ariston was simply confused," Damiskos said.

"Ariston?"

"Tash. He calls himself Ariston—at least he did to me when we met last night."

"Ah. That's new." Marzana looked at Varazda, eyebrows raised. Varazda shrugged. "Right. Well … Ariston … kills this other man, doesn't take the time to check who it is—"

"Perhaps he can't because the body ended up in the river. No, you don't have a river here."

"In the harbour," Marzana supplied. "Good thought. So he doesn't actually know who it was, but he knows he's dead, and he races off to turn himself in to the watch." He looked over at Varazda. "You're very quiet. What do you think?"

"I think all that makes sense." He'd been quiet because he was listening raptly to his friend and his lover finishing each other's sentences. "Personally, I'd have thought he was protecting the person who really did kill Themistokles. But if Themistokles isn't dead, obviously that won't wash."

"Quite," said Marzana.

"Exactly," said Damiskos at the same time.

"In any case, we need to find him," said Marzana. "Do you have any idea where he'd have gone if he didn't come back here?"

"He spends most of his time at Themistokles's studio. I suppose you've been back there?

"He's not there. Is there … " Marzana hesitated delicately.

"A girl?" Dami supplied. "Or a boy?"

Varazda sighed. "A girl. There's always a girl. Sometimes there's more than one girl. At the moment I believe there is very much only one—she's a goddess, apparently, the lodestar of whatnot—but I've absolutely no idea who she is. Except … I can't remember why, but I've formed the distinct impression that she's older than T—than Ariston." Dami's courteous attention to referring to Tash by his chosen name reminded Varazda that he should do the same. "Less a girl, in fact, than a woman."

"That's … not a great deal of help," said Marzana, giving him a look.

"I know. Sorry."

"I wonder," said Dami, "if he'd have gone to this woman when he's on the run from the law, though, if he worships the ground she treads on."

"Good point," said Marzana.

"Not my area," said Varazda shortly. "But I suppose he might have gone to one of his friends. I know a few of them. I can go look for him."

"If you would," said Marzana. "I'd like to get this cleared up."

"Of course. I'll track him down. If he's out there wandering around—I'm worried about him."

Marzana nodded. "I apologize for … " His gaze flicked toward Damiskos, his expression slightly guilty. "I mean, you have a guest to entertain."

Dami cleared his throat. "Perhaps I can help. I feel it's partly my fault he got away last night."

"You needn't feel that," said Varazda firmly.

"I'd just as soon not have to put any of my men on this,"

Marzana said. "We've a lot of work to do before the Asteria tomorrow."

"Tomorrow," Varazda repeated. "It *is* tomorrow, isn't it? I believe I'd actually forgotten."

"You're Phemian, aren't you?" Marzana said to Dami. It was obvious enough from his looks and his accent. "Are you … a newcomer to Boukos?"

"A visitor," Damiskos explained equably. "It is not my first time in the city, but I have never been here for a festival before."

"We take our festivals very seriously," said Marzana. "And how did you come to meet Varazda?"

"At Laothalia in the summer," Varazda supplied before Dami had time to worry what to say.

At that the pieces obviously fell into place in Marzana's mind. He looked at Damiskos with a sudden, startled respect. "You're the Phemian officer Varazda spoke of. Of course! First Spear of the Second Koryphos?"

Dami smiled embarrassedly. "I, uh, gather Varazda has talked about me."

"You saved his life," said Marzana gravely. "All his friends are indebted to you."

"No, he—" Damiskos started to correct him, then stopped. "Did I save your life?"

"Several times, I think," said Varazda. "One doesn't keep track."

"Some do," said Marzana. "In any case"—He gave Dami a rather military nod of his own.—"it is an honour and pleasure to meet you."

After Marzana had left, Varazda went upstairs to dress, while Dami went to his room to do the same. Varazda was fastening his belt when he was startled by loud goose noises from downstairs, followed by a thump, and Damiskos's voice calling, "Oi! A little help?"

Feeling that this was beginning to become a habit, Varazda tore down the stairs to find Selene in the kitchen, flapping and hissing and making determined lunges at Dami, who had tidily barricaded himself behind the table, which he had flipped on its side.

"Holy God, I'm sorry—how did she get in the house? Let me get Remi."

"Please."

He ran to the front of the house to find the door mysteriously closed. Opening it, he shouted out into the street for his daughter, who came running, wide-eyed with surprise.

"Will you please get Selene out of the house?"

"But—but Maia told me to put her in the house."

"What? Well—get her out again, please. She and Damiskos aren't friends yet."

Remi scurried obediently into the kitchen and quieted her pet. Varazda looked across the street at Maia, who was still sitting on her doorstep with Yazata. She nodded at him with a strange expression that almost looked like reassurance. Not feeling up to analyzing what that was about, Varazda retreated into the house to supervise the removal of the goose and help Dami right the kitchen table.

"I wish I could promise you that won't happen again," he said.

"No," said Damiskos, "I quite see that you can't. I may have overreacted." He gestured to the table. "Do they—I'm not familiar with pet geese—do they eventually stop doing that, or am I going to have to learn to defend myself? I couldn't help but notice that you didn't approach her yourself."

"No, well, she doesn't go for everyone like that, just people she doesn't know in the house, especially if they're

66

near Remi. But I have been bitten a few too many times to approach her when she's angry."

Dami nodded gravely. "I see. I will continue to be on my guard."

"I'm afraid that's wisest."

He didn't mention that this attack seemed as if it might have been premeditated. Perhaps he was imagining things.

CHAPTER 6

"One of the places I think he goes to meet his friends is a local bath-house," Varazda said. "If we find him there, we can kill two birds with one stone and get a bath too."

Varazda got his sandals fastened. For the second day in a row, he was dressed in a plain tunic, without makeup or jewellery, and all he had done with his hair was to hastily braid it. He wondered again whether Tash had arranged all of this especially to ruin his time with Dami.

"It's not where you usually go?" Dami had got his own sandals on and was eying his cane by the front door, evidently trying to decide whether to take it or not.

"No, I usually go to the Baths of Soukos. They're a little further, but they have the best pool in the city. I've never been to this place Ariston goes. I assume it's fashionable."

"Well," said Dami, picking up his cane, "lead the way."

Out in the street, Varazda blew a kiss to Remi and one to Yazata, and each returned the gesture in their own way. Maia was gone from her stoop by this time, and the door to her house stood open. Dami was focussed on putting a comfortable distance between himself and Selene as quickly as possible.

"We're going to look for Tash!" Varazda called across the street.

"Why?" Yazata half started up from the step, clutching his bowl of peas. "Where is he?"

"Well, we don't know. But Themistokles isn't dead—"

"Marzana told me. What happened?"

"We don't know," Varazda repeated patiently. "But Tash doesn't need to hide from the watch. And, obviously, he has some explaining to do."

Yazata sat back down. "I see." He darted a worried glance at Dami, then looked down at the peas before adding, "God guard your coming and your going."

As soon as Varazda had known the date on which Dami would arrive, he had cleared his schedule as best he could for the days immediately following. It had meant cancelling one dance class, postponing a non-urgent piece of work for the Basileon, and finding someone to cover for him in the music shop, where he had been helping a few days a week since Gia's husband got sick. All this meant that he had a free day, but it had come at some cost, and he was not pleased to have to use it searching for Tash.

Dami was subdued and stern, and Varazda wasn't sure how to cheer him up without flippancy. He was probably worried about slowing Varazda down, and Varazda wished he would say something about it, so he could be appropriately reassured. Though of course Varazda *was* walking slower than he would have if alone, whether it was strictly necessary or not.

Tash's usual bath-house was not at all what Varazda had expected. It was small and dingy, the slave at the door sleepily contemptuous.

"Ariston? Which one? I know a dozen. Most of 'em foreigners. Aristons and Demoses and Nikos. That'll be one obios each, sirs."

Varazda paid for both of them, and they went in. He was

beginning to doubt he had the right place, but then he saw the sign painted on the wall of the small, dim entry hall. FOREIGNERS, it said, above an arrow pointing to the left, and for the benefit of the illiterate there were a couple of very poor drawings of men in trousers and hats.

When they followed the arrow, they found themselves in a steamy hallway with a gutter running down the middle, flanked by rows of private bath cubicles.

There was nothing wrong with it. The place was clean and respectable, if a little shabby, a small business catering to the city's growing population of Zashians and Shandians who liked their privacy while they bathed. But it wasn't the smart, fashionable establishment Varazda had imagined Tash frequenting, and he knew why. It made him sad.

Dami was looking at him with one of his quiet, penetrating gazes. "The Baths of Soukos, where you go—they don't have a section like this, do they?"

Varazda shook his head. "They're ordinary Pseuchaian public baths. But I'm not twenty-one."

They loitered a few minutes in the foreigners' section, but there was no good place for waiting or meeting anyone there, and they drew suspicious glances from the few patrons who passed. There was no sign of Tash, and frankly it seemed unlikely that he would be there. It was obviously just a place to bathe, not to socialize.

"Tash—Ariston—he's not really a foreigner. He's lived in Boukos since he was a child. He never wears Zashian clothes, doesn't have any Zashian friends apart from Yazata and me. He's given himself a Pseuchaian name. I know he doesn't come here because he *wants* to bathe in private. He used to come to the Baths of Soukos with me until a couple of years ago, and then he told me he was going to some new place his friends had introduced him to."

Dami made a sympathetic face. "I'm glad you don't. Come here, I mean."

They left the bath-house, under the suspicious eye of the doorman, and in the street outside Varazda was surprised to hear his name called—his real name, not the Pseuchaian version. He looked up to see his friend Shorab, a clerk of about his own age, hurrying down the street toward the bath-house.

"Varazda, I wondered when I would run into you here," he said, sounding delighted. "But I see you're on your way out, so I can't invite you for a drink. Maybe another time?"

"Of course," said Varazda, smiling. "My house is not far from here."

"Oh, really? Such a nice part of town!"

Shorab smiled and nodded at Dami, but did not offer his name or give Varazda the chance to supply Dami's. Shorab was still very Zashian, from his felt hat and silky beard to his manners. He spoke Pseuchaian scrupulously and correctly, as did everyone at the embassy. On formal occasions he wore a sword, a more modern, steel version of Varazda's.

"They're not very good baths," Shorab was saying, "but I'm not brave enough to face the Pseuchaian bath-houses, myself. Farhata used to try to talk me into it … " For a moment his face fell, then he collected himself. "But he never succeeded. Well—I shall see you around soon, I'm sure. God guard your coming and your going."

"And yours," said Varazda with a bow.

Shorab went into the bath-house, and Varazda and Dami walked on down the street.

"I'm sorry for not introducing you," Varazda said, knowing it was not necessary but still feeling he should say it.

Dami smiled. "I remember it took me a while to get used to the way Zashians do introductions—or *don't* do introductions. I would meet people and tell them my name, and they'd look at me as if I'd made a rude noise and they were trying not to notice."

Varazda laughed. "Shorab is his name. I've no objection

71

to telling you. He works at the embassy, as you might imagine. The other name he mentioned … Farhata. He was one of the ambassador's aides, the one who was killed a month ago when the embassy was set on fire. He and Shorab were old friends."

"I'm sorry."

"Shorab has been very angry about how little justice has been done in that case."

Dami nodded and did not ask for details. Perhaps he already knew.

They went next to a bakery in the square at the end of the street, in search of one of Tash's former girlfriends with whom he seemed still to be friendly. They found her cutting squares of syrup-soaked cake behind the bakery counter.

"I've no idea, haven't seen him for *ages*," she replied cheerfully when Varazda asked about Tash. "You're his brother, right? Do you know about his new girl?"

"No, not really," said Varazda warily. He wasn't sure how much old girlfriends and new girlfriends were supposed to mix, and whether this was a fishing expedition on her part, or an offer to share information, or what.

"Oh, I don't know anything either—he's been very secretive lately—but I think she might work in Temple Walk. I mean," she added, giggling, "as somebody's maid or something."

"Right," said Varazda, keeping his eyebrows from rising with an effort. "Thanks."

"Tell him to come visit when you see him—we all miss him. Would you like some cake?" She smiled winningly at Dami, who, Varazda realized, had been eyeing the cake throughout their conversation.

"We'd love some," Dami said promptly. "Oh, I mean—can we spare the time?" He looked doubtfully at Varazda.

"We can spare the time," said Varazda.

"My treat." Dami dug in the wallet on his belt for some coins.

Tash's ex-girlfriend put two generous slices onto a plate and set them on the counter. She took Dami's money and walked back to put it in the cash box, affording them a view of her belly, round as a melon under her dress.

"Oh," she said suddenly, looking down at herself. "I hope you're not thinking—" She laughed. "This isn't Tash's!"

Varazda managed to maintain a neutral expression, and Dami stuffed a large chunk of cake into his mouth, presumably to stop himself saying, "Of course not!"

Perhaps she'd just forgotten—or perhaps she had never known. Either way it made Varazda sad, in rather the same way as the foreigners' section of the bath.

Dami was halfway through his square of cake by this time, so Varazda hurried to catch up. It was delicious, definitely an improvement on the bath-house.

"Where to now?" Dami asked when they emerged in the street, full of cake and somewhat sticky-fingered.

"There's a wine shop Ariston frequents—it belongs to the family of one of his friends, one of his more reliable friends. We should ask in there."

"Lead the way."

The shop, at the sign of the laurel leaf in the Vintners' District, was probably their best bet for finding Tash—the bakery had been a long shot but conveniently close—and it was also in a scenic part of the city. Varazda pointed out the landmarks to Dami as they passed.

"That's the Sanctuary of Terza, down there." A plain white building stood at the foot of a long flight of shallow steps. "You can get there from the other side too, off New Philadion Street." Without the stairs. He didn't say that.

73

He realized he didn't know how often worshippers of Terza had to visit their temple. Perhaps he should have asked Marzana's son about that, at the same time as he had asked about where they put their portable shrines.

"That's good to know. I usually go to the Bread Day ceremonies," Dami said.

"I realize you can't tell me about those," said Varazda with a smile.

"Oh, no, I can. And I will, if you're interested. Though it's very … I don't know how interesting it is, from the outside."

"I'm sure I can manage to stay awake," said Varazda lightly. "Since it's an important part of your life."

"It is," Dami said slowly, and left it at that.

They reached the Vintners' District, with its wine shops and warehouses and heady, grapey aroma, and found the sign of the laurel. It was a small shop on a corner, its shutters gleaming with a fresh coat of sky-blue paint, vines cascading down above the door. The morning was pretty far gone by this time, and the shop was open, though empty of customers. Tash's friend Stratos was sweeping the doorstep with an apron on. He looked up at their approach.

"Pharastes, hello! What can I get you?" His glance flicked to Dami, and his eyes widened a little, then his smile widened to match.

"We're looking for Ariston, actually. Have you seen him today?"

"Who? Oh, Tasos! Shit, I forgot we're supposed to call him Ariston now. Yeah. I mean no. I haven't seen him, but Dad said he came by looking for me while I was out getting pastries. We've got fresh pastries, by the way—what kind would you like? The cheese ones are really good with the Kastian red we've got right now."

If the pastries were still fresh, that meant Tash had been here not that long ago.

"Can we speak to your father, please? We need to find out where Ariston went."

"The Kastian red is really good too, sir."

"Stratos. Can we speak to your father, please."

"Sure thing, sir."

Stratos dove back inside the shop, his broom clattering to the floor. He was a long time coming back. Varazda began to think that they might as well have ordered wine at this point. There were no seats in front of the shop, and he didn't like to make Dami stand for so long. He reminded himself that Dami was tough—almost as tough as he looked—and would be furiously embarrassed if he knew Varazda was worrying about him like this.

Finally Stratos returned, followed by his father, wiping his hands on his own apron.

"This is Tasos's friend Pharastes." Stratos waved an arm, presenting Varazda.

"Ah yes," said Stratos's father. "We have met, I believe. Young Tasos was here early this morning."

So apparently the pastries were not all that fresh. He should have known.

"Do you know where he was going?" Varazda asked. "It is somewhat urgent that we find him."

"I couldn't say, no. He wanted to see Stratos, said something about—oh! He said something about the theatre." Stratos's father looked pleased with himself. "Perhaps he wanted Stratos to come to the theatre with him, I couldn't say. He seemed in a rush, though. Unkempt. Not like him," he conceded. "I'm sorry I can't help you more."

"No, that's very helpful, thank you."

Stratos, who had gone back inside the shop again, had returned by this time with two of the not-exactly-fresh cheese pastries in a dish, a wine jug under his arm, and a couple of cups dangling from his fingers. To his obvious chagrin, his father handed the pastries over to Varazda and

75

Dami for free, and did not press them to sit down and drink.

They walked away down Little Bridge Street.

"Not as good as that cake," Dami remarked, scrutinizing his half-eaten pastry. "But it would probably be better with a cup of Kastian red. Are we headed to the theatre?"

"If you're up for it. It is a longish walk."

"I'm prepared." Dami flourished his cane with a wry grin.

Varazda smiled gently back at him. He could think of a variety of things to say, but a friendly nothing seemed the best of all.

They pressed on to the Theatre of Polykratos, a half-circle of pink stone set into the side of a hill on the edge of town, in what had until a few years ago been a wooded park. The theatre was unfinished; the niches in the wall behind the stage stood empty, and the imported pink stone had a raw, unworn look to it. But plays were already being staged here. Varazda had gone with some friends to see a really biting satire of Boukossian politics, back in the spring.

There was a rehearsal underway when they arrived at the top steps. Actors without costumes or masks were declaiming their lines from the stage.

"To the palace! The vizier must be stopped!"

Two of the actors rushed in opposite directions at the same moment, turned in confusion, rushed the other way, collided with perfect timing, and tumbled to the stage.

Dami chuckled, and Varazda glanced at him in surprise. He wasn't sure what he had expected Dami's taste in theatre to be, but somehow he hadn't imagined him laughing at a straightforward farce. It was a pleasant surprise, though. Varazda took a guilty pleasure in low comedy himself.

Besides the actors, there were only a few people in the theatre, mostly workers sweeping fallen leaves from the ranks of marble seats. From where Dami and Varazda stood, they had a good view of the whole place, and Tash was nowhere to be seen.

"It was a long shot," Varazda said gloomily. "He may not have come here at all if he couldn't get Stratos to come with him."

"What would they have come here for, do you think? When there's no performance on. Is he friends with one of the actors?"

"Not that I know of, but ... ah! He does have a friend who works in the park. He's the head gardener. An old man —I've no idea how Ariston comes to know him."

This meant wandering the park in search of the gardener's house, which was of course well hidden to avoid detracting from the beauty of the carefully maintained wilderness. It was in fact very beautiful: a style of garden that was popular in Boukos but also felt very Zashian. They talked about that as they walked. Dami seemed to have an interest in gardening, and knew more about the varieties of plants and trees than Varazda.

Then they reached the head gardener's cottage, and there was the old man himself, sitting on a bench outside his door, and beside him, hunched over a wine-cup, in the clothes he'd had on last night, was Tash. Relief made Varazda feel a surge of affection for him.

Luckily, Varazda and Dami came around the corner of the cottage, so they were quite close when Tash looked up and saw them. He made no more than a token attempt to rise from the bench.

"Hello," said the gardener, eyeing them speculatively. He was white-haired and weatherbeaten, but still sturdy, his shoulders broad, his hands strong. "Can I help you?"

"It's my housemate Pharastes," Tash supplied sullenly, before Varazda could speak. "And his—whatever." He flapped an unenthusiastic hand at Dami. "They've probably been *looking* for me."

77

"Did you want to be found?" asked the gardener, looking up at Dami and Varazda as if considering whether he should chase them off with his pruning hook or not.

Tash mumbled something into his wine cup. The gardener seemed to come to a decision, and got to his feet, but only to walk to the other side of his door and bring back a couple of wooden stools, which he set down opposite the bench.

"My name's Giontes," he said, resuming his seat.

"Damiskos Temnon." Dami offered his hand. "You have a beautiful park here." He pulled one of the stools closer to the gardener's side of the bench and sat. Gesturing to some plants near the cottage door, he said, "How do you get the rosemary to grow so well in pots? I've never seen it do so well potted."

"Ah," said the gardener. "I can tell you about that."

Tash sat and stared with a look of astonished disgust as his friend launched into an animated discussion of the way to grow rosemary in pots. Then he glared up at Varazda.

"What the fuck did you come here for? To talk about fucking rosemary?"

"Not exclusively," said Varazda, pulling up his own stool and dropping down onto it. "Marzana wants to talk to you."

"I've got nothing to say to him."

"I know, but I think maybe you should come up with something to say. Something other than 'I killed Themistokles Glyptikos,' because we all know you didn't."

Tash swirled the wine in his cup and stared bleakly at it.

"You want me to tell Marzana the truth, don't you."

"I do."

"Because he's your friend."

"Because he's the chief of the public watch, mainly. But because he's my friend—and your friend—I know you can trust him. If you killed somebody … " He let that hang there, gently.

"I didn't kill anybody," Tash replied irritably. "Nobody's dead. I mean—I guess a lot of people are dead, but ... "

"Not Themistokles."

"No, I guess not."

"Which is a good thing, right?"

"Of course it's a good thing!" Tash looked up, his face full of conflicting emotions. "Holy shit. I can't even tell you. When I thought he was dead—God, I'm glad he's not dead. He's—he's—I mean, I ... " He trailed off, unable to put his feelings for his master into words.

The gardener had got up and fetched another wine cup and filled it for Dami. The two of them had moved on to discussing fruit trees.

"Why did you think he was dead?" Varazda asked.

"I ... " Tash hesitated a long time, then tossed back the remainder of his wine and said, "I thought I heard somebody say they'd killed him."

So I was right after all, Varazda thought. *He was trying to protect someone.* Things were beginning to make a tiny bit more sense.

"Do you think," he said with the utmost gentleness, "it's possible that you misheard?"

Tash dropped his head into his hands. "Not misheard, just mis ... misinterpreted. Like an idiot. There wasn't even *time* for them to have killed him, if I'd have stopped to think about it. I don't even know why I was so sure that's what they meant, I just—something about the way sh—they—said it ... "

"How was that?"

"So, so *violently*."

"It was something about ... harming Themistokles in some way?"

"Yeah, I guess. Yeah. But I don't know why—I mean, I thought, if they'd done it, they must've had a good reason, you know? That's why I ... "

"That's why you tried to protect them."

Tash nodded miserably.

"Do you know who … this person … was talking to, when they said this?"

"No. I never heard him clearly. Just a male voice. It doesn't matter now, though, does it? Themistokles isn't dead, or even—whatever."

"Even threatened?"

"What?"

"He isn't even threatened? Are you sure of that?"

"I, uh … " Tash whimpered. "No, I guess I'm not. But I don't think so."

"Maybe we had better let Marzana make up his mind about that. You did involve the watch, and he is personally concerned about you."

Tash groaned. "I just—I was trying—immortal fuck, why do I even try to do anything?"

At that point the gardening conversation that had been going on at the other end of the bench hit a lull, and Dami caught Varazda's eye with a questioning look.

"We do owe Marzana an explanation," said Varazda firmly.

"But—we don't have to tell him what really happened, do we?"

"That's usually what's meant by 'an explanation,' yes. He thinks you might have killed someone else by accident. You'll need to disabuse him of that notion, and it will need to be convincing. I'd suggest the whole truth."

"Oh. Well, I'll tell him, but … I mean, I'll tell him." Tash looked shifty. Varazda was not satisfied, but he left it at that.

"Let's go home, Ariston," Varazda said, unfolding himself from the stool.

Tash looked up at him, wide-eyed, for a moment confused by his chosen name.

"Oh. Right. I guess we'd ... we could. I don't—I mean, I don't have anything else to do right now."

Dami thanked the gardener for his hospitality, the gardener said, "If you ever want any cuttings, come see me," and they shook hands like old friends.

Tash's gaze flicked warily to Dami, then back to Varazda. "Is he all right?" he asked in an undertone, in Zashian. "Yaza didn't—with the frying pan—did he?"

"Yazata almost broke his own nose," Varazda said, in Pseuchaian, "and Damiskos speaks Zashian, so that's not an effective way to talk behind his back."

"Oh," said Tash, chastened. "Sorry."

"Maybe say that to him?"

"Right. Yeah."

And he did, fumblingly but sincerely, as the three of them walked back through the park toward the theatre.

"It's all right," said Dami, with one of his serious smiles. "I understand that you were distraught."

"Yeah, but ... I was lying, too. I didn't think I'd killed my master. I thought somebody else had, and I ... "

"You wanted to protect that person," Dami supplied after a moment, when Tash seemed to have run out of momentum. "Varazda guessed it was that."

"Yeah. I just ... It was like a nightmare." Tash shuddered, and didn't pull away when Varazda put an arm around his shoulders and gave them a slight squeeze.

"So," said Varazda, "Ariston. How do you feel about going to talk to Marzana?"

Ariston sighed. "I don't really want to. Could it wait ... until tomorrow?"

"Tomorrow's the Asteria," Varazda reminded him.

"Shit, yeah. I forgot."

"Which one is the Asteria?" Dami asked. "Is that the festival where everybody, uh, gets drunk and has sex?"

"That's the Psobion," Ariston supplied. "The Asteria is in honour of Kerialos."

"Oh, right, of course. The one where the women take over the city."

Varazda nodded. "And men are expected to stay home unless they have a chaperone."

"I've heard they can be quite strict about it." After a moment, looking at Varazda thoughtfully, he said, "What do you do?"

The question pleased Varazda. He liked that Dami didn't take it for granted that he knew which side Varazda would fall on, when the city divided itself by sex.

"I usually dress up and go out," he said. "I have to be a bit careful where I go—some people think of it as cheating. But I have friends who understand, and I generally go out with them. This year, of course, I'll only go if you want to come."

"I wouldn't want to cramp your style—but I don't particularly want to stay home with Yazata's cooking and the murderous goose, either. I'll come." After a moment he added, "I look forward to seeing you dressed up."

"What did Yaza cook?" Ariston asked curiously.

"Labash," said Varazda.

Ariston wrinkled his nose. "That stuff's disgusting."

"I quite like it," said Dami, "but it was *very* spicy."

Ariston laughed a little wanly. "Varazda, can we wait until after the Asteria to tell Marzana?"

"No … why?"

"He's not going to be able to do anything about it today."

"He might. It depends what he has to do. Who, for instance, he has to look for."

"It's no one, it's … I mean, look. Suppose we just wait. They wouldn't be able to find h—the person—today, because I know where they are, I tried to get to them today, and they just wouldn't."

"What?"

"Marzana and his watchmen wouldn't be able to find the person who was—or is—planning to kill Themistokles," Damiskos translated. "Who Ariston thought had succeeded, and whom he wishes to protect."

"No, no, nobody's planning to kill Themistokles! It was all a misunderstanding. I just—I want to talk to somebody first, before Marzana finds out."

"Warn them, in effect?" Varazda raised an eyebrow at him.

"Find out what really happened," Dami suggested diplomatically.

"That," said Ariston. "Yeah."

"Right," said Varazda. "And when you say 'we' will be able to go out tomorrow, just what do you mean?"

"You know. Whatever. Dressing up. If you can get away with it, so can I."

Varazda didn't bother to point out that he could pass for a woman because he had long hair and hips and pierced ears and in fact *looked* reasonably like a woman, and that Ariston didn't.

"Ariston, when I dress in women's clothes and go out for the Asteria, I do it because it means something to me. Not because I 'can get away with it.'"

Ariston rolled his eyes. "I'm not you, Varazda. I'm a man, all right? But I can pretend to be a woman. It doesn't have to *mean* anything."

"Ariston," said Dami gently, "this person we'd be going out to find tomorrow. Are you sure you'd like to show up dressed as a woman—considering that you'd prefer people know you're a man—when we find them?"

It was a master stroke. Varazda would never again accuse Dami of lacking subtlety or being awkward with people. He'd got the measure of Ariston, he'd put the suggestion tactfully, and he'd got through to him.

"Yeah," said Ariston. "I mean no. I mean, if I'm with you, Varazda, I can dress however, right?"

Varazda nodded. "Right."

And if he was dressed in men's clothes, he couldn't wander off by himself, Varazda realized. Brilliance. Sheer brilliance.

"I was thinking," said Dami, as they reached the street at the edge of the park, fronting the theatre, "that I might give the two of you a chance to talk privately. I'm going to take a chair home, if that's all right."

"What?" said Ariston. "That's not—"

"That is perfectly all right," said Varazda, smiling.

CHAPTER 7

"Papa," said Remi, climbing up onto the divan beside Varazda, "Why does Yaza call me the wrong word?"

Varazda looked up from the note he was trying to write to Marzana. "You mean Umit?"

"Mm-hmm."

He sighed. "Well, my sweet, in Zash, where Yazata and Tash and I used to live, sometimes girls have two names, and so Yazata wanted you to have two names: Remi, and Umit. But Remi is your real name."

She was silent for a moment, frowning. "But why did he call me the wrong word *in the house*?"

Oh, God. She'd understood more than Varazda had given her credit for. "You mean because Umit is the name he usually calls you outside the house, right?"

Should he lie? He tried never to lie to Remi if he could help it. He wanted her to learn to value honesty herself. So perhaps he ought to explain that when Zashian girls had two names, one was for use within their own families, the other for strangers, so that the girl's true name would not be spoken by unauthorized lips. He could explain that Yazata had wanted Remi to have a public name because it was traditional, but that even he rarely used it because nobody else did, and that he used it now, in their own home, as a deliberate insult to Damiskos. Remi could probably have understood some of that.

Damiskos almost certainly understood all of it already.

"I think," said Varazda in a conspiratorial tone, "that maybe he forgot."

"Forgot my *name*?" Remi squeaked.

Varazda nodded solemnly. "I think maybe."

Remi laughed her sweet, silvery laugh, and bounced down off the divan to run out into the kitchen calling, "Yaza, my name is Remi! *Remi*! Yaza, did you forget my name?"

Varazda looked across at Dami, seated in the corner of the divan, and shrugged apologetically. Dami smiled, but it was a rather sad smile.

"This is what I've written," Varazda said, tapping his stylus on the edge of the tablet. "*Ariston has been found safe and assures us that he has not killed anyone. He was trying to protect someone.* What do I say after that?"

"'We do not think there is any cause for alarm but will brief you as we learn more.'"

"Will what you?"

"Brief. It's a military term."

"How do you spell it?"

Dami spelled out the word for him, then scooted over on the divan to put his chin on Varazda's shoulder and look down at the tablet.

"It looks like a child's handwriting, I'm sure," said Varazda sourly.

"It's beautiful," said Dami, nuzzling up into Varazda's hair. "Just like you."

It was such a silly compliment, so glibly delivered, that Varazda had to laugh.

"I have prepared food for lunch," Yazata announced loudly from the doorway.

Dami sat bolt upright, and Varazda dropped the stylus, which rolled onto the floor.

"I don't think we're hungry," Varazda said, thinking of all the cake and stale pastries that they had eaten that morning. He looked at Dami, who looked stricken, as if he wanted to contradict Varazda but couldn't. "We're not hungry."

Yazata looked at them as if he suspected the phrase of some lewd double meaning. "I have prepared soup," he informed them, and turned majestically back into the kitchen.

Varazda went to pay Maia's older son to deliver the note to Marzana, and returned to find Dami sitting at the table with Remi, politely nibbling some slices of pear, while Ariston, groggy after being woken from a nap, mechanically spooned soup into his mouth. The only conversation in the room was provided by Remi, who was telling Damiskos a long story about someone named Poobos, who may not have been real. Presently, at a pause in the narrative, Dami excused himself and beckoned to Varazda.

"Is it safe for me to go out in the yard?" he whispered. "With the murder goose, I mean."

"I'll check."

Varazda preceded him out the kitchen door. Selene was indeed wandering loose in the yard, along with several of the chickens. He shooed them back into their enclosure and shut the gate.

"It's all yours," he said to Dami, gesturing toward the privy.

"Thanks."

Yazata was at the sink washing dishes when Varazda came back in.

"A word?" Varazda said, leaning against the counter beside Yazata.

"Of course."

"Did you and Maia put Remi up to setting Selene on Damiskos this morning?"

Yazata swished his dish-mop unnecessarily through the water for a moment. "We told Remi that Selene would not attack him—please do not blame her."

"I wasn't thinking of blaming her!"

"I can see now it was unworthy of us."

"Setting an angry goose on a lame man? Yes, I think I'd call that unworthy of you."

Yazata stood there looking at him as if he expected Varazda to say something more.

"Please don't do it again," said Varazda, pushing off from the counter and stalking back across the kitchen.

"Walking halfway across the city is well and good," Dami said when Varazda met him in the yard, "but I could use some real exercise. I don't suppose you'd care to … "

"What?"

"Spar with me."

"God, I'd love it." Varazda grinned. "Out here?"

Ariston and Remi burst out through the kitchen door and began tearing around the perimeter of the yard.

"Ah, maybe not. How about inside in your practice room?" Dami cocked an eyebrow. "An interesting challenge?"

Varazda felt an anticipatory shiver chase down his spine. Sparring with Damiskos was thrilling. Almost—well, not almost, but very nearly somewhere in the same region—as good as sex with him.

They went inside and through to the practice room, shutting the door behind them. Varazda caught down his swords from the brackets where they hung, in the fashion of his ancestors, while he wasn't using them. He tossed one to Dami and tucked the other under his arm to fold back his shirtsleeves, watching from under his lashes the way Dami hefted the blade, reacquainting himself with its weight and balance. God, he was lovely when he was in his element.

They stretched, each in his own way; Dami was much more businesslike, less delicate about it.

"Can I show you something you may not know?" Varazda said daringly. "As a warm-up?"

"Sure … " Dami looked half-intrigued, half-sceptical.

"Can you do this?"

Varazda held the sword lightly for a moment, balancing it in his fingers, and then he spun it, just a simple half-twist.

Dami gave a shout of laughter. "No! I can't do that."

"I'll teach you. Here."

He came around behind Dami, tucking his own sword out of the way in his sash, and reached around, his arm following the curve of Dami's.

"That's a ridiculous way to hold a sword," Dami said sternly as Varazda repositioned the hilt in his grip.

"Hush." He stepped away and drew his own sword again to demonstrate the beginning of the twist, as slowly as possible. "Try it."

And of course Dami got it on the first try, though he was never able to make it look particularly graceful. He was too economical in his movements, too inclined to brandish the sword instead of toying with it. Still, his big hands were more nimble than you might think. Varazda had known that, of course. He remembered watching Dami play the lute at the Hapikon bonfire. He remembered other things, too.

Then Dami turned the warm-up into the actual bout by spinning around, sword up, and catching Varazda's blade mid-twist. Varazda sprang back a step, then bounced forward again, swinging with both hands on the hilt and all his weight behind the motion. His sword clanged against Dami's, and Dami pushed it relentlessly back, a distinct gleam in his eye that told Varazda he hadn't found it too easy.

Varazda darted around him, ducking and spinning, more of a dance move than a sword-fighting one, and Dami's blade hissed delicately against the sleeve of his shirt, like a caress.

It was like being batted by a lion's paw with its claws drawn in. Except that with a beast you would never know how long you were safe, and with Dami you were *always* safe. Varazda would never have said he craved this kind of excitement, but there was something about it—the closeness of danger combined with the absolute absence of it—that stirred his blood in a way he had never known he wanted.

It *was* like sex, actually.

They fought with a mixture of laughter and serious concentration. Dami had been right that the room would present challenges, though they were mostly, as it turned out, challenges for Varazda. He found himself backed against walls, manoeuvred so that the sun from the window was in his eyes, and ducking around the chair. He got in a few blows, and he was pleased to find he remembered parries and attacks Dami had taught him a month ago.

Mostly he just revelled in watching—participating in—the glory that was Damiskos with a sword in his hand. He was neither flashy nor rough. He was strong and wickedly fast—except when his bad leg came into play—but most of all he was precise. Unerring, almost, in a way that Varazda knew took thought and long practice.

They sparred until they were both exhausted. Or, at any rate, until Varazda was exhausted, and Dami doing a good job of pretending the same state. Varazda liked to think he had at least tired him out a bit. Dami sank onto the one chair in the room, and Varazda lay flat on his back on the floor.

He looked up at Dami. "How is that so much fun?"

Dami chuckled slightly. "It is, isn't it?"

"For you too?"

"You know it."

He did, but it was still nice to hear.

"Can I ask you something?" said Dami.

"Of course."

90

"Are you … " He was leaning with his forearms on his knees, and his voice went low and a little rough. "Are you nervous about going to bed with me again?"

Varazda pushed his hands into his hair, feeling his face go still, his defenses come up. It was quite a Damiskos type of question, really. And when Varazda did not immediately answer, it got some even more Damiskos additions:

"I'd understand if you were. I don't mean—not that anybody *should* be nervous about going to bed with me, and you absolutely don't have to be, but if you are, maybe there's something I can say that will help? The thing is, I get the impression there's going to have to be some, uh, strategizing involved if we're ever to be alone together in a room with a bed, and so if there's anything … I just want you to know that I'm up for that. I don't mind talking about it."

"I'm not nervous, Dami." Varazda rolled up off the floor to his feet and held out a hand. "Let's go."

They were both sweaty, and it would probably be nicer if they weren't. But afterward, after … whatever they were going to do … they would be messy in a different way, and so they'd need to wash then, and there was only so much water in the cistern in the yard, and some of it needed to be saved for Yazata, who didn't go to the public baths, and none of this was ideal stuff to be thinking about while on the way to your lover's bed. Varazda knew that.

It was better than thinking about what he was going to do in his lover's bed and worrying that it was not going to be good enough.

Dami followed him into the bedroom, and Varazda latched the door behind them.

"Is this all right?" he found himself saying, at the same moment that Dami said, "What do you want to—"

"Oh," they both said.

"It's fine," said Dami. "Maybe a little abrupt, but … if you're in the mood. We're not being watched by philosophy students, so I'm good to go."

Varazda did his best to laugh, but the remark just brought him back to that night on the beach at Laothalia, himself nearly out of his mind with tension, throwing himself into what he imagined was a necessary public tryst with Damiskos with all the fatalism of a soldier throwing himself on a wall of enemy spears. And Dami being so gentle, so perfectly considerate. Barely touching Varazda, totally unconcerned with making good his boast to the students that he didn't mind being watched.

He shouldn't have to be so considerate every time they went to bed together. Anyone would tire of that.

Varazda swept one braid over his shoulder, untied the ribbon that held it in place, and shook it out with a careless gesture. He did the same to the others, combing his fingers through the mass of his hair. Dami liked his hair, he knew. Most people did.

He unbuttoned his shirt at the throat, pulled it off over his head from the hem up, the best way to get it off elegantly without getting tangled up in the fabric. Shirts that unbuttoned all the way down the front were better for that, but more buttons made them more expensive.

He stood in front of Damiskos no more undressed than he had been last night, feeling beautiful but ill-at-ease. He reached for one of Dami's hands, brought it to the ties that held his trousers closed at one hip.

Dami's expression was unreadable. He fumbled with the fabric for a moment, as if reluctant to touch Varazda too much, and when the second tie came undone, he caught the waistband of the trousers to keep them from sliding down too quickly. The fabric whispered over Varazda's skin, and he felt cold. He was not remotely aroused.

"Come." He reached for Dami's hand again and drew him toward the bed. Dami followed almost meekly.

They got Dami's clothes off—not complicated, really—and got on the bed together. Some dispassionate observer in Varazda's skin told him that it was not badly done, slithery and seductive without being overwhelming, and Dami could have nothing to complain of.

But Dami was still watching him intently, almost warily. This was the hard part. You couldn't fake it with Dami.

They ended up with Dami on his back and Varazda settled astride his thighs. Dami caught Varazda's hands and brought them down to his chest.

"Touch me?" he suggested with a little hopeful smile.

Varazda managed an answering smile and drew his hands down Dami's chest, lightly tickling the roughness of wiry hair with his nails, exploring the planes of muscle lower down. Dami threw one arm half over his face as if embarrassed, but he was still smiling. Varazda felt filled with affection for him.

He went on touching, mapping his lover's skin with his fingertips. The stubble along his jaw, the shape of his throat, the ridges of collarbone and shoulder, and the bulky muscles of his upper arms. He nudged one of Dami's thighs to the side so that he could move to kneel between Dami's absurdly gorgeous thighs.

He rubbed his thumbs over Dami's nipples, and Dami flinched and tensed with a low, appreciative sound. Varazda moved down again, thumbing the soft skin at the inside of Dami's hips, stroking his inner thighs, tangling his fingertips delicately in the dark curls of his private hair. He had not yet touched Dami's genitals. They were almost intimidatingly magnificent: big and beautifully formed, his member flushed with arousal, long and thick and straight.

"All right, love?" said Dami, reaching down to stroke Varazda's hair.

Varazda laughed.

He knew what he should do. He knew how to do it, too. He leaned gracefully down and swirled his tongue around the tip of Dami's manhood. His mouth filled with the familiar salty taste, and he felt Dami draw in a sharp breath, muscles stiffening under him. He pushed down onto Dami, tongue sliding over his length, relaxing his throat to take it all in. He knew how to do this.

He gagged. He couldn't get Dami out of his mouth fast enough—might even have scraped him with his teeth on the way up. He twisted away, coughing, tears stinging his eyes.

"I'm sorry," he said hoarsely when he could get his voice working. "I had intended … But I don't seem to be able … " He coughed again. "Did I hurt you?"

"No." Dami's own voice was rough. "Uh—close, but no."

Dami's erection had wilted almost completely. Varazda's hadn't quite come to fruition in the first place. He kept his face turned away from Dami, clamping his teeth shut on all the things his pride wouldn't let him say.

Not even a competent whore. You couldn't even go through with it.

Dami sat up, and Varazda waited for the solicitous question, for the consideration that he shouldn't need yet again. It didn't come, at least not in the form Varazda had been expecting. Dami said nothing, just sat there, his posture a little vulnerable, with Varazda still kneeling between his legs.

"Are you all right?" Dami said finally.

"Fine. I—"

There was a rush of air from the bedroom door opening. They both started and looked up to see Yazata in the doorway.

"What," Yazata cried breathlessly, "is going on?"

"Yazata!" Varazda growled, propelling himself off the bed and making for the door. "Get out."

Yazata flinched, averting his gaze but not moving from the doorway. "What were you—"

Varazda grabbed the edge of the door and held on, his arm shaking with the effort of not shoving it closed in Yazata's face.

"Yazata." He tried to keep his voice calm. "Please leave. Please don't ever do this again."

"But I thought … " Yazata murmured, wincing.

"Everything is fine. Please let me close the door."

"I heard sounds of violence!" Yazata blurted out finally. "What was he doing to you?"

As gently as possible, Varazda pushed the door closed, forcing Yazata back out into the sitting room. He clicked the latch into place and turned back toward Dami, who was sitting on the edge of the bed with a look of dismay on his face.

"I think … " Dami started.

"What?" Varazda snapped.

Dami's eyebrows twitched. "I think you're sexy when you're angry—but, uh, what I was going to say is I think that killed the mood pretty effectively."

"Which?" Varazda could hear but not control the savagery in his voice. "Yazata breaking down the door, or me nearly biting off your manhood?"

"I could do without either," Dami said mildly. He reached for his tunic, which lay across the head of the bed, and shrugged into it. "I'm starting to feel nostalgic for the drunk philosophers."

Varazda didn't know whether that was intended as a joke or a criticism, or which would be worse. He gathered up his own clothes and dressed at lightning speed.

"You know," he said, "in the king's household, 'dancer' is a euphemism. Like everything in Zash. You knew that, didn't you?"

"I … what? No?"

"I was a pleasure slave, really. I danced, but that wasn't really what I was for."

"I didn't know that." Dami's voice was suddenly hard.

"Now you do."

Now he did. And he was angry about it, clearly. Not angry because of what Varazda had been, surely, but angry that Varazda had kept it a secret.

There was another tap at the door.

"What. Now," Varazda snarled.

"Sorry," said Ariston loudly. "I—uh. There's a boy at the door with a message. He said you're needed at the embassy, like right now. I don't know, they've got a dancing emergency or something? Sorry."

"That's fine," said Varazda tightly. "Thank you."

"Uh. It's just that, you know, I should give the boy a tip, but I don't have any money."

"Did you look in the jar in the kitchen?"

"Ohhhh, you mean the jar in the kitchen where there's always money? No, I didn't. Thanks."

Ariston's footsteps receded into the kitchen. Varazda pinched the bridge of his nose. "Right. I have to go out. It's not a 'dancing emergency.' It's the Basileon."

"I see," said Dami. "'You're needed at the embassy' is a code."

"In a rudimentary sense." He looked back toward the bed. Dami was dressed by this time, his belt fastened, sitting on the edge of the mattress. "I'm sorry, Dami. This isn't going as well as I had hoped."

"It's just how these things go," said Dami. "Don't worry about me, I'll be fine. I have a book to read. You attend to your dancing emergency."

CHAPTER 8

IT WAS early evening when Varazda came back to the house. His mood was not greatly lightened by the meeting he'd had, but he had visited the embassy library and borrowed several books, which he carried under his arm. He heard voices in the kitchen: Remi monologuing in her three-year-old way, and Ariston trying to talk over her.

And then: "These look done. What do you think?" Damiskos, in his kitchen, talking to his family. Varazda smiled.

Dami was cooking, in fact, Varazda saw when he came through to the back of the house. Dami and Ariston had between the two of them cobbled together a quite reasonable dinner. Remi was sitting at the table messily peeling a hard-boiled egg, while Dami was at the stove making griddle-cakes, and Ariston was tossing a salad of chickpeas and cucumbers. They all looked up at Varazda as he entered. Dami smiled.

"Sorry I was so long," Varazda said. He put down his bundle of scrolls.

"Yazata's sulking in his room and won't come down,"

Ariston informed him. "What did you guys do to do to make him so mad?"

"Nothing," said Varazda. "Never mind."

"I think," said Dami tentatively, "that it was a misunderstanding. He heard us sparring—"

"Sparring?" Ariston repeated, looking mystified. "You mean fighting? With—with swords?"

Dami nodded.

"Varazda doesn't know how to *fight* with a sword." He looked at Varazda. "Do you?"

"You'd be surprised," said Damiskos, before Varazda had a chance to reply.

"Yeah," said Ariston. "Wow. So Yazata heard this, and what? He thought it was some really rough sex, or what?"

"I don't know what he thought," said Varazda quickly. "He overreacted."

Ariston gave Dami a sympathetic look. "Want me to talk to him for you?"

"No!" said Varazda. "That wouldn't help. I will talk to him."

"Just trying to be helpful," Ariston said sullenly.

"It's good of you," said Dami. "These are all finished," he added, sliding the last of the griddle-cakes onto a plate. "Let's eat."

"So this sculpting master of yours," said Dami to Ariston, after they were all seated at the table and had filled their plates, "the one you didn't kill. Who is he? What's he like?"

"Themistokles Glyptikos. You haven't heard of him?"

"Sculpture is not really my field." Dami shrugged apologetically. "He's well-regarded?"

"Famous," Ariston corrected him. "He studied in Kos, under Tellephoros. He works in marble—life-sized, naturalistic, he has a way of rendering draperies that's beyond anything anyone is doing today. Demostikos from the

Marble Porches called his *Soukos and the Dolphin* 'miraculous.'"

"He's young," Varazda added, looking up from cutting Remi's griddle-cake for her. "Well, young-ish. Our age."

Ariston made a face. "He's not young-young, but he's not some grizzled old-timer either. He's in the prime of his life. He's brilliant. I'm his only apprentice."

"Good for you," said Dami with sincerity.

"Papa," said Remi, "can I give Selene some cheese?"

"No, my sweet, Selene doesn't eat cheese."

"Hello, Selene," said Damiskos, moving warily down the bench away from her.

"He's going into politics, too."

"But if I give Selene some cheese, then she will eat it. Please?"

"Who's going into politics? See, sweetheart, Selene doesn't want it. You eat it yourself."

"Themistokles."

"Is going into politics?"

Ariston groaned. "Yes!"

"That's new."

"Yeah … maybe I wasn't supposed to talk about it yet. He's going to run in the next election. He's got … " Ariston flapped his hands. "Opinions about stuff."

"Can you be more specific?" Dami suggested.

Ariston gave a snort of laughter, which Dami's tone of friendly exasperation had invited. "No? I'm really just in it for the sculpture." He straightened up. "No, look. I'm not that stupid. But Themistokles is a brilliant artist, really brilliant, and a great teacher too, and I'm learning so much from him. And I like him, I do, but he can also be kind of an asshole? I don't know what his political opinions are because I don't *want* to know. Just in case, you know? He could be—I don't know—anti-Zashian or pro-slavery or something—I don't think he is, but he's the kind of guy that you just never

99

know. But so long as he's willing to teach me, I just want to learn as much as I can. Does that make sense?"

Dami nodded. Varazda nodded too, and so did Remi, who went on nodding longer than was necessary and nearly fell off the bench.

"That doesn't make *me* an asshole, does it?" Ariston asked anxiously.

Everyone shook their heads. Remi shook her head so hard that her pigtails flicked her nose, and she nearly fell off the bench again.

"What's a *asshole*?" she asked when she had righted herself.

"A word that Tash isn't supposed to use in the house."

"He's Amistron now, Papa," Remi informed him earnestly.

"Yes, you're quite right, and I'm sorry." He had thought that Remi might not yet have adapted to the new name, but of course she had. Even if she couldn't quite pronounce it.

Dami said thoughtfully, "You don't think this … threat, if it was a threat, that you heard someone utter against Themistokles, might have had something to do with his politics?"

"No! The person who—the person I thought might have killed him, they're not an enemy, or in politics or anything. I thought … " Ariston picked fretfully at his hard-boiled egg. "Honestly, what I thought was that if they were driven to those lengths, it must have been because of something he did—I don't know what, but he could have done something—and I still think maybe he did, so I just want to make sure this person's all right."

Varazda considered that for a moment, and from Dami's expression he was doing the same. Their eyes met briefly across the table. Varazda thought they were both reaching the same conclusion.

"That seems quite reasonable," Varazda said, and Dami

nodded. "We'll help you make sure you get to see them tomorrow."

Ariston nodded awkwardly. "Thanks. So—earlier, Yazata interrupted you guys sparring, or … "

"Something like that," said Dami. Varazda could have kicked him.

"*Something* like that?" Ariston repeated.

"What's sparring?" asked Remi.

"Play-fighting," Varazda supplied.

"Yeah," said Ariston, with a salacious emphasis, "*play*-fighting."

Varazda did kick him.

"*Play*-fighting," Remi repeated, with an exaggerated eye-roll.

"I'll take care of the dishes," said Varazda, getting up from the bench.

"I can do that," Dami offered.

"You made dinner."

Ariston brought out a bottle of wine, and he and Dami were soon deep in a technical discussion of how to sculpt drapery. At least, Ariston was deep in the discussion; Dami was doing his thing, listening as seriously as if he were being briefed on the strategy of some important campaign. Remi played under the table with the wooden horse Dami had brought her, and Varazda washed dishes. By the time he was finished, Dami was on his feet, demonstrating with a pot lid how to hold in a shield in combat, in answer to some question from Ariston, while Remi danced up and down and feinted at him with a wooden spoon.

Varazda took Remi up to bed, thinking to make some sort of joke—*don't let me find you fighting again when I come back,* or something—but finding he didn't have the heart for it. Dami and Ariston were in the sitting room when he came back, now discussing politics.

"I'm going to take Yazata up some food," Varazda said, putting his head in the door.

"Want me to—" Ariston started.

"No, thank you. I should talk to him."

He went up Yazata's staircase with a dish of leftovers and knocked on the door of Yazata's room.

"Who is it?" came Yazata's voice, sounding wary.

"It's Varazda."

After a moment, "What do you want?"

"I'm sorry about this afternoon. Sorry that you were alarmed, and that I got angry with you." He drew a breath. "Look, Yaza. He's only staying a week. Then he's going back to Pheme. Not because you've made him unwelcome—" *Though God knows you have.* "—but because that was the plan all along. He has a job and a family to go back to."

Yazata pulled the door open suddenly, staring. "A family?"

Varazda sighed. "Parents. A half-brother." He thrust the dish of food into Yazata's hands. "You should have some dinner."

"Ah." Yazata glanced down at the food as if confused by it. "Where did this come from?"

"Tash and Damiskos cooked. Apparently Tash's ex-girl-friend, the one who works in a bakery, taught him to do a few things in the kitchen. It was a surprise to me too. And they teach cookery in the Phemian army, I suppose." The joke, unsurprisingly, failed to land.

"I thought he was going to stay longer." Yazata looked up from the dish, brow furrowed. "The room—I thought you intended for him to live here."

"I did—I won't say, 'I do,' because if this is how it's going to be, if you dislike him this much, it's not going to work. He'll see that as well as I do. When he goes back to Pheme, you'll be rid of him."

"*You'll* be rid of him," Yazata breathed.

"*I* don't want to be rid of him! For God's sake, Yazata." He unclenched his jaw. "Sorry. I understand you think he's not good for me, but … " *But he is. He is so good for me, and I wish you could see that.* "I don't want to be rid of him," he repeated.

Yazata flinched, but then he nodded. "I understand. But … that's what Maia said you would say, too."

"What? No offense to Maia, but what does she know about it? I don't confide in her."

"I do."

"I guess you do. And she is entitled to her opinion of Damiskos. As are you. But if the two of you could stand to be civil to him for the short time that he is here, I would count it a favour."

"Of course. I would do anything for you. You know that."

"I—" *I'm the one who is making a sacrifice here*, he wanted to say. "I know that, Yazata. I've always known that. I'm—sorry that I asked too much, this once." That sounded too bitter, so after a moment he made himself say again, "I'm sorry."

"Time I called it a night!" Ariston announced stagily, bouncing up from the divan when Varazda reappeared in the sitting room. "Well! See you both tomorrow!"

Varazda waited for his footsteps to recede up the stairs before he subsided onto the divan, not too close to Damiskos. Dami nudged a full cup of wine along the table toward him.

"Poured one for you."

"Thank you. I hardly think I deserve it."

"It is your wine."

Varazda reached for the cup and took a long swallow. "You were justifiably angry with me, this afternoon."

Dami had to pause for a minute, perhaps trying to remember what Varazda was talking about. "Oh. I don't know about justified, but I was angry. I was angry that you don't care enough for yourself—you tried to do something to me that you obviously hate and have every reason to hate, you couldn't do it, and you made me … you made me party to that. You made me into a stick to beat yourself with. That's not what I want."

Varazda digested that for a moment, taking another swallow of wine. "You weren't angry that I concealed from you what I had really been?"

"No! Fuck euphemisms. You were a dancer. You *are* a dancer. If some assholes in some provincial palace couldn't see that, that was their mistake. You shouldn't have to carry any guilt over that."

"Thank you. I don't, very much, any more. And Gudul was a sleepy place. You shouldn't imagine there were ever very many … "

"Yeah, but fuck them. You were a boy—"

"A eunuch."

"—a young person, and you shouldn't have had to endure that. I've never wanted to hurt anyone as much as I want to round those men up and … " He squeezed Varazda's shoulder slightly. "But I wouldn't if it would distress you. Or I might, but I'd make sure you didn't have to watch."

Varazda laughed. "You're a marvel, First Spear, you really are."

He wished he could say that as sincerely as he meant it.

"So we've sorted that out, then, right?" said Dami.

"I suppose so." After a moment he admitted, "It does trouble me that there are things—like the Stalk of the Lily—that I can't do for you. You'll … miss them."

"I'll live," said Dami sternly. "If you can't take pleasure in it, I don't want it."

"Did you take pleasure in doing that for me, at Laothalia?" Varazda's mind took him back to that bedroom in the slave quarters again, Dami's mouth on him, the impossibly thrilling intimacy of it.

"Gods. Yeah. Of course."

"Oh." That was a revelation, actually. He hadn't thought Dami had *hated* it—clearly he had not—but he had assumed … what had he assumed? Just that Dami was very generous. He forgot for a moment that this was all ending in a week, and said, "In that case, it may be that I could learn to like it too. But—you would have to let me practice."

Dami laughed. "If you insist. Later, though. Not today."

Varazda nodded. "I got some books for you from the embassy." He pulled the scrolls across the table and flipped over the tags that showed their titles.

"What's this one?" Dami pulled one out of the pile.

"Oh, that's—I thought you might like that. It's fables from Suna. For children, really, but I thought, if you haven't read Zashian in a while, it might be good practice."

Dami picked up the scroll and untied the ribbon. "Want me to read to you?"

Varazda looked at him for a moment in the lamplight. Maybe he had grown too used to having his own way, he thought, because he could not reconcile himself to losing this man. He wasn't going to let him go back to Pheme and stay there. He didn't know what the solution was, but if there *was* a solution, he was going to find it.

"I'd like that," he said.

He arranged himself on the divan with his head in Dami's lap. Dami unrolled the scroll of fables. In his low voice with its thick Phemian accent he began to read: "Long ago in the city of Suna there lived a poor shoemaker … "

On the morning of the Asteria, Varazda was up early. It was a crisp, bright day, the kind of fall weather that he loved. He pushed open the shutters in his room to let in air and sunlight.

Remi was asleep in her little bed, on her stomach, one leg stretched out and the other drawn up as if she were executing a gazelle leap in her sleep. She had tossed her blanket off as usual; he went and gently replaced it.

He picked out clothes for the day. He had a couple of Pseuchaian-style gowns, one a pale blue that didn't really suit him, but was useful for times when he wanted to impersonate a certain type of woman—the other a deep, rusty orange. He would stand out more in that one, certainly, and that might not be wise on the Asteria. But he wanted Dami to see him in that orange gown. He unfolded it from the chest and shook it out.

He sat before the mirror at his dressing-table to do his make-up—kohl, lip-rouge, powder, and a hint of gold on his eyelids—and put in his earrings, a small pair of hoops that matched the gown better than any of his others. He put up his hair in a simple twist, held in place with a filmy scarf in the style that many of his female friends favoured these days.

For himself, he liked the way that the bodice of the gown draped, but it did show off his lack of breasts. He picked out a dark red mantle that harmonized interestingly with the colour of the gown, and wrapped it in a style that accentuated his waist and disguised his flat chest. He picked up the mirror and held it up and at arm's length to get the best view he could of the whole.

In truth, Varazda didn't think he made a beautiful woman. When he dressed in women's clothes he began to notice how bony and stern his face was, that his hands, for all their delicacy, were rather large, the muscles of his arms developed from a lifetime of dancing. And he was tall, reasonably tall even for a man. He looked like the sort of woman who would be described as "striking rather than beautiful," and honestly he liked that.

He wondered what Dami would think.

Remi was stirring by this time, and woke to exclaim and laugh delightedly over Varazda's clothes. She had been too young to understand what was going on last Asteria, and Varazda didn't know if she would remember what he had worn. He occasionally dressed in women's clothes for work, but she didn't usually see that.

They went out to the landing and found Dami at the bottom of the stairs, looking up. He gasped.

"Oh, darling! You look so lovely."

The endearment seemed to have burst out of him against his will, and he looked ready to be cringingly embarrassed of it. Varazda wanted to run down the stairs to him and ask to hear it again.

"He's wearing a dress," Remi explained in case Dami had missed it.

"She *is*," Dami agreed. "Don't you think she looks pretty?"

He looked tentatively up at Varazda, who felt rather breathless. Of course they were going out in public, where Varazda would be passing as a woman, and Dami would have to remember to say "she" then. But for him to do it now, so seriously, when he didn't need to, felt like a little gift.

"Oh, Papa's a 'she' today," said Remi, as if that were a normal thing.

Varazda came the rest of the way down the stairs as Remi went pattering off down the hall, calling out, "Yaza, Amistron—Papa is wearing a pretty dress!"

"Here, I got something for you." Dami held out a tiny cloth bag. "I … I forgot to give it to you earlier." He wore his usual mortified-Damiskos expression.

"Shocking. I'll add another item to the quest you're going to have to undertake to prove your devotion."

Varazda undid the drawstring of the bag and poured out into his palm a pair of impossibly delicate gold earrings. They had strings of tiny gold beads and pendants in the shape of adorable, big-eyed owls. And pearls, small but perfect. He looked up at Dami, wide-eyed as the owls and a little dismayed. Dami had represented himself as barely getting by on a miserable salary. How much had he spent on these?

"I didn't buy them," said Dami, half-admission, half-reassurance. "I inherited them. My grandmother—my father's mother—left me some of her jewellery a long time ago, for my future wife. I thought you'd like these."

"I—I like them very much. They're perfect—so feminine."

My future wife, my future wife, my future wife. The phrase clanged in Varazda's head like a bell.

"I'll put them in right now," he said, reaching up to unfasten the hoops he was wearing.

He didn't know what he felt. Terrified that Dami was giving him things intended for his *future wife*? Pleased that he was? Heart-sick at the thought that there were other pieces of jewellery that Dami might be keeping back for the *actual* future wife?

"I wanted to buy you something," Dami forged on. "But then I remembered I had these, and I thought they would suit you. I think they belonged to my grandmother's mother-in-law. She was a famous socialite in her youth."

So they had been in his family for generations. They were practically his ancestral jewels. Fucking hell.

"Oh, they do suit you!" Dami looked ridiculously pleased.

"Thank you," said Varazda. "They are lovely."

They went through to the kitchen for breakfast. Yazata was there, frying salt fish on the stove. Remi was standing on a stool at the workbench near him, carefully dismembering some mushrooms with her fingers. Yazata glanced up, surveyed Varazda's outfit, and an affectionate smile flashed across his face. He always liked it when Varazda dressed up. But he said nothing, just turned his attention back to the fish. Ariston came down shortly, dressed for the day in one of his plain, Pseuchaian-style outfits. Remi helped Varazda and Dami set the table.

"So how does this work?" Dami asked as they sat eating pickles and fried fish. "What do I need to know to avoid being stoned in the street or torn limb-from-limb or whatever it is that happens to men at the Asteria?"

"I don't think they actually do that any more," said Ariston, but he didn't sound very sure.

"They've *never* done that," said Varazda. "Outside of plays. All it is, is … " He ticked off items on his fingers as he recalled them: "You have to stay in the house unless you have a female escort, you have to cover your head with your mantle when you go out in public, and you're not allowed to speak or look any woman in the eye without permission. You can't go in the theatre or the council house of the Basileon, most temples, that sort of thing. Places women used not to be allowed in on ordinary days."

"Women still aren't allowed in the civil assembly in Pheme," said Dami.

"Right. And supposedly some of these other rules applied to women in Boukos in the distant past. You can't buy or sell without the consent of your male relatives … I'm trying to think if there are any others."

"Basically we have to behave like Zashian women," said Dami.

"Exactly."

"*Respectable* Zashian women." Yazata added in an undertone.

"I've met a few of those, believe it or not," Dami

returned with a smile. He inclined his head. "Probably not as many as you."

Yazata looked back down at his plate. Varazda wasn't sure whether the exchange had been friendly or not.

"And what goes on?" Dami pursued. "For the festival."

"Well, men aren't allowed to work, except in businesses owned by women. So most shops will be closed for the day, but you know Marzana, whom you met yesterday? His wife owns a sweet shop—the one we stopped at on our way up from the harbour—so he'll likely be working there while she goes out.

"As for what you do when you go out—there are rites at the Temple of Kerialos, but of course I've never participated in those. They also dance in the Basileon and put on a play in the theatre, though that's less popular these days because women are actually allowed to perform in regular plays now. And there are a lot of local traditions. The sandal-makers' wives host a picnic that I always try to get to. Today, of course, our first priority is finding Ariston's friend."

"Perhaps," said Dami, "it's time we knew who that was."

CHAPTER 9

"She works at a house on Temple Walk," Ariston said, staring fiercely at the table. "Owns it, actually."

Varazda glanced at Dami to see if that meant anything to him. Evidently it did.

"Her name is Kallisto," Ariston went on. "She's … she's Themistokles's mistress."

"I see," said Varazda neutrally. "And you think she might have had reason to wish Themistokles harm."

"Well, I don't—I mean, I hope not. I just … I can't think of any other explanation. That's why I went looking for her yesterday. But she wasn't in the city. I went to the theatre—she sings in the chorus there, and the groundskeeper is a friend of hers, used to belong to the same household, and he told me she was in the country visiting their patron and wouldn't be back until tomorrow. I mean today."

"And today, where will she be?"

"I don't know," Ariston admitted. "I was just planning—I mean, I was hoping that we could go to her house and see if she's there, or if we can find out where she's gone for the festival."

Varazda sighed. "We'd better hope it's somewhere we can

get into. And we'd better leave now, if we want to have any hope of catching her at home."

He got up and began gathering dishes. "You'll be all right here on your own with Remi, Yaza?"

"What? Oh, yes, of course. You're going to—to call on someone's mistress?"

Varazda patted Yazata's shoulder. "I'll explain later."

Dami looked adorable with his mantle pulled up over his head. It was a dark, forest-green mantle that complemented his eyes, making them look more green than brown. He tucked his arm through Varazda's as they headed out the door with Ariston trailing behind them, trying to get his own mantle to stay over his head.

Somehow—probably because he was putting a lot of thought into it—Dami struck what Varazda thought was exactly the right note for a man going out on the Asteria. He couldn't have imitated a woman if he had tried; everything about his physical presence was masculine. But he could be quiet and rather sternly meek, eyes downcast, following a half-step behind Varazda as if acting upon orders. He had brought his cane and leaned on it when necessary rather than on Varazda's arm.

They turned out of Saffron Alley into Fountain Street and met a group of women in short tunics, bare-legged and with their hair down, on their way to a rite or a procession, with ornamental spears and sistra in their hands.

"Wow," said Ariston, with what Varazda thought was unnecessary emphasis, when they had passed the women. "I'd heard you could see things like that on the Asteria, but still—just, wow. It's wasted on you." He rolled his eyes at Varazda, and then Varazda saw him glance at Dami.

Dami evidently saw it too. "It's not wasted on me," he

said mildly. "Though I'm aware it's not intended for me, either."

"Right, yeah. I just wondered. I mean I thought maybe you only had eyes for Varazda or whatever." Clearly Ariston wanted to talk about this, and was going at it in his usual awkward way. Varazda wished himself elsewhere, or dead, or both.

"Ariston," said Dami, "you love this woman Kallisto enough to try to take on a murder charge for her, and *you're* still noticing other women's legs. Though, you know, if she reciprocates your love, you should probably stop *mentioning* them."

"Yeah. Right, yeah." Ariston looked slightly flummoxed. "I didn't mean—that. I just meant, you know, because Varazda's a man. I thought maybe you didn't like women."

Dami gave Varazda's arm a discreet little squeeze. He didn't say, "Varazda's not a man." He must have realized you couldn't say that to Ariston, because if Varazda wasn't a man, perhaps Ariston wasn't a man either. And Ariston was a man.

Instead Dami just said, "I like a lot of things." He nudged Varazda. "Do you remember me saying that to you before?" he asked in an undertone.

Varazda did remember that. Oh, he remembered it. He thought about it all the time, worried about what it meant for the two of them, because he knew he *didn't* like a lot of things.

Temple Walk was very quiet on the morning of the Asteria. It was probably always quiet in the mornings; Varazda never came here. It was the street of the city's most exclusive courtesans, who sold refinement and conversation as much as—often instead of—sex. To tell the truth, Varazda avoided the place more or less on purpose. The whole thing hit a little close to home.

It was a very pretty street, though, with its elegant frescoes and potted fruit trees, culminating in the pink-and-white confection that was the Temple of Orante. Ariston seemed to have decided that Dami needed a guided tour, so he was explaining the hierarchy and nomenclature of the different houses, detailing their specialties as if he had visited them all. He hadn't, Varazda knew for a fact; he didn't have the money, for one thing, or the time, for another.

"Of course, they could open today," Ariston explained. "Most of the houses are owned by women. But then most of their clients have to stay home, so what would be the point?"

"They could have women clients," Dami pointed out reasonably.

"Oooh, I hadn't thought of that. Do you think so?"

"I think it would be none of our business."

"Yeah, no. Obviously. You're right."

Dami was being a very good sport about all this, treading a fine line between humouring Ariston and encouraging him, and between offending Varazda by being too interested in the courtesans and embarrassing him by insisting too much on his disinterest. He made it look effortless, but Varazda suspected that was like the way he compensated for his ruined knee: a lot more work than it looked. Varazda wished it wasn't necessary.

"Kallisto's house is the last one on the right," Ariston said, pointing. "With the sea-blue shutters. She's kept the name of the previous owner, but it's all hers now." He sounded proud.

The house, which was at the end of the street nearest the temple, had a pair of gracefully posed swans carved in high relief on either side of the door and the name Kykne painted above the lintel.

"Themistokles designed those." Ariston pointed to the swans. He still sounded proud. "But I carved them, actually."

"Really?" Dami leaned in to inspect one, drawing Varazda with him. "They're great! Aren't they, darling?"

"They are beautiful," Varazda agreed, not really looking at the swans. Dami had called him "darling" again, this time in public.

"Thanks," said Ariston. "That was how we, you know … how Kallisto and I met."

He squared his shoulders and reached up to knock on the door. Varazda stopped him with a hand on his arm.

"I think that's my job today. You concentrate on keep your eyes demurely on the ground."

"Oh, right." Ariston shuffled back, tugging his mantle back up over his head.

Varazda knocked twice before the door was answered by a slender girl of about Ariston's age, in a modest white gown, with her damp blonde hair pulled over one shoulder and a comb in her hand. Behind her, for only a moment but very clearly, Varazda caught sight of a man he knew—the spice merchant, in fact, in whose house he was engaged to dance the day after tomorrow. The man had a distinctive square jaw and steel-grey hair. He ducked out of sight. It was an interesting coincidence, and Varazda wondered if he might make something of it.

"Oh, hello, Ariston!" the girl trilled. "I mean," she corrected herself with a giggly attempt at gravity, looking up at Varazda, "greetings, Sister. Blessings of the Asteria and all that. Thanks awfully for bringing Ariston by! And—" Here she looked Dami rather baldly up and down, paused on the cane, and settled for an unenthusiastic, "Hello."

Varazda decided that he hated her.

"Hello, Leto," said Ariston without much more enthusiasm. "Is Kallisto in?"

Varazda was so busy being relieved that this girl was not

Kallisto that he almost forgot to feel disappointed when she said, "I'm afraid you just missed her. She's gone out."

"What a shame," said Varazda. "We had hoped to talk with her. Do you expect her back soon?"

"I couldn't say, I'm sure."

"You don't know where she's gone?"

Leto appeared to weigh whether or not to tell them. She shrugged. "To dance at the Palace of Art? I'm not sure. Will you come in?" She stepped back from the doorway, and gestured with her comb. "We've got some nice Kastian wine."

"It's very kind of you," said Varazda, "but I'm afraid we have no time to stop."

"Oh, well." She looked speculatively at Ariston a moment longer, as if she might have been considering asking Varazda to leave him with her. On the Asteria it would not have been an inappropriate request from one woman to another. But she appeared to think better of it, shrugged, and shut the door in their faces.

"Well," said Dami as they turned away from the door, obviously suppressing laughter. "She was charming."

"Oh, I *can't stand* her," said Ariston passionately. "She's always like that. If you're not swooning and drooling over her she's got no use for you. She's Kallisto's freedwoman."

"So," said Varazda, bringing them back to business. "The Palace of Art. Do you think that's true?"

"Oh, yes, I expect so," said Ariston. "I know she does like dancing. That's Eudia's," he added to Dami, pointing out a house on the opposite side of the street. "It's too bad we can't go in. There are some amazing frescos in the atrium."

"I've seen them," said Dami, "actually."

"Oh, you have? Gosh." Ariston looked distinctly as if he wanted to ask Damiskos more about that, and then thought better of it. Possibly because Varazda was looking daggers at him. Varazda himself wasn't sure.

He wanted very much not to care. He wanted to be able

to laugh and raise an eyebrow and say something arch, calling Dami "First Spear." Instead he found himself feeling painfully awkward: too tall, too angular in his flashy gown and heirloom earrings. How absurd, he chastised himself.

They walked to the Palace of Art, Ariston and Varazda on either side of Damiskos, Ariston playing tour guide the entire time, pointing out the sights importantly and making sedately appreciative comments about the women they passed. Varazda thought Ariston would have tried to take Dami's other arm if it hadn't been for the cane.

Finally, apparently deciding that he had talked enough and should encourage Dami to talk about himself, Ariston asked earnestly, "So how did you injure your leg?"

"Ariston … " Varazda said in a warning tone. Or what he wished were a warning tone—in fact it just sounded angry.

"It's all right," said Dami mildly. "I get asked that all the time."

"Oh, God, I'm sorry," Ariston gabbled. "I didn't think."

"It's all right," said Dami again. "I just meant that because I get asked often, I have an answer prepared. I was injured in a campaign on the Deshan Coast. I was captured by a hostile warlord and had my legs broken as punishment for the trouble we'd caused him. The other one healed better."

Ariston looked sick, all the colour draining from his face. "Shit. I'm—I'm sorry. Uh. Wow. Yeah." He had stopped in the middle of the street, and his mantle had fallen back onto his shoulders. He gave Varazda a beseeching look as if perhaps hoping he would say it wasn't true. "You, uh. You tell people that?"

Dami gave a low, gentle laugh. "No," he admitted. "Usually I don't. I say I was injured on campaign but not in battle, and I leave it at that. But you are Varazda's brother, and I felt I owed you the truth."

"Oh. Uh. Thanks." Ariston looked a little stunned.

Varazda reached out and pulled Ariston's mantle back up. "Let's walk. We don't want to miss Kallisto."

"Right. Right." After they had walked a little further, Ariston undisguisedly staring at Dami's lame leg, he said, "Well, you know my thing, I guess."

"Your thing?"

"My thing that I don't like to talk to people about?"

Dami nodded crisply. "Yes, I know that thing."

"Right," said Ariston. "Well. Good."

"Ariston," said Dami, "I have been thinking. About what you overheard Kallisto say. What is her specialty? Does she have one?"

"Specialty?"

"Yes, in the sense of ... " His gaze flicked to Varazda, and he seemed to revise what he had been about to say. "What she does for her clients."

"Oh, I ... I don't think so. That is, I don't know. I only know about some of the others because people talk about them," Ariston admitted reluctantly. "You know. Why?"

"Hm. No, just thinking."

Varazda wasn't quite sure he followed that. From the look on Ariston's face, he hadn't done much better.

"Never mind," said Dami cheerfully, smiling at both of them. "On to the Palace of Art."

CHAPTER 10

THE PALACE OF ART was a beautiful building, modern but built in an ancient style, with fat red-painted columns across the front and a flight of shallow steps leading up to the porch. Its name always amused Varazda. Only in a democracy like Boukos would anyone think to call such a welcoming building, wide open to the public every day of the year and virtually unguarded, a "palace."

Today garlands of late-summer flowers had been looped between the red columns, and greenery strewed down the steps. The dancing was well underway when Varazda, Dami, and Ariston arrived. It was all women, of course, with a few men seated demurely on the steps of the Palace of Art, amateurishly minding a group of children. The women were whirling and stamping in the wide, sunlit square, to the accompaniment of loud drums and horns. It was a dance that Varazda knew.

"You want to join them, don't you, babe?" Dami leaned toward Varazda to whisper.

"That's not what we're here for," said Varazda repressively. "And I don't recall giving you permission to call me 'babe.'"

"You don't?" Dami's eyes were shining with mischief now.

This was a side of him that Varazda adored, one that didn't seem to come out very often. Perhaps if he were happier it would.

"There she is!" Ariston was pointing into the crowd of whirling women. "Kallisto," he clarified, giving them a look. They had been too obviously distracted. "There. Do you see her?"

Varazda looked out at the dancers. Even if he'd known what Kallisto looked like, it was hard to spot anyone in the fast-moving crowd.

"I'll have to take your word for it," he said. "As I recall, this dance can go on for a long time. Why don't we wait with the men and children."

"Why don't Ariston and I wait with the men and children," Dami amended, "and *you* dance."

"You do look like you want to," Ariston said assessingly. "Go on."

"Ariston gets to watch his girlfriend dance," Dami said, looking Varazda in the eye, the mischief tempered with warm affection. "I want to watch mine."

Varazda nodded, grinning. She, Dami's girlfriend, tossed the loose end of her mantle over her shoulder and set off toward the dance.

"Kallisto's not my girlfriend," she heard Ariston saying wistfully behind her. She was too far away to hear Dami's reply.

Dancing among women as a woman was not something Varazda got to do often, and there was something both familiar and foreign about it. It was a simple round dance: in, out, spin, clap, stamp, rather martial and masculine, and then some very feminine shimmies and twists.

Some of Varazda's friends were there and waved to her across the circle. She curled her fingers in the gesture known as "rose-hands" in the court dances of Gudul, and spun in unison with the other women. She rode the tide of exhilaration raised by the communal dance, the easy flow of it, the mixture of masculine and feminine that might have been made for her, but was really a high mystery of the Boukossian women's festival. She looked for Dami on the benches, and there he was, watching her.

And this suddenly was new, and disconcerting, and Varazda almost missed a turn in the dance. She had never actually danced for Dami. On the beach at Laothalia, at a different festival whose name she had shamefully forgotten, she had danced before an audience that included Dami, and Dami had watched her practice in the slave's yard before that. But neither time had it been *intended* for him. Nor was it now, if Varazda was honest. She'd wanted to join the dance because it was something she always did at the Asteria, part of her enjoyment of the festival—because she dressed as a woman often enough, but it was not often that she felt like a woman down to the marrow of her bones like this. Besides, her friends were here and would expect to see her dance.

Dami deserved to see Varazda dance *for him*.

The musicians began a new tune. This one was a dance for pairs, and some of the women began dancing with each other while others twirled alone. A few went to draw in men from the sidelines. Varazda saw Ariston dancing awkwardly with a tall, dark woman who looked as if she could have picked him up and slung him over her shoulder if she'd wanted to. Ariston wasn't much of a dancer. Varazda hoped he had not lost sight of Kallisto in his concentration on the steps.

Dami sat by himself on the bench in front of the Palace of Art. When Varazda looked at him, he smiled. He probably didn't mean for it to look wistful.

She walked through the dance toward him, intending at first to sit down by his side. But if he had asked, "Don't you want to go on dancing?" she would not have been able to answer honestly, "No." She held out her hands as she approached.

He looked up questioningly.

"I thought you might like a dance," she said.

It took him only a moment to work out what she had in mind. As he allowed himself to be pulled to his feet, a grin slowly dawned on his face.

She pulled him forward a few steps away from the bench, so that she could move around him. She raised her hands and swayed her hips, provocatively close. She reached out and brushed the draped fold of his mantle back slightly from his face, sliding the fabric between her fingers.

She toyed with the end of his mantle; she spun around him, laying her wrist over his shoulder and trailing her hand across his back. She took his hand and twirled and shimmied at the end of his outstretched arm. He remained more or less fixed in place the whole time, letting Varazda dance around him as if he were a cult statue. From his grin, he loved every moment of it.

The music changed to a dance he obviously knew, and then, almost seamlessly, they were really dancing together, hands clasped, moving in unison in a highly modified form of the steps which they fell into with ease. Dami had a good sense of rhythm and moved easily; he would have been good at the martial, masculine dances when he'd had the full use of both knees. But he could still do this, though Varazda thought that perhaps he hadn't realized it until now. He looked like he might cry, but the tears stayed in his eyes, sparkling.

The music changed once more, and they stopped and stood, hand in hand, foreheads resting against each other for a moment. Varazda thought of their sparring the day before, and how that had been like the mirror-image of this.

They were interrupted by the arrival of Ariston, rather

breathless, announcing, "These are the friends I told you about. Damiskos, uh—Varazda—this is Kallisto."

Kallisto, it turned out, was the woman Ariston had been dancing with.

She was in no way what Varazda had expected. She was older than Ariston, perhaps in her late twenties, and taller than Ariston, her skin the colour of copper, her curly black hair pulled severely back from her face. "Kallisto" could not have been the name her mother gave her—if her mother had had the opportunity to name her at all. From what Ariston had said, she was a freed slave. She was big-boned without being voluptuous, her shoulders rather broad, her face strong-featured. She was the kind of woman you might call "striking rather than beautiful."

"Delighted to meet you, Varazda," Kallisto said, leaning in to give Varazda a firm handshake, as appropriate between women on the Asteria. She pronounced his name with care and precision.

Varazda shook her hand, although with the end of the dance, like the breaking of a spell, he had gone back to being a non-woman in women's clothes. He tried not to feel too annoyed by the interruption.

"So, uh." Ariston wiped his hands down the skirt of his tunic. "We should go somewhere and talk. We have to—uh, ask you about some things."

"Of course," she said, smiling at Ariston and reaching out to readjust the fold of his mantle which had once again fallen back around his shoulders. "Lead the way—or rather, let your friend Varazda lead the way." She shot Varazda a smile.

They went up the steps of the Palace of Art and into its cool, quiet interior. There were few people looking at the pictures today, and it was easy to find seats on a bench in a corner where they could be assured of not being overheard. Kallisto settled herself and arranged her mantle with a careless grace.

Ariston cleared his throat loudly and began. "The other night—Orante's night—I came over to see you, late, around the second hour. I'd just come from a party, and I was a bit ... well, Themistokles said he was going to show some people one of my sketches, but he never did, which wasn't his fault, there was never an opportunity, but still I felt a bit ... uh. You know.

"Leto said you were busy, but ... she says that sometimes even when you're not. So I went around to the window at the back, I was just going to knock and see if you wanted to ... " He glanced miserably at Varazda and Dami, then forged on. "If you wanted to have a game of robbers. But I heard you inside talking to someone. You said, 'I'll do to you what I did to Themistokles.' And I thought—somehow—it meant you'd killed Themistokles."

"I didn't!" A woman of her poise could not really be said to yelp, but she came close.

"We know," Ariston assured her, actually putting a hand on her arm. "We know. The public watch has been—"

"The public watch?" she repeated in dismay. She shook off Ariston's hand. "Holy Waters. You were eavesdropping on me, Ariston. What business did you have being back there? I showed you that back gate because I *trusted* you."

"I'm sorry. I know I shouldn't have been there, I know I should have left as soon as I heard voices."

"You should have."

"I know that. But I did hear you say, 'I'll do to you what—"

"Which was none of your business. And didn't mean I *killed* him."

"Well, uh, it's just that then the man said, 'What did you do to Themistokles?' And you said, uh, something about, about holding him by the throat until he couldn't breathe." Ariston cringed. "At least that's what I thought I heard. Probably—I mean obviously—I heard wrong, but I ... it was just, there was just something about the way you said it. You sounded so, so—not even angry, just *fierce*. You sounded like you could have killed someone. And I thought—I was just worried about you."

Kallisto had been gritting her teeth through this new revelation, but she unclenched them to say, "You what? You heard that, and you were worried about *me*?"

"Yes, because I thought—I thought you'd killed Themistokles, and I thought if you had, you must have had a good reason. I thought maybe he'd done something to you."

Kallisto looked at Ariston for a moment with an unreadable expression that might have been tenderness. "Oh. I see. No. It is not that at all."

"I'm so glad."

She heaved a sigh. "It was very sweet of you to worry, Ariston."

"He turned himself in to the public watch to protect you," said Varazda.

"Ariston, you didn't! What did they do?"

"Held me in a cell while they went and found out Themistokles wasn't dead."

"Do I need to clear *your* name now?"

"No! They'll just think that I was drunk or something." Ariston gave Varazda a pleading look.

"The chief officer of the watch is a friend of ours," said Varazda. "We will be able to smooth things over. Indeed, in large part we already have."

"But you're telling me this now … " said Kallisto. She looked away for a moment. "I will tell you why I said what you heard me say, Ariston. I think that I owe it to you for your heroism." She turned back to Varazda. "Here is what it is. I am a courtesan. I get my living by making men feel however it is they want to feel with me. Mostly, the way men want to feel with me is … how to put it? Mastered. Powerless. It's like the Asteria in a way. They just want to feel that way for a little while and then go back to their regular lives, where they *are* the powerful ones.

"Themistokles Glyptikos is my main client these days, but he isn't a rich man, and he has other concerns—he wants to marry and is seeking patrons—so I have always seen other men besides him. One of them was with me on Orante's night, when Ariston heard us together. I said that I would *do to him what I did to Themistokles*." Her voice dropped into something like a growl, suggestive of big cats, and her eyes fell half-closed, menacingly. It was remarkably effective. "It was part of the game," she added in a normal tone. "As for what I did to Themistokles, well—that too is part of the game. Some men like it."

"Oh," said Varazda blankly. He glanced at Dami, who was not looking surprised. Dami, in fact, had guessed this. This was Kallisto's "specialty."

"I have shocked you," Kallisto said, with just a hint of archness. "You are a respectable Zashian woman. Please forgive me."

"What? No, no, I'm not—a respectable Zashian woman. Not at all."

He *was* shocked, though, so he didn't know what else to say. It didn't help that he had noticed Ariston's expression now, and it was different from either his own or Dami's. Ariston looked entranced.

"Why the reference to Themistokles, specifically?" Dami asked.

Kallisto sighed. "It's part of the fantasy for him. He … he considers Themistokles a rival and enjoys being chastised by Themi's mistress. He proposes specific scenarios. I can't tell you more. Likely I have already told you more than I should."

"We will be discreet," said Varazda. "Do not worry. It seems this was a misunderstanding, and we will all forget it ever happened."

"We're glad to know you're all right," said Ariston fervently.

They parted ways on the steps of the Palace of Art. Kallisto walked out to rejoin the crowd of women, tall and regal in her red gown.

"What are we going to do now?" Ariston asked anxiously, as they stood watching her.

"Ah," said Varazda. "Well." He looked to Dami.

"We don't have to tell Marzana that I thought Themistokles was dead because I eavesdropped on a sex game, do we?" Ariston squeaked.

"I don't think we have to tell him that," said Dami. "But *were* you eavesdropping?"

"No! No. It was like I said. I stopped outside the window, because … because I thought she might be in there with someone, and I wanted to hear her voice. I've—I've done it before," he admitted in an abject whisper. "I guess—actually, that is eavesdropping, isn't it?"

Varazda put an arm around Ariston's shoulders.

"I never heard anything like *that* before, though," Ariston went on, "and I didn't know that was, you know, what she did. Though … " He looked off into the middle distance. "It does make sense. I mean, a woman like Kallisto? Why wouldn't you want her taking, taking charge of you? Who wouldn't want that? R-right?"

"Nothing wrong with wanting it," Dami said quickly. "In my view. Or doing it, either, if she's agreeable—which it seems she is. But that's *my* view, and I may not be the person to ask."

Ariston laughed. "You mean because you've got a thirty-year-old boyfriend?"

"That's what I mean. My view may not be typical."

127

Varazda released his hold on Ariston and gave him a thump on the back instead.

They walked on down the street away from the Palace of Art.

"Where should we go now?" Ariston asked. "If we're not, uh, going to go tell Marzana everything."

"There's the sandal-makers' wives' picnic," said Varazda, still feeling somewhat distracted. "It would be starting soon. We will need to tell Marzana something, though, eventually."

"Yeah yeah." Ariston waved a hand airily. "Plenty of time. Don't want to miss the sandal picnic."

They bent their steps in the direction of the leather market where the picnic was always held. Ariston began walking ahead, and Varazda fell back to keep pace with Dami.

"Does it appeal to you?" Varazda asked in an undertone.

"Does … you mean what Kallisto does? No, it does not." He shuddered slightly. "Divine Terza, no. The thought of being powerless doesn't turn me on—never has. In fact … "

"In fact?"

"Well, all things being equal, I like being in charge. Not that … "

"I like it too. You, in charge."

"That means a lot."

"It does, yes."

They smiled privately at one another for a moment.

"Ariston," Varazda called, "slow down, will you? Remember you're not allowed to go about without a chaperone."

"Oh, yeah." He glanced back and saw how far he had gotten ahead of them. "Gods, yes. Sorry! Sorry," he repeated to Dami, when they had caught up to him. "I forgot."

"Lykanos Lykandros," said Varazda, changing the subject but to some purpose. "Does the name mean anything to you?"

"Eh?" said Ariston. "To me?"

"To you, yes."

"Um, sure. I haven't met him, myself, but he was Themistokles's old patron."

"Was he really?"

Ariston nodded. "When Themistokles was really young, before he went to study with Tellephoros in Kos. Lykanos was a sculptor himself, but he gave it up years ago. They're still friends, though, him and Themistokles."

"Indeed?"

"Why? That came out of nowhere."

"Not really. I saw Lykanos at Kallisto's house just now."

"Wait, you know him?"

"Not to speak to. He's a spice merchant," Varazda added, to Dami. "A very wealthy man and a patron to a lot of artists in the city."

"You don't think he's Themistokles's rival?" said Ariston excitedly. "The one she was talking about, who—with the— you know?"

Varazda shrugged, disingenuously. "I just wondered."

"What would he have been doing at Kallisto's when she was out, though?" Ariston pursued. "D'you think he'd spent the night?" He grimaced.

"With the Asteria the next day?" Varazda was sceptical.

Dami shook his head. "Didn't sound like they have that kind of relationship. More likely he's got something with the servant, Leto, too."

Ariston's eyes widened. "When he gets to be with Kallisto any time he wants? No way. And Leto's so ... so *ordinary*."

"I can't say I disagree," said Damiskos, flashing Ariston a rather roguish smile. "Kallisto's something, though."

"Isn't she wonderful?"

"Does she know how you feel about her?"

"Wh ... I mean ... " Ariston wrinkled his nose. "Probably. She's very smart."

After the sandal-makers' wives' picnic, which was chaotic and enjoyable as always, they headed up to the sea wall—in hired chairs, this time, at Varazda's suggestion—to Chereia's sweet shop. The sky soared dazzlingly blue out over the harbour, the breeze off the water strong and chilly. But the benches which Chereia had recently added outside her shop were packed with women, wrapped in warm mantles, chatting and eating under the brightly-painted new sign. Inside the shop's honey-scented interior they found Marzana and his elder son behind the counter, dealing with a mob of female customers. Marzana spotted them by the door and spared them a harried wave.

"This is such a weird festival," said Ariston, who was being very chummy with Damiskos again. "You don't have anything like it in Pheme, do you?"

The spectacle of Marzana with his beard and military bearing doling out fritters and making change behind the sweet-shop counter was definitely an odd one. His son Sorgana, who was seven and took prizes at school for rhetoric and geometry, was not a tremendous amount of help when it came to the practical tasks of running a shop. As they watched, he dropped a tray full of sesame sweets, began gathering them up one at a time, and was putting the ones that had rolled across the floor back on the tray with the ones that hadn't until a grandmotherly woman swooped down and scolded him.

"Not remotely," Dami answered with a grin.

"I think about moving to Pheme sometimes," said Ariston. "When I've finished my studies. Though Kos would probably be better for my career. Have you ever been to Kos?"

"Ariston," said Varazda warningly. "Not now, if you don't mind."

"Why don't I go spell Marzana off," Dami suggested, "while you and Ariston talk to him?"

"Oh, I can come help you," Ariston said eagerly.

"Sure," said Dami before Varazda could intervene to protect him.

Varazda led the way through the packed shop, Dami remembered to follow meekly behind him, and Ariston got elbowed in the ribs by a woman with a large basket and made it to the counter by clinging to the back of Dami's mantle and frantically squeaking "Excuse me, excuse me!"

"No time to talk now, I'm afraid," said Marzana when he saw them arrive. He reached around Varazda to make change for a group of girls.

"I'm here to offer you some assistance so you can take a break. Damiskos and Ariston here are good workers."

Marzana glanced sceptically between Dami and Ariston, shrugged, and lifted up the hinged section of counter to let them all come through.

"Everything's one obios for a half dozen," he said by way of instruction. "Good luck."

Marzana led the way into the back room, which was the sweet shop's kitchen. A half-full tray of fig fritters lay on the counter, and he pulled it toward himself as he sat on one of the stools.

"Thanks for the rescue," he said. "I assume you've something to tell me?"

Varazda perched on another stool and helped himself to a fritter. "Yes, but I don't know what you'll think of it." He explained what they had learned from Kallisto, though without mentioning her name.

"I believe it," said Marzana when Varazda had finished. He licked honey off his fingers. "I wouldn't have ten years ago, though I'm sure there are men in Zash who like their concubines to play-act like that. It's just that in Boukos one talks about it."

"The woman in question is free, if that makes a difference."

Marzana looked up. "A difference in what?" he asked rather sharply.

"A difference in how you feel about the play-acting," Varazda clarified. "It would be one thing if she were a slave or a concubine, but she's a freedwoman making her living as a courtesan. She's not absolutely powerless."

"No. And you're right, that does make a difference. I thought you meant, did it make a difference to whether I believe her or not—and of course it doesn't. Though I suppose I should ask if you believe her."

Varazda nodded. "I do."

"She didn't tell you the man's name."

"No, but that's as one would expect. She can't go around revealing her clients' fantasies, even in Boukos."

Marzana laughed. "No, you're right. Even in Boukos. Strange thought."

The back door of the shop opened just then, and Chereia came in.

"Varazda!" she gasped as the door swung shut behind her. "Look at you! That gown—it's stunning!"

Varazda had almost forgotten what he was wearing. He looked down at the rust-coloured gown and laughed.

"You look lovely yourself, as always," he said truthfully.

She was dressed for the festival in leaf-green, her brown hair simply and elegantly swept back from her face. Varazda thought she radiated a kind of wholesome beauty, in manner as well as appearance. She was a few years older than he.

"And those earrings," Chereia said, coming around the table to inspect them. "They're new, aren't they?"

"Hello, darling," said Marzana dryly. "Lovely to see you."

"Oh, yes, yes," said Chereia, leaning over to give him a teasingly perfunctory kiss on the cheek. "But let me get a look at the earrings. They're just exquisite. Where did you get them?"

"They are nice, aren't they? They were a gift."

"From ... your soldier?"

Varazda nodded.

"He's here, you know," Marzana put in, with a glint in his eye.

"Where?"

"Out front. Minding the counter with Sorgana and Tash. Ariston, I mean."

"You put him to work?"

Marzana shrugged. "It was Varazda's idea."

"Actually, it wasn't," said Varazda. "It was his own idea. Damiskos's."

"I'm going to go take a look at him," said Chereia. "May I?"

"Of course. Be my guest."

"Why did she ask your permission?" Marzana asked, looking confused.

Chereia went to the door and opened it to peek out. Varazda, following her, saw Dami behind the counter, running the sweet shop with military precision. He had got Sorgana making change and Ariston packing orders while he dealt with customers, and the milling crowd had somehow coalesced into an orderly line.

"Well!" said Chereia, turning back to Varazda with raised eyebrows. "If he wants a job ... "

"What?" said Marzana, coming to the door himself. "I was doing all right myself." He looked critically at Dami's operation. "That's all very well, but now there's no one to refill the dishes or put the trays back until the crowd dies down. They're sacrificing everything for speed."

"Why don't you go out there and help them?" Chereia suggested. "I want to talk to Varazda."

Marzana gave her a kiss and obeyed, and she closed the shop door behind him. She rolled her eyes.

"I can run that shop by myself," she said. "And it takes four of them?"

"Only two of them have elite military training," Varazda pointed out, to be fair. "The other two are Sorgana and Ariston."

Chereia laughed, then looked thoughtful. "We were surprised, Marzana and I. When he met Damiskos at your house."

"Yes," said Varazda a little stiffly. "Everyone has been surprised."

"He looks very nice—and I do mean *very nice*—but more importantly, Marzana had nothing but good to say about him. We just didn't know you were ... well. Quite frankly, we didn't know you were in the market for handsome soldiers —but perhaps you didn't know that yourself?"

"I ... I did and I didn't." He wasn't surprised, or particularly disappointed; he knew he'd always kept that aspect of himself secret. But it was still a somewhat lonely feeling, realizing that even Chereia and Marzana, two of his most perceptive friends, had not guessed the truth. "I've always liked men, actually, and I've always liked *that type* of man— don't ask me to explain exactly what I mean by that, please— but I never thought I wanted a lover. I didn't even really like ... " Could he truly talk about this, even to Chereia? No, he decided, he could not. "I'm still not sure that 'having a lover' is something I can do properly."

"Oh, nonsense—you can do it brilliantly. You're a wonderful friend, and it's all the same skills, all the important parts. What do Tash—Ariston, I mean—and Yazata think of him?"

Varazda considered various ways he could answer that, none of them quite honest.

"Ariston has taken to him," he said finally. "Yazata is being very odd."

"Odd how?"

"He's trying very hard to be hostile—it's not really in his nature, but he's putting a lot of effort into it. And it's also as if he thinks he's doing me a favour, somehow? As if he thinks I need protecting. He won't explain himself—he just keeps giving me significant looks."

"That *is* odd."

"Perhaps I failed to prepare him adequately—probably I did. But I told him my plans nearly a month ago, and if he had objected then, I would not have gone ahead with any of it. The work on the house ... " He spread his hands hopelessly. "He had plenty of time to talk to me about it, if he had misgivings. But instead, a couple of days before Damiskos's ship was expected, he suddenly seemed to come to the realization that I was making a terrible mistake and he couldn't be a party to it. On the day Dami's ship was due, Yazata made sure to be out of the house."

Chereia sighed. "And he won't have it out with you, of course, because he's much too Zashian. Blessed Orante. That's miserable. I don't know how to advise you, except ... no," she corrected herself, "I've really no idea."

"What were you going to say, though?"

She hesitated. "Just that I think there's usually a lot of negotiating involved in anything ... anything permanent, even when passion is involved. In a marriage, for example. Marzana and I had to do a *lot* of negotiating, and we started off as a love affair that we didn't really expect to last." She smiled. "You didn't know that about us, did you? We were lovers for two months—a little more than two months—before we were married. All the while thinking that Marzana could be summoned back to Zash any day."

Varazda's eyebrows had risen in spite of himself. He had known that Marzana stayed in Boukos for Chereia's sake, having come to the city on the first diplomatic mission from Zash. It hadn't occurred to him that they might have been lovers before they were married. It wasn't the sort of thing he spent much time thinking about, in relation to his friends; and besides, Marzana was such a model of rectitude, and Chereia, for a Boukossian woman, so wholesome and matronly. He wondered if it would have changed his opinion of them to have learned this a month ago instead of now.

CHAPTER 11

WHEN THEY CAME BACK out into the shop, custom had died down and the men were chatting behind the counter while Ariston and Sorgana refilled and rearranged dishes of sweets.

"And of course in the summer," Marzana was saying, "there are plenty of good beaches for sea bathing. I'll introduce you to my trainer."

"I have to go fetch Sandy from Audia and Phoros's," Chereia told her husband, "and then Audia and I are going to the temple just quickly before dinner. Varazda, do you want to leave Ariston with us for the evening? You and Damiskos might like to walk home together."

"Hey," said Ariston from the kitchen, "I'm not a kid."

"It's the Asteria," Varazda and Marzana reminded him in chorus.

"Yes," said Varazda to Chereia. "Thank you. Shall we?" He looked at Dami.

Dami nodded and retrieved his cane. He said a warm goodbye to Marzana and his family.

"I like your friends," he said when they were out in the street.

"Marzana and Chereia are wonderful," Varazda agreed.

It felt a little awkward to be alone again after all the events of the day. Varazda had to look at the sky to remind himself what time it was. Only early afternoon; it felt as if it should have been much later.

"Marzana was telling me I should take up swimming," Dami said. "Apparently it's excellent exercise—he says it's his main way of keeping fit. I've never swum much myself, not living near a good pool or having a coastal villa or anything."

"If you want to practice, I can take you to the Baths of Soukos—they have the best pool in the city."

"So you said."

"Ah, I did, didn't I."

After a moment, when Varazda didn't come up with anything more to say, Dami went on talking about exercise regimes. Varazda had never thought much about what people who didn't dance could do to keep their bodies fit, or how much work went into maintaining a physique like Dami's when anything that involved much bending of the knees had to be avoided.

He wanted to say that Dami need not worry on his account, that much as he enjoyed Dami's muscles, he didn't expect Dami to be able to keep them up forever. He didn't expect himself to be able to stay fit enough to dance forever; it was something he had thought about a lot and had made his peace with.

He wanted to say, "I'd love you even if you got fat." But he'd never told Dami that he loved him, and that would decidedly not be the right way to say it. Supposing that he decided to say it at all.

"I don't expect to be able to stay fit forever," Dami said, as if he'd heard Varazda's thoughts, or some of them. "I've known that at some point I'll have to sacrifice my vanity if I want to keep walking at all—almost everything I do wears away at my bad knee, and it'll only get worse over time. So I suppose swimming might be good."

"I'll take you," said Varazda firmly. "Tomorrow, after I finish work. Oh. I have to work tomorrow. A dance class in the morning, and then a shift in the music shop in the afternoon, and in the evening I have an engagement at the embassy."

"Of course," said Dami. "I won't be a burden. I can go sightseeing. I've a list of places I want to visit."

That was very sensible of him, knowing that he would be left on his own in the city because Varazda worked for a living, and Varazda should not have felt aggrieved at the thought that he would miss showing Dami the sights himself. But he'd imagined his lover spending the time when they weren't together relaxing at the house, getting to know Yazata and the neighbours, playing with Remi, and generally becoming a member of the family. He swallowed his disappointment and listened to Dami describe the places he hoped to visit and offered suggestions.

The next three days passed in a very strange kind of normalcy.

Yazata had taken Varazda's request to heart and was being entirely civil to Dami. They even had a few conversations—initiated by Dami—which might have been described as friendly. As for Ariston, he continued to hang on Dami's every word. The reading aloud from the *Tales of Suna* became a family event, with Ariston and Remi competing for space on the divan with Dami and Varazda, and Yazata, though officially remaining aloof, lingering in the kitchen and rather obviously listening.

Varazda taught his dance class on Moon's Day morning in the studio next to his house, and Dami tagged along, sitting on the floor out of the way to watch Varazda warm up and put his students through their paces, and chatting with Hanem, their hired musician, after the class was over. They ate with Yazata and went out again to the music store with Remi in tow. Hanem was there eating his lunch, and he and Dami spent a long time talking lutes and comparing fingering techniques on the shop's instruments, while Remi ran around dusting things that didn't need to be dusted and distracting the customers. Eventually, when custom seem to have died down for the day, Varazda turned over the shop to Hanem, sent Remi to play with Maia's children, and he and Dami went to the Baths of Soukos. Varazda showed off in the water, and Dami swam workmanlike laps and then got out of the pool and did his usual exercise, which was quite enjoyable to watch.

"I wish you could come with me to the embassy tonight," Varazda said as they walked home in the early evening.

Dami slipped his hand into Varazda's and gave him a gentle smile. "I've enjoyed spending the day with you."

Varazda bumped his shoulder lightly against Dami's. "So have I."

"I thought I might go out and get my dinner at a restaurant, then take a walk. Where do you recommend?"

"Tono's place, at the sign of the olive tree in Ironmongers' Street, is excellent," said Varazda. "And near the agora, which is a nice place to walk at dusk. I can give you directions."

"Perfect." Dami leaned over and gave him a brief, casual kiss, his lips soft and warm against Varazda's.

"I might not be home until late," Varazda said regretfully.

"I'll be fine. I trust Remi to keep me safe from the goose."

All the same, Varazda hoped he might be able to slip out of the embassy party early. But as it turned out, the thing ran even later than he had anticipated, and it was late enough by the time Varazda could get away that Shorab offered him a couch to spend the rest of the night, and insisted on arranging an escort for him when he was determined to return home. Varazda walked home listening to the embassy guard, a big Pseuchaian man, chat vacuously about politics, and found the house dark and silent. He dragged himself upstairs and fell into bed without changing his clothes.

His first engagement on Market Day was in the afternoon, and he was dancing with a troupe and needed to rehearse with them in the morning, so he could not afford to sleep late. He crept downstairs to the kitchen, half-dressed and with tangled hair and smeary makeup from the night before, hoping to sneak out to the yard and wash before anyone else woke. Instead, he found Dami at the table, drizzling honey on a bowl of porridge that he had made himself.

"Terza's head. Do you need a drink? Or, uh, raw egg? Pickle juice?"

Varazda gave him an arch growl. "I am not hung over, First Spear. I never drink when I'm dancing."

"Sorry," said Dami very cutely. "Do you want some porridge?"

"I do. As soon as I've washed."

He splashed water on his face, scrubbed off his eye makeup, and ran wet hands through his hair until he felt almost presentable. There was a second bowl of porridge steaming on the table with a spoon beside it when he returned to the kitchen.

"This is the sort of thing *I* should be doing for *you*," Varazda complained as he slid onto the bench opposite Dami. "I am supposed to be the host here."

"I'm not going to be recommending this establishment to any of my friends, it's true. Too many frying-pan attacks, *and* you have to make your own breakfast." Dami shook his head.

Varazda pulled the spoon out of the honey pot and watched the golden liquid slide off onto his porridge. He realized he felt very happy.

Market Day was a long day, especially coming on the heels of a late night. Varazda had to rehearse, dance in the afternoon, and then present himself at Lykanos Lykandros's mansion not only fit to dance to his usual standard (in case he needed to get invited back) but also alert enough to gather information on Lykanos. The dancing went well, the merchant's guests were duly impressed, and Varazda learned absolutely nothing of any use. He was beginning to wonder if this was because there was nothing of any use to be learned.

The third day was Xereus's Day, and the Saffron Alley household had a longstanding tradition of hosting friends for dinner on Xereus's Day. Varazda had forgotten to mention it to Dami, not thinking he would have made other plans, but he had; he had already accepted an invitation from Chereia, whom he had met in the market the previous day. Yazata, apparently, had told Dami that Varazda would be busy Xereus's night.

"You'd better go," said Varazda gloomily. They were standing in the hall by his front door. He leaned back against the wall, feeling defeated. "Yazata must have made a mistake."

"I'm sure that's what it was," Dami said, in a toneless voice that must have served him well in the army, for instance when relaying orders that he knew to be ridiculous. Something caught his attention, and he looked sharply at the row of pegs on the wall by the door. "By any chance, did you move my sword?"

"No."

"It was hanging there, wasn't it?"

Varazda moved the cloaks that were hanging on the pegs and looked under them.

"Yazata must have … " Varazda started.

"Tidied," Dami finished for him quickly. "It's quite all

right. I only wear it out of habit. And I'm sure it will turn up."

"I'm sure it will."

They looked at one another. Varazda wasn't sure whether he wanted to laugh or cry, and from Dami's expression, he was feeling much the same way.

Dami sighed and ran a hand through his hair. "Look, I've no desire to come between you and your family—if he truly can't live with me—"

"You'll go back to Pheme. I know. Do *not* say 'I'm afraid I'm ruining your family'—I can see it in your eyes that you are a moment away from saying it. *Do not.*"

"I—But I—" He looked as though the effort not to say it would physically break him.

"Damiskos. I have held my family together through worse than this. And I will do it again if I have to."

After a moment, as if with a great effort, Dami gave one of his curt nods. "If I can't live here," he said slowly, "there are other ways … I won't go back to Pheme and stay there just because Yazata doesn't like me. We'll work it out."

That was incredibly comforting. Varazda leaned in and kissed him. "Thank you," he said. "We will."

"Perhaps, at the moment, we could discuss strategy?"

"Mm. Could we arrange to have you save Yazata's life somehow?"

"Defend him from the murder goose, maybe?"

"No, Selene likes him. He claims to have trained her not to shit in the house—which I don't believe, because everyone who's ever kept a goose tells me it isn't possible, but it is a fact that she doesn't shit in the house."

"Fascinating. Not germane, but fascinating."

"You could … " A genuine idea occurred to Varazda. "You could make yourself useful around the house in some way."

"I'd love to. I can wash dishes. I can help cook."

"Dishes, yes. Cooking, no. Yaza likes cooking—that's his domain, and he guards it jealously."

"Yes, of course. I ought to have realized that's why you don't know how to boil water."

"Exactly."

"There must be something else I can do. Does he grow any vegetables? I know something about gardening. Of course it's another one of those things I can't really do with my bad leg—too much kneeling. But that gardener at the park was saying you can plant rosemary in jars, like strawberries, which I didn't know, and I could manage that. You could make quite a nice garden that way, actually. And vines and trees, of course, would be manageable."

"Do you want to plant some jars of rosemary in our yard?"

As soon as it was out of his mouth, he realized it was an absurd thing to say. Dami wasn't settling in for good; it didn't make sense for him to plant things in their garden.

"Sure," said Dami easily. "If you have any idea where I could get jars big enough. And, you know, you have to plant it in the spring."

"Right."

"Beets and turnips you can plant in the fall, though. Yazata might like to have some of those growing in the garden. Or perhaps he does already? I, uh, didn't see any in the yard, but I haven't looked around much—just some quick goose reconnaissance."

"Come look at it now. I'll defend you from Selene."

He led the way back through the house to the doors, which already stood open. Dami looked out into the yard.

"It's a little sad."

The yard was a long strip of land behind the two houses and the music shop, badly cobbled in places, packed earth and patchy grass in others. On Yazata and Ariston's side an area was fenced off for the chickens, with a muddy pond for

Selene. Remi was in there now, scattering grain. She waved furiously at Dami, dropping half the grain in her excitement.

Along the back wall, which screened them from their neighbours' yards, a couple of blocks of inferior marble, with preliminary chisel-marks, stood on wooden trestles. Cast-off tools from Ariston's master were jumbled up under the work-bench and across the yard.

"None of us has the least idea about planting things," said Varazda. "We had almost no useful skills when we were freed. Palace eunuchs—what could you expect? Yazata set himself to learning to cook and keep house. But agriculture was beyond even him."

"Horticulture," Dami corrected him. "That's what you call it when it's a garden."

"You see what I mean." Varazda headed for the chicken enclosure to rescue the rest of the grain from Remi. "I think they've had enough, sweetheart."

"You could do a lot with this yard, though," Dami said, following him, careful to keep the gate between himself and Selene. "It gets good sunlight, even with the high wall on that side—and the wall would be good for training vines. What's that, under the tarp?" He pointed to the far corner where the music shop met the neighbours' wall.

"Clay. Belongs to Ariston. I don't know where he got it or what he plans to do with it."

"Have you thought about putting in an ornamental pool?"

"Uh. No?"

Dami gestured, walking down the middle of the yard. "Yes, you could put something in right here. Tiled, you know, in Zashian style. The goose would like it."

"Are you thinking of trying to win her over by making her a pond?"

"You don't think it would work?"

They spent some time discussing what Dami thought

they could do with the yard, until Remi lost patience and insisted Dami come play with her, stamping into the house and returning with a jointed wooden doll which she thrust into his hands.

"You have to be a giant," she told him firmly. "And I am a centimaur."

Varazda retreated into the house, leaving Dami to his fate. Yazata was in the sitting room, darning a hole in one of Ariston's tunics with ferocious concentration, the needle clenched in his big fingers. Varazda stood in the doorway looking in at him. He wondered if Dami knew how to sew. It was possible; perhaps Phemian soldiers needed to be able to repair their own clothes on campaign, just as they apparently needed to be able to cook their own dinners.

"Yazata," Varazda said, "did you happen to see Damiskos's sword? It was hanging up by the front door."

Yazata looked up with that resolute expression and nodded once.

"It's just that it's not there any more."

"No."

"Did you, in fact, hide it?"

Yazata drew a deep breath and nodded again.

"Yaza, what is going on? Why are you doing this?"

Yazata glanced past Varazda at the kitchen, obviously making sure they were not overheard. "I'm worried about you," he said finally. "I think you are getting in over your head."

Varazda took a moment to consider what that could mean. It wasn't particularly flattering. "I don't want you to worry about me," he said carefully, "but as for 'getting in over my head,' perhaps I can better be the judge of that?"

"I know how it seems to you. You go out in the world while I stay at home, you know the customs, and of course you have your sense of duty. But I have my own knowledge of people, and I know *you*. You are very strong, but you are not invulnerable. When you came back from Pheme, you had been so badly hurt. I don't mean your arm—"

"You mean my nerves, I know. I was in a state. But Yaza, when you say, 'my sense of duty'—"

Remi, in the character of a centaur, came pelting into the kitchen, whinnying and shrieking with laughter. Dami came stamping in after her, giving leisurely chase.

"You won't get away!" he called.

"Yes, I think the weather will continue fine," Yazata said loudly. "But if you'll pardon me, I have work to do."

"Oh for the love of … " Varazda turned away from the doorway, rolling his eyes.

Remi barrelled into his legs, and he scooped her up and tossed her in the air, to her surprise and delight.

"Papa, are you going to play with us too?"

He wanted to hug her and bury his face in her soft hair, but instead he set her down with a flourish and said, "I am, and you'll never get away from me!"

If only the same could be said of everyone in the household.

CHAPTER 12

DAMI'S INVITATION to Chereia and Marzana's was for an hour earlier than dinner in Saffron Alley, so Varazda walked with Dami part of the way to the sea wall.

"This is where we part ways," Varazda said when they reached the agora. "I've an errand to run in this direction." He nodded across the agora to the south. "You'll be able to find your way?"

"Of course," said Dami, with an amused smile. "It's not that big a city."

Varazda remembered one of the hand signals Dami had taught him on their night reconnaissance in Nione's villa. He held up a hand with forefinger and thumb pinched together. *Message received.* Dami laughed and leaned in to kiss him on the cheek.

When Varazda knocked at the door between the swan reliefs, it was opened by Leto again. Her hair was pinned up this time, her makeup half done; she seemed to make a specialty of answering the door in a state of deshabille.

She gave Varazda an irritated look before turning to call into the house: "Mistress, that Sasian woman is here again— dressed as a *man*. Do you want me to get rid of her?"

Kallisto emerged from a door halfway down the hall. "Of course not. Varazda, come in. Leto, will you bring us wine?"

Leto tossed her head and wandered off toward the back of the house.

"Come in," said Kallisto warmly to Varazda. "I've been hoping you would come back, my dear. I see you've left your man at home today."

"Today he can fend for himself," said Varazda, returning her smile.

"I love your coat," Kallisto said, reaching out to finger the fabric of his sleeve as he came inside. "I have often wanted a coat like that."

She led him into a private sitting-room, elegant and unfussy in its decor, where she offered him a seat and brought out a plate of biscuits without further troubling Leto. Her manner was very warm but not at all flirtatious. On the surface, it might have made Varazda's job here easier. In fact, it made him wary.

Leto returned with the wine, and Kallisto met her in the doorway. Instead of handing over the bottle, Leto beckoned her mistress into the hall and pulled the door closed.

"I hope you know what you're doing with that," Varazda heard Leto say from behind the closed door. He wondered if she thought she was speaking quietly enough not to be heard, or just didn't care.

"Excuse me?" said Kallisto.

"I said I hope you know what you're doing. It won't be good for business if it gets out that you entertain women."

Kallisto gave a contemptuous snort. "It won't be good for business if anyone finds out you were seeing that young man who was executed."

"Do you have to keep mentioning him all the time? He was just a friend."

"You're not still keeping company with the others, are you? The group of them."

"How could I be, when they've all been exiled?" She made a disgusted noise. "Honestly. If you wanted to keep me from choosing my own friends, you should never have freed me, should you?"

Nothing more was said, and Varazda could only assume that in the ensuing silence, Kallisto snatched the bottle of wine from her servant, who was gone by the time the door reopened.

"I beg your pardon," she said to Varazda as she resumed her seat. She looked genuinely embarrassed.

"Not at all."

She poured wine for each of them. "Ariston is well?" she said. "I haven't seen him since the Asteria. I hope he hasn't suffered any lasting harm from that episode. It was such a mess."

"It was," Varazda agreed. "But he is fine. I don't think he suffered anything worse than embarrassment."

"Oh. Oh good. I hoped you hadn't come to give me bad news of him. You must tell him to come visit me soon. Will you? Of course, as his sister—"

"I am not Ariston's sister."

Kallisto smiled. "I know you and he are not related by blood—he has told me that—but you *are* his sister, aren't you?"

Varazda gave her a long look. "Why," he asked finally, "are you pretending not to know what I am?"

She widened her eyes at him innocently. "*What* you are?"

"You're Zashian, *Kallisto*. You know 'Varazda' is a man's name."

"I know you're not a man."

"You know that doesn't make me a woman. And I'm very sure Ariston has never called me his sister."

She laughed, a little like a cat purring. "You might well be a woman. Who am I to judge? I have known women whom all the world called men. I thought you might be one.

But I see that's not what you are. All right, you win. Ariston calls you his brother, and I am Zashian. How did you know?"

There had been several clues, but he chose one. "You have a tiny scar, just here." He touched the side of his own nose where he wore the little flower-shaped stud. "I don't think a girl born in Boukos would have had her nose pierced."

"I shouldn't have thought that a person named *Varazda* from the Deshan Coast—by the look of you—would either." She shrugged her broad shoulders. "But I see so many things in my work that nothing surprises me any more."

He smiled, letting it reach his eyes this time. "I am delighted to hear it."

He wanted to know, but did not want to ask, exactly what kind of person she had thought he might be. Was there a name for these women whom the world called men? He had known boy brides in Zash, who had given up their status as men when they married their husbands—but they didn't have anything like that in Boukos. And it wasn't quite what he was, anyway. He had never, to his knowledge, met anyone whose understanding of how they fit into the categories of male and female was as slippery as his own.

"So," she said. "What do you want with me, then?"

He recalled himself to the matter at hand. "Your client Lykanos Lykandros … "

"I never told you that was his name." She paused, then winced. "Not until just now, I suppose."

He kindly let that pass without comment. "Do you think that he knows you're Zashian?"

She gave that a moment's thought, eyebrows raised. "Yes," she said decisively. "Yes, he does."

"Is that unusual? You don't advertise the fact, do you?"

She shook her head. "I grew up in Boukos, or nearly. I was twelve when I was brought here—a slave, in one of the bigger Pigeon Street houses. That was, as you will have guessed, before the trade agreement. There were very few

Zashians in Boukos in those days. My quaint ways, my thick accent, they served me well enough while I was in Pigeon Street, but as I saved money to buy my freedom, I began to see that if I wanted to rise in my profession, I would do well not to seem like a foreigner. It would limit my appeal. So I changed my name and worked hard to lose my accent."

She paused. "But you were not asking for my whole history. You want to know whether I keep a secret of it. I don't these days, not as much as I used to. I don't need to, since the embassy came to Boukos. Themi knows my origins, because he asked once about my past. Lykanos … " She smiled slowly, privately amused. "Oh yes, with him it was because he wanted me to dress up once. He'd bought this dreadful gown at the market, with doves on it. I told him it would be ridiculous for me to wear it because where I'm from, doves are for a young, marriageable girl. He asked where that was, and I told him."

"How did he react?"

"Embarrassment, mostly. And he seemed surprised. He's brought it up a few times since—silly things, you know. 'I didn't think Sasians bathed,' and 'But you speak Pseuchaian so well.'" She rolled her eyes. "All quite sincere. I don't think he's much accustomed to thinking of anyone's feelings but his own."

"Quite," said Varazda, who knew the type well.

"Why do you ask?"

Varazda leaned back in his chair, recrossing his legs and smoothing out the skirt of his coat.

"About Lykanos. I've met him. I danced at a party at his house. He didn't seem to me to be a man who hates Zashians, though I can believe what you say of his ignorance. I got the usual comments, 'I thought you would be fatter,' and so on. But I've heard that he has been involved in something more troubling. Do you remember the riot in the Month of Grapes?"

Her eyebrows went up. "You mean that business when the Sasian embassy was burned? I heard about it of course, but no more than that. You're not, surely, saying that Lykanos had anything to do with that?"

"It would trouble you if he did?"

"Well ... " She had to give that some thought. "No, I suppose not, really. I wouldn't fear for my own safety, if that's what you're thinking. But he is a valuable client. I'd be sorry to have to give him up."

"Of course. I haven't heard that he was directly involved in the riot, but he may have approved of it, because he helped some of the culprits escape from justice."

"I thought they'd never caught the men who did it."

"I've a friend in the public watch who says they did." It was strictly true, though that was not where his own information came from. "But they weren't able to prosecute." He shrugged as if naturally he did not know more about it than that.

She frowned. "I see. And Lykanos is supposed to have had something to do with that."

"That is what they say. What do you make of it?"

She gave him a long, thoughtful look. "I might ask what your own interest is in the matter."

"You might, and I might say that I'm wondering whether to accept any more invitations to dance at his house."

"You might," Kallisto agreed. "And I might think there was more to it than that. But then, I might choose not to ask. I should say, from what I know of Lykanos, that if he's exerting himself in any matter, it's because money is involved. He tells me often how well his business is doing. Apparently he has some lucrative thing going on involving safflower." She shrugged.

"Is he generous with you?" Varazda asked.

"Generous enough. He's not a miser. Before you ask, though, the reason I'm not exclusive with him is because I don't like him very much. And I do like Themi. I'll miss him when he enters political life."

Varazda nodded sympathetically. "What are his views, by the way?"

"He favours the Sasian alliance, in general, and he's not a radical, but he has sympathy for the abolitionists."

"Really? You should tell Ariston. He said he doesn't know what Themistokles's views are, and he was afraid he might not like them."

She winced slightly. "I try not to talk to Ariston about Themi. I don't want him to feel jealous."

Varazda didn't really know what to say to this. Here they were far outside his field, and he felt it. He should know more about this now, shouldn't he? After all, he was in love himself. Probably.

"I'm sure that's wise," he said evasively.

She looked at him thoughtfully for a moment. "Does he talk about me much?" she asked suddenly.

"Who—Ariston?" Ugh, that was amateurish. "Well. He's mentioned you, but not by name—not until, you know, the other night, with the misunderstanding."

"The misunderstanding, yes. He tried to protect me, didn't he. It's rather touching."

"I'm sure."

"He is a very nice boy. I don't want him to get hurt. You would tell me, I hope, if you thought he might be hurt by our acquaintance?"

Varazda thought about that for a moment. "No," he said finally. "No, I don't think I would."

"No?" Kallisto looked curious rather than offended.

"I don't have enough experience of that … side of life … to advise anyone, much less to go to work behind anyone's back."

"I see."

"I do love Ariston like a brother, though, and I would defend him by any means from anyone who *had* hurt him."

She gave her purring laugh again. "I am glad to hear it." After a moment she added, in a different tone which Varazda could not interpret, "I like him very much."

She leaned forward to refill Varazda's cup.

"This business about 'What I did to Themistokles,'" he said.

She looked wary again. "Yes?"

"Pardon me for returning to it. Was it normal for Lykanos to want details about what you'd done to some other man?" He needed her to confirm for him that Lykanos was the man Ariston had heard her with.

"Oh, for him, yes, very normal. Only about Themistokles, though, as I said." She stopped, realizing what he'd just made her say. He gave her an innocent look. She went on, wearily: "He has a fixation on Themistokles. They were lovers at one time, when Themi was a boy. Lykanos keeps asking me if he can watch the two of us." Another eyeroll. "I've never said yes to *that*."

"Oh, God, I should think not. I once had to—" He snapped his mouth shut. What on earth had he been about to reveal?

She gave him a smile so comradely and conspiratorial that it made him smile in return.

"Free men want the strangest things sometimes, don't they?" she said. "But there's no shame in it, I think. In Zash, everyone is taught to hate themselves for wanting things, but I like the way they're not like that here."

"I know what you mean," he said.

"Themi's not ashamed of what he wants," she said thoughtfully, "but Lykanos … I wouldn't call him 'ashamed,' either, but there is something secretive about him. Something darker."

He was glad she had returned to the topic of her own accord. "Jealousy, maybe?"

"Of Themi? It could be. On the surface they are friends, but there is certainly something there … Well, it is not for me to speak of, especially not to a stranger. Though I feel as if I know you. Tash—" She put her fingers to her lips. "I mean Ariston—I must remember to call him by the name that I encouraged him to take. Ariston has talked of you often."

"He has?" Varazda raised his eyebrows.

"I don't believe he ever mentioned your name—it was always 'my brother' this and 'my brother' that. 'My brother looks after all of us, my brother works three different jobs to support us, my brother would do anything for his family, he's so good with my niece, he cares for everyone in the neighbourhood … '"

"Well … " Varazda found to his surprise that he was genuinely embarrassed.

"What else did he say? Oh, I remember. 'My brother is so comfortable being himself. I wish I could be like that.' I remember wondering what he meant by that, but now I think I see."

"Do you?"

"I think he meant that you don't try to blend in. Not even a little bit. I admire that."

CHAPTER 13

LATER THAT NIGHT, Yazata and Varazda stood in the corner of the hall near Varazda's dining room, looking through at the people inside but trying to stay out of sight.

"What are we going to do?" Yazata asked, twisting his hands together.

Varazda pinched the bridge of his nose. "I don't know. Yes, I do. We'll have to keep him here as long as we can and try to prevent him drinking too much."

Yazata nodded mutely.

"I wish you hadn't sent Damiskos away," Varazda said bitterly.

"What do you imagine he would do?" Yazata made it sound like a genuine question.

Varazda gave him a sour look. "He was First Spear of the most famous legion of the Phemian army—that's like … " He cast about for a Zashian equivalent that might make sense to Yazata. "It's a little like the Gilded Blade of the Undying Band. He's a strategist. He comes up with plans and organizes people. And he's physically intimidating—as you may have noticed. He'd be able to deal with Stamos. And he'd want to. He'd see as well as you and I do that it's only a matter of time before Stamos hits her, if he's not doing it already."

"And would that concern him?"

Varazda stared at him. "Can you ask me that? Do you think I would care for him, would have invited him into our lives, if I thought he *wouldn't care* that my friend's husband might be beating her?"

"He's a man," Yazata said simply. "They don't care about that kind of thing. They think it's right."

"Were you not listening when I told you what he did at Laothalia?"

"Of course I was listening. He saved your life. You feel indebted to him. He's still a man, and I know what men are like."

Yazata swept back out into the dining room to rejoin their guests, and Varazda trailed after him.

Varazda was sitting at the kitchen table when Dami let himself in the front door. It was dark, a lamp on the table casting the only light on the ground floor of the house. Varazda could hear Dami propping his cane in the corner and hanging up his cloak. Then he appeared in the kitchen doorway.

"Dinner party go all right?" he said, leaning against the doorpost.

"Ah, no. I wouldn't say that."

"Oh. What happened?"

"Maia, our neighbour from across the street, was here, and her husband showed up."

Dami slid onto the bench opposite him. "Is he violent?"

"Mostly he's loud and rude, especially when he's been drinking, which of course he had. Maia claims he doesn't hit her, but I don't believe it. She's afraid of him. He's a sailor, away from home for long stretches, which suits everyone well. When he does come home, I'm never sure what's best to do. Tonight I thought I'd keep him here as long as I could and hope when he went home with Maia he'd just pass out and not give her any trouble." He shrugged discontentedly. "Ariston took the children out to play, to get them away from him, which was a help. But Yazata's friend Maraz was here, and she's just recovered from an illness and not been out of her mistress's house in a month, and it was hardly the pleasant evening we'd hoped for her." He levered himself up from his seat. "Do you want a drink? I was just thinking about getting myself a drink."

"Yes, please."

"I haven't asked how your evening was," Varazda said, as he pulled a bottle of wine from the shelf where they kept them.

"It was ... I'm afraid it was delightful."

"Bastard," said Varazda without heat.

"Except, of course, that I wished you could have been there."

"Naturally."

"I had a long conversation with Sorgana about the cult of Terza. Learned a few things, actually. And I played knuckle-bones with the younger boy and lost. We had delicious lamb ... "

Varazda growled, and Dami gave an abashed laugh. Varazda passed him a full cup of wine and poured one for himself.

"Chereia interrogated me about my past," Dami added, "and said she approves of me."

"Good! Not that I had any doubt—I know her to have excellent judgement."

Varazda took a gulp of wine. He slid onto the bench next to Dami, and Dami's arm came around him to pull him close. It felt so good.

An hour later, the wine bottle was empty, and they were still sitting at the table, on opposite sides now. They had somehow ended up deep in a discussion of horses. Varazda, as the son of a Deshan warlord, had learned to ride before he was old enough to remember, and was still comfortable on horseback, but his actual knowledge of the animals was sketchy. Dami of course was full of information, had opinions about breeds and gaits and types of saddles, and could list the names of all the horses he had owned in his career and describe their qualities and what had become of them. It was a little like hearing him list a series of departed friends. Varazda told him so.

"I could do that too," said Dami. "And I could do departed lovers … there have been a fair number of those."

Varazda looked into his cup to check whether there was any more wine at the bottom. There wasn't. "Other soldiers?"

Dami nodded. "Mostly. It brings you together, and then it's what tears you apart, in the end." He tapped a finger on the table. "Poetic."

"Mm." Varazda checked his cup again, just in case. There was still no wine in it. "Does the man of higher rank always get to be in charge, in bed?"

"Uh. I mean, not always. Depends on your personality. Also a lot of times you're equals. When I was a captain in the Fourth Darian, I had a brief thing with another captain, and I let him fuck me one time, just because he wanted to. Only time I've actually done that. It was … I'd say mediocre. He didn't really know what he was doing.

"But then a couple of years after that, I visited this courtesan in Pheme, and she did this thing with her fingers, and … " He dropped his head back, eyes closed. "It was so good." He opened his eyes, wine-warmed gaze on Varazda.

"I could probably do that." Varazda heard the words

come out of his mouth and wondered how that had happened.

Dami snorted. "You could do it the regular way, honey. If you wanted. From what I've seen, you've got a perfectly serviceable prick. It just takes a little while to warm up."

"That's ... that's very sweet of you to say." He felt as if he might tear up and wasn't sure why. "I couldn't ever do it to you, though. I don't think I could. I hate it so much."

"Oh, yeah." Dami's expression clamped down into military seriousness. "Don't even—it won't happen."

"But if you ... "

"I said 'if you wanted,' and you don't, so we're done. Dismissed."

"There's a chapter in *The Three Gardens*," Varazda pursued doggedly, "called the Cinnamon ... the Cinnamon Forest? No, Grove. The Cinnamon Grove."

Dami cocked an eyebrow. "Do cinnamons grow in groves?"

"It's trees, it comes off of trees, of course it grows in groves. Shh. It's in *The Three Gardens*, in the Garden of Roses, and it's all about ... "

"Spicy stuff?"

"Mm."

"Is the finger thing in there?"

"I think so. I never really studied that section."

"Well, I'm up for anything you are. I don't suppose you could get a copy of *The Three Gardens* here."

"Are you kidding? This is Boukos. The city's awash with them. Somebody's translating it into Pseuchaian—Ariston knows a fellow who painted frescos in somebody's country house based on the Garden of Jasmine."

Dami sputtered with laughter, smacking his palm on the table. Varazda was suddenly overcome by a hot wave of longing, like an indescribable hunger.

"Dami, I—I want to go to bed with you, so badly. But I think I may be a little drunk."

"Varazda? Not to come over all coarse and soldierly on you, but you're shitfaced."

"I'm a little bit drunk," Varazda pursued, "I think, and I can't get hard when I'm drunk. I know, I used to do it on purpose, at Gudul, when I had to go to bed with men who didn't want to know I even had it in me—and why did I mention that, that's not romantic at all. What I meant to say is, can we do something even if I'm not … you know. Can you handle it being one-sided like that?"

"That may be the sweetest thing anyone's ever asked me. Darling. Yes. I could handle that. If you were tired or something. But you're not, you're drunk."

"You're drunk too."

"Oh, sweetheart. We shared a single bottle of wine. I'm not drunk."

"Please, Dami. We could do what we did in that vineyard at Laothalia. You liked that."

"Marble-Porches style, that's what that's called."

"Is it?"

"Yeah, but the Marble Porches is a philosophy school. I didn't want to mention it at the time."

"A philosophy school? I like the Zashian style of naming sex acts better."

"We're not doing it. Varazda. My sweet. You have inhibitions, we've already established that, and they're lowered because you're drunk, and the name for what I'd be doing if I took you to bed like this is *taking advantage*."

Varazda dropped his head onto his outstretched arms on the table. "Why are you *like* this?" he groaned, muffled by his hair.

"Because secretly you love it."

Varazda swept his hair out of the way and peered up from the table. "I wouldn't say it was all that secret."

Dami grinned. "Do you know what we should do?"

"What?"

"I should go next door and borrow one of the lutes, and play for you."

"God, yes. You should do that. Why haven't you done that already?" Varazda rolled his head to one side on the table and waved a hand in a less imperious gesture than he intended. "Go, go."

"You're going to have to get me the key. Or do you expect me to break a window?"

"I expect you to command the door to open to you." Varazda sat up, raking back his hair. "Very well. I shall accompany you."

"Think you can find the way?"

Varazda leaned across the table to swat at Dami, who ducked away, swinging his legs over the bench, and slipped, and nearly tipped the bench over before he caught the edge of the table and righted himself. He glared at Varazda.

"Do not speak. I am sober as a fucking funeral oration. I can drink all the King of Zash's eunuchs under the table, any day."

"That is pure bravado, First Spear. You have no idea how much some of the King of Zash's eunuchs can drink."

Dami made a show of coming around the table and helping Varazda to his feet, and Varazda made a show of getting up gracefully—drink never made him uncoordinated, the way it did some people—and then he was wrapping his arms around Dami and kissing him hungrily.

"This—doesn't count—as taking advantage?" he asked anxiously when they parted for air.

Dami's hands slid up his back and into the cascade of his hair. Holy angels. Dami really did have such beautiful eyes, especially when they were filled with that almost painful intensity.

"No," Dami said very gently. "I don't think so. You don't have inhibitions about kissing me."

"No," Varazda breathed. He felt again as if he might be close to tears.

"I want to stand between you and harm," Dami said, his voice still incredibly soft. "I will always try to do that. Even —*especially*—if the harm might come from me."

Varazda kissed him again, gripping his strong shoulders, clinging to him. Not caring how weak it might make him look.

They parted finally and swayed together down the hall, bumping each other teasingly and leaning unnecessarily on one another. They made it out the door but hadn't closed it behind them when they heard a crash and shouting from across the street.

Maia's door flew open, and Maia and her eldest daughter, Aula, burst out and stumbled down the steps. Stamos's voice followed them: "Come back here, you whores!"

Maia looked up and saw Varazda in his doorway, and she smoothed her skirts, preparing to pretend there was nothing going on—as she had always done when things like this had happened in the past. She froze, looking past Varazda at Damiskos, her expression startled, even a little alarmed.

Stamos came storming out of the house into the street, barefoot, a wine bottle dangling from his hand.

Varazda was first down the steps. Dami ducked back inside the house, reaching for something that wasn't there, reappearing without the sword that Yazata still had.

"The fuck you looking at, Sasian?" Stamos growled. "Get inside your house before I drag you there by the hair like you deserve."

This was the most aggressive Stamos had ever been with any of his neighbours, to Varazda's knowledge. It might have been because he was drunker than usual, but there was also a controlled, animal ferocity about him. He was a big man, slightly top-heavy, with arms as thick as tree-trunks and shoulders like an ox. He was normally crude and sneering without uttering actual threats.

"I tell you what," said Varazda cheerily. "Why don't *you* get back on your ship, you obscene ape-man, and take the first opportunity to fall headfirst into a barrel of piss?"

God, but that felt good. He'd been wanting to say something like that to Stamos for years.

Stamos was staring at him in disbelief. Maia was still standing frozen in the street, with Aula clinging to her arm, as if she couldn't make herself say her usual lines: *Don't worry, it's nothing. Just a disagreement.*

Dami came down the steps into the street. He had his cane, and it was obvious he needed it going down the steps. Stamos spared him a contemptuous glance and looked back at Varazda.

"What did you just say to me, you dickless goat-fucker?" Stamos's voice was low and menacing.

"Sooo … quite apart from how you think I'd fuck a goat without a dick, or at any rate why I'd bother, that's *actually* not the part that they cut off anyway—I would have expected you to know that, a well-travelled man like yourself."

"What's going on?" Damiskos asked casually. He had put his hand on Varazda's arm. Varazda wasn't sure why, but it was nice to have it there.

"None of your business, old man." Stamos sneered pointedly at the cane.

"I'm Damiskos." He gave Maia and Aula a curt half-bow. "You seemed to come out of your house in some distress. Is there anything we can do?"

"Fuck off back into your house," Stamos replied.

"Other than that," said Dami, cutting off something very witty that Varazda knew he was going to have thought of in a moment. Varazda realized he was feeling slightly light-headed. Dami might have been right about how drunk he was.

"I—I—" Maia glanced between Dami and Stamos.

"No," Stamos said for her, taking a step closer, wine bottle swinging in his fist. "We don't need any interfering cripples or Sasian *cunts*—"

"Mm, still not … " Varazda started.

"I'm sure there's no need to speak that way of your neighbours," said Dami, in a mild tone that nevertheless managed to cut through Stamos's obscenities and silence him for a moment.

"Tell them it's nothing," Stamos ordered Maia, giving her an unfriendly nudge.

"I won't," said Maia tightly. She gripped her daughter's arm. Aula looked terrified. "Not this time. I won't let you—"

Stamos grabbed her arm. "You shut your mouth." To Damiskos he explained, his voice rising as he lost control of his anger:

"She lost me a captain's place because she wouldn't make nice with the ship-owner's wife and kids. That's all I asked, but no, it's too much for this ungrateful bitch!"

Maia wrenched her arm out of his grasp and took a step back, drawing Aula with her. "Their grown son laid hands on our Aula! Was I supposed to stand by and let that happen? Is that what you wanted?"

"Damn fucking right that's what I wanted! What other good is she? I'd've been captain of my own ship instead of slaving on Dromo's tub another season. If you didn't want him to touch your precious Aula, you should've slept with him yourself! I know you're whore enough. But you don't want me to get ahead—you've never wanted me to get ahead."

Maia turned toward Varazda. "He tried to get into Aula's room to punish her—he was going to beat her, for refusing to go with that awful boy. I—I—" She still didn't seem to be able to admit it: that she had, finally, been trying to get away.

Varazda stepped between the women and Stamos. He was feeling much more sober.

"I really do think you need to be back on your ship," he told Stamos.

"You fucking what? You—" He stopped with a grunt as Dami stepped in front of Varazda and planted a hand in the middle of Stamos's chest.

"He's right," Dami said. "Leave the women alone and go back to your ship."

"Yeah?" Stamos sneered, swatting at Dami's hand without managing to dislodge it. He stepped back instead. "Who's going to make me?"

Damiskos looked at him. "Is that a real question?"

Varazda almost laughed. Aula, with a startled gasp, did.

Stamos growled and swung the heavy wine bottle he still held. Dami caught his arm as it came up, gave him a shove, and the bottle crashed on the pavement, shards of pottery flying.

"The only thing you can hope to do here," said Damiskos conversationally, "is outrun me. I suggest you do it."

There was no protest from Maia or Aula, no attempt to come to Stamos's defense. Varazda was glad of that.

"You've got some fucking—" Stamos began.

Damiskos, who had disarmed Stamos without letting go of his cane, now swung it with both hands like a fighting staff and hit Stamos on the side of the head.

"Try again," he said crisply.

"Who the fuck ... " Stamos stumbled back, shaking his head. "Don't know who the fuck you think ... I'm gonna fucking ... I swear on fucking Orante's fucking ... " And he turned and ran out of Saffron Alley.

Aula and Maia were hugging one another, and Maia

began to cry. When Varazda turned toward them, she pulled him into their embrace.

"I'm so sorry," she gulped. "So, so sorry."

He hugged her back. "You didn't do anything wrong."

"I hope my interference wasn't, uh, unwelcome," said Dami.

Aula looked up sharply. "He's made our lives a hell for as long as I can remember. I pray to the gods he stays away."

Maia cried harder.

"We'll all do what we can to make sure of it," said Varazda, before Dami could try to reply—because what could he say? He would only be here for a few more days.

CHAPTER 14

IN THE END they did go to the music store and get the lute. Varazda offered to take Maia and Aula in and feed them, but they went back to their house to see to the younger children. Maia kept looking at Dami as though she wanted to say something to him but couldn't work up the courage.

They brought the lute back to Varazda's sitting room, and Dami played and sang. His voice was deep and rough as his stubble, the low notes sounding almost growly. Varazda fell asleep curled up next to him on the divan.

He woke before dawn, feeling clear-headed and alert. The room was bathed in a cold, grey light. He uncoiled himself and sat up to look at Dami, who had fallen asleep with the lute still in his lap, legs stretched out, leaning back against a pile of cushions in the corner of the divan. His sleeping face was stripped of its sternness, as if he might be having pleasant dreams.

As Varazda watched, Dami stirred, arching his back slightly and moving his head against the cushions. A smile twitched at his lips. The lute slipped across his lap. Varazda reached out and caught it before it fell, but Dami was already blinking awake.

His gaze, warm and slightly disoriented, was on Varazda, who slid the lute away onto the table and moved toward him. Dami pulled him onto his lap, hands firm on Varazda's waist, with an eagerness that sent a thrill through him. Varazda straddled his thighs and moved against him. Dami was already impressively hard, and Varazda felt his own desire rising to meet him. Dami's mouth was hot and urgent against his, and his hands were everywhere. It was exactly what Varazda had been wanting all night.

He pulled back, rising up on his knees and bracing one hand on the wall above Dami's shoulder. They breathed for a moment.

"You're quite awake?" Varazda said. "Because—there's more than one kind of 'taking advantage,' isn't there?"

"Mmm." Dami rubbed his eyes and scraped a hand across his stubble. "I'm—waking up." He squinted at the lines of weak light coming through the shutters. "It's not morning yet, is it?"

"It's not. Do you ... want to go to bed?"

"Divine Terza. Yes. Let's."

They scrambled off the divan and headed for the bedroom. Varazda latched the door.

"Do you want me to go down on you?" Dami asked.

"Go where?"

Dami made an indicative gesture, from his lips to Varazda's groin. "Has to be on the bed, though. Can't literally go to my knees for you, sorry."

"No, no, you don't have to ... Holy angels. Yes, I want you to do that, but ... " He looked down helplessly. "You're already ... so ..." It didn't seem polite to make him wait for his own gratification.

Dami chuckled, low and beautiful. "I have an idea." He put his hands on Varazda's belt. "May I?"

"Yes."

It felt different to be undressed when he was wearing

Pseuchaian clothes—a little awkward and perfunctory—and he realized no one but himself had ever done it before. He wondered if Dami had much experience undressing his male lovers; if they'd all been soldiers together, perhaps they just unbuckled their armour and stripped off their tunics and got to it.

They both broke down giggling when Varazda's hair got caught in the neck of his tunic and ended up all over his face. He shook it back and attacked Dami's military-style belt, which had a strangely complicated buckle that he couldn't immediately undo. Dami meanwhile was trying to push Varazda's loincloth down without properly undoing it, and they both ended up leaning into each other, nuzzling affectionately, on the edge of laughter, until their clothes were scattered on the floor around them.

Dami firmed his grip on Varazda's waist and lifted him, and Varazda wrapped his legs around Dami and held on, doing his best to make himself easy to carry. Dami did carry him, all the way to the bed, where he tumbled him down the wrong way round, with a little grunt of effort. Something about that—the way he'd done it, the fact that he hadn't tried to make it look easy—brought a great swell of affection to Varazda's heart.

He started to sit up to rearrange himself the right way around on the bed, but instead he lazily watched Dami take down the reservoir of oil from the lamp stand and come back to the bed. In the thin shadows of early morning, his body, naked and roused, was like something out of a dream.

"Hold out your hands," Dami said.

Varazda obeyed, uncomprehending, and Dami poured a little oil into them. He took Varazda's hands in his and smoothed the oil slowly over both palms with his thumbs. He sat on the bed by Varazda's hip.

"What am I supposed to do with these?" Varazda asked, holding up his slick hands.

"You'll think of something," said Dami, and he drew up his legs and stretched out on his side, right way around on the bed.

"Oh," said Varazda. This was so far from what he had expected that he was actually rather shocked. For a moment he froze, oily hands awkwardly out in front of him.

"So what you do … " Dami began drily.

Varazda growled. "I know what to do."

He dropped his head back to the mattress, and Dami's beautiful cock was in front of his face, Dami's strong hands were on his thighs, and Dami's mouth gently touched the red-hot centre of his own desire.

He caressed Dami's manhood with his slippery palms, pressing his face into Dami's thighs, all the technique he had ever known forgotten. He was on fire from the waist down, his flesh crying out for more everywhere Dami touched with his mouth and hands. He begged aloud, in the dialect of his childhood, which he knew Dami didn't understand.

"Ah, Dami, my heart, I … " He was molten, reforming under Dami's touch. "I'm—I'll—almost—" was all he could manage by way of warning.

He heard that throaty chuckle again, and Dami drew back with a slow lick, and held Varazda with one big hand, balancing him on that precipice for a long, aching moment before, with a gentle swirl of his thumb, he tipped him over. Varazda tried to muffle his shout of pleasure against Dami's thigh, and it didn't quite work.

His head was full of Dami's scent, his cheek and lips pressed against the rough hair of Dami's body. Pleasure sang through him, sparking like fire and warming as wine, and he nuzzled between Dami's legs and opened his throbbing lips on Dami's flesh as if he was hungry for the taste of him. He licked clumsily, making no attempt to take Dami's manhood all the way into his mouth. Dami might despise him for this abject display, but just then he couldn't help it, didn't care—he wanted this so much.

Dami rolled over and spread his thighs with a groan to give Varazda easier access, and Varazda's fingers slipping daringly into the warm, muscular cleft below Dami's balls. That sent Dami over the edge, and he came with a long shudder.

They lay top-to-tail, sprawled and entangled, for long minutes after Dami's climax. Dami had his arm around one of Varazda's legs, and stroked lightly along thigh and knee and up to his ankle.

"You have the most incredible legs," he said drowsily. "I don't know if I've mentioned that before."

Varazda smiled absurdly up at the ceiling. He was rather proud of his legs. "I'm glad you like them."

"And I'm glad you get to show them off." He kissed Varazda's ankle.

"You … that was all right? You liked it? I'm afraid I wasn't very attentive—I … got caught up."

"Are you kidding? I love that. You can get caught up with me any time, sweetheart. And you know, as I may have said before—I like a lot of things."

Varazda disentangled himself slightly from Dami in order to push up on his hands into a sitting position. Dami looked so good sprawled there, sweaty and mussed, with his arm twined around Varazda's leg. Varazda had a fleeting thought of asking just what "I like a lot of things" meant, but the moment was so good, and he didn't want to risk it. He flopped back down on the bed with a happy sigh.

Varazda woke much later that morning feeling warm and beautiful and slightly sticky. He was alone in the bed, but it was Dami's bed; he was lying by the window, and there was a rumpled space in the bedclothes and a squashed-down pillow next to him showing where Dami had slept for the last few hours of the night.

He rolled over under the covers and snuggled into Dami's side of the bed, breathing in the familiar scent of his lover. Last night had gone pretty well after all, he thought. Or ended well, anyway. He smiled to himself.

All right, Varazda, he told himself sternly. *This is no time to luxuriate*. He still had work to do if he wanted Dami in his life for more than a few days. And he did, because he was in love with Dami. Had he ever seriously doubted that?

He'd meant to spend the morning practicing, but more importantly, he had not been there when Remi woke. He was always there when Remi woke—usually she woke him, in fact—and she would be upset. He rolled out of bed and grabbed the first item of clothing that his hand fell on, hauling it over his head and tugging out his hair. It was a white tunic of Dami's, and it was large and shapeless on Varazda. He headed for the door.

Remi was in the kitchen, sitting on a bench and feeding pieces of lettuce to Selene, who was strutting back and forth under the table.

"Yaza, look, Papa's up!" she announced happily.

Yazata turned from the sink with a dripping bowl in his hands and a stricken expression on his face.

"I'm sorry," said Varazda, rubbing his eyes. "I … uh … should have … "

"No, no," said Yazata quickly, clutching the wet bowl. "I got Remi up. It's no trouble."

"Oh."

"No, no trouble. You deserve to—to be able to lie in bed with your—" He drew himself up bravely. "With your lover. From time to time."

Varazda's mouth felt dry, and he wondered if he had a headache coming on after all. "Do I?" he said blankly.

"Oh, Varazda," Yazata moaned. "I am so sorry."

Remi looked between them with mystified alarm. "Did you do something bad?"

"It's nothing, Remi my sweet," said Yazata, "it's nothing. No! It's not nothing. I have been foolish, and unkind to your father. I have been most terribly foolish."

Remi looked like she might begin to cry. So did Yazata, for that matter.

"Yaza ... " Varazda began. Could he go back to bed now? he wondered. Where was Dami?

"Here," said Yazata, hastily putting his bowl back in the sink and drying his hands on his robe before reaching for a basket of saffron buns on the workbench. "You must be hungry. Sit down."

"Thanks. I'm actually thirsty ... "

"Of course! And I made fresh kilf!" He plopped the basket on the table and dove back to the workbench for a covered jug.

"Are you friends again?" Remi wanted to know.

"Yes, Remiza," said Varazda. "We always will be. We've never not been friends."

"But, but Yaza said ... "

Varazda rubbed his eyes. "He said that he'd made a mistake and he was sorry. That's what you say, isn't it, when you make a mistake—that you're sorry?"

"Oh."

"Even adults."

Remi laughed as if that was a good joke. "Can I go out and play with Dori and Opi?"

"Yes," said Varazda, "that's an excellent idea. Why don't you take Selene with you."

Yazata set a cup of kilf in front of Varazda and sat down at the table opposite him. He twisted his big hands together.

Varazda sipped his kilf. "Thanks. You've had a change of heart about something?"

"I heard noise in the street last night and looked out my window. I saw everything that happened."

Varazda gave a wry laugh. "You regretted taking away Dami's sword, because you noticed he could have used it? By the way, where has he gone?"

"I don't know," said Yazata quickly. "I shouldn't have hidden his sword, no, but I should also have trusted you from the beginning. I should have trusted you to know your own mind and not to be deceived. But you see, back when you first told me about meeting Damiskos on Pheme—you were in such a bad state when you came back from Pheme. I think all I heard was that he was someone who'd been in this trouble with you—perhaps he'd gotten you into it, I thought. Well, I convinced myself that was the case."

Varazda nodded. "Yes, I was in a bad way. I can see how you would have worried. I'm sorry."

"It is *not* your fault. Nor his fault, I can see that now. Holy God, don't think I can't see that now. But I'm always so quick to believe the worst of men."

"You have good reason. And Dami didn't make a good impression, what with attacking Tash on his first night here."

"That's … yes. That was unfortunate. Though even I can see that he was only doing the right thing. I could see that at the time, once I heard what had happened. But … " He heaved a large sigh. "You see, I thought, when you invited Damiskos here, when I knew you were still working on something to do with the affairs in Pheme, I thought … "

"You thought Dami was work, didn't you?" Varazda supplied. "You thought I was sleeping with him for work."

Yazata nodded mutely.

"And that I invited him to live with us because I was still on the job?"

Yazata nodded again.

"I was beginning to suspect that's what you thought. Holy God. It's a wonder you didn't do more than steal his sword and set the goose on him, Yaza, if that's what you thought. Did it not occur to you that if he were work, I would have told you?"

"Well, I … but … Do you mean to say he *wasn't*? I'm sure I remember you saying that you had to pretend to be in love with him or some such."

"Ye-es. That's true. We pretended to be a couple for a little while at Laothalia. But that was him doing me a favour, because Aristokles had disappeared and taken my cover story with him. Dami was never part of my assignment. And when we went to bed together, it was because we both wanted to. Both, um, both times."

"Angels of the Almighty. I had no idea. I thought … I thought you were *becoming* fond of him, certainly I could see that, but you had been so, so businesslike before he got here—"

Varazda groaned. "I was trying to spare your feelings. I didn't want you to worry that you were going to be displaced, that I was becoming someone different just because … " He gestured vaguely. "This new thing had happened to me."

"Yes, yes," said Yazata, nodding, "that makes perfect sense, now that you explain it." He took a discreet swipe at his eyes with the sleeve of his robe.

"And you weren't entirely wrong," Varazda forged on. "We did start out as … well, reluctant allies, and then became fond of one another. And of course I'm not experienced in these things, so I was less sure of what I wanted than he—if you've seen that, you've seen the truth."

Yazata wrinkled his nose sceptically. "I don't know. You seem pretty sure to me."

"Do I?"

"Yes. That's why I was so worried about you. I didn't like the idea of your having to entertain this man, of course." He shuddered. "I felt I needed to protect you somehow, but I didn't know how. Then when I saw that you didn't seem to be pretending to like him—you may think I can't tell, because no one else can, but I have known you a long time, and it seemed to me you were becoming truly attached, and *that* made me fear for you. Because who was he? Someone connected with the riot and that bad business on Pheme, that's all I knew.

"Then I saw what he did last night, and I realized I had no reason to be afraid for you. I—you see—I had spoken to Maia about it, and of course I could not tell her exactly what I feared, because she cannot know about your work, but I told her that I was afraid the man you were bringing here would not be good for you. Of course she thought she knew what I meant by that."

"Someone like Stamos," Varazda supplied.

Yazata nodded. "I told her he didn't seem so bad, but she said they don't, at first. They charm you, and then they reveal their true nature." He shuddered again. "My first master was like that. I remember how he was with the women and children … " He trailed off, because this was a story he had no need to rehearse for Varazda. "Well, last night when I saw Damiskos in the street, I thought I had seen his true nature, and it was nothing like what I had imagined."

"I'm so glad, Yazata. I'm so very glad."

"And you are truly in love with him?" He asked it not with reluctance but with an almost childlike wonder.

"I … I don't know. Do you think that's something I'm even capable of?"

"Do I think … Varazda, I think you are the most loving person I know."

"Don't be absurd."

"I am not being absurd. Look at how you keep bringing people into your household. First it was me: 'Yazata,' you said, 'you should come live with me. I'll work, and you can keep house.' Just as if that was the sort of thing that friends do for one another all the time. Then, 'Young Tash has nowhere to go, he should move in with us.' I took some convincing, as you will recall. Then Remi was going to be taken in by that horrible family, and you said, 'Yazata, I think we could raise a child. Don't you think so?' You had to convince me again, and every day I thank God that you did. So you see, it's entirely like you to want to take in a lame soldier and add a room to the house for him so he doesn't have to climb stairs. And if you get something from him that you've always wanted and never got to have, well, you deserve it."

"How do you know that I've always wanted … "

Yazata shrugged uncomfortably. "It—it always seemed obvious to me. You like men."

"Mm. I hadn't thought it was obvious."

"I'm sorry—I really was so convinced that you were courting him for the sake of your job, you know. What a terrible fool I have been. And now … "

"And now?"

"He's left."

"He's *what*?"

"There's—there's a note." Yazata hauled himself up from the table to fetch a tablet which was lying on the workbench. "He left it on the table. Tash had already gone, or I would have asked him to read it. I … I'm so sorry."

He put the tablet gingerly down on the table in front of Varazda, who looked at it in cold incomprehension for a moment. Then he began to laugh.

"What?" Yazata demanded, alarmed.

"It's Bread Day. There's some religious observance. He's gone to the shrine of Terza. That's all." He rested his head in his hands. "Holy angels, Yazata, you nearly stopped my heart for a moment there."

"You mean—he's not gone? He's—he's coming back?" Yazata stared at the tablet as if he thought the words might suddenly become plain to him. "You're sure?"

"I think if he'd meant, 'I'm going to the shrine and then I'm off home to Pheme, thanks for last night,' that's what he would have written. He's a pretty straightforward man."

Yazata groaned. "I have been thrice a fool—one hundred times a fool! What can I do to make amends?"

"You've already done it. All that stuff about me being the most loving person you know … If you're happy for me, if I haven't made your life intolerable … " Tears were sliding down his cheeks. "I love you so much, Yazata."

"And I love you! Never doubt it."

"I know," said Varazda, wiping his eyes. "I know." After a moment he added, dryly, "There are one or two things you could apologize to Damiskos for."

"Hello, can I come in?" called Maia's voice from the front door.

"Maia!" Yazata bustled off to the hall. "Are you all right? I saw the terrible scene last night. He didn't come back, did he?"

Maia joined them in the kitchen. "No, he didn't come back. Thanks to your friend. Is he here? Your friend. I wanted to tell him—how grateful I am."

"He's gone to do his devotions at the temple of Terza," Yazata explained importantly. "I have been telling Varazda how sorry I am for believing the worst of him."

Maia winced. "I'm the one who should apologize, Pharastes. I'm afraid I put ideas into Iasta's head."

"Nonsense," said Yazata stoutly. "It was no one's fault but my own."

"No, I can't let you say that." Maia turned to Varazda. For a moment she seemed distracted by what he was wearing. Varazda realized he was still in Dami's unbelted, oversized tunic. "I, uh. I imagined he was someone like Stamos—I told Iasta he should do whatever he could to get rid of him, for your sake. And then—and then *he* was the one who got rid of Stamos, and I'm so very grateful, I can't tell you. So you see I'm terribly sorry. Can you forgive me?"

"Of course. My dears, of course I forgive both of you. You were trying to look out for me."

Yazata gathered them both into an embrace, and Varazda had just finished kissing him on the cheek when the front door opened again and Dami came in.

He wasn't alone. A woman followed him in whom Varazda recognized after a moment as Kallisto's servant Leto. It was the first time he had seen her fully coifed and ready to go out.

"Hello," said Dami, leaning his cane in the corner by the door. "You got my note?"

"Yes," said Varazda, disentangling himself from Maia and Yazata, who were both looking at Dami with expressions so overflowing with pathos that after a moment Dami noticed and began to look alarmed. None of them was quite dry-eyed, but only Varazda had obvious tear-tracks down his face. He rubbed them away hastily.

"I met Leto coming up the street," Dami explained awkwardly. To her he said, "I assume you're looking for Ariston."

Leto gave the group in the kitchen a smile so half-hearted it was more like a sneer. "No."

"Who's Ariston?" said Maia.

"Tash," Yazata explained. "He is calling himself Ariston now."

"Oh, I didn't know that."

"It's not him I want to see," said Leto impatiently. "It's —" She flicked her fingers in Varazda's direction. "—that one."

Dami gave her a hard look, which she didn't notice.

"Come inside then," said Varazda unenthusiastically, gesturing toward the sitting room.

Yazata bustled Maia off to his side of the house, and Leto

came in, scanning the rooms as she passed through them with unconcealed—and unsympathetic—curiosity. Varazda beckoned to Dami, who was standing sternly in the hall as if awaiting orders. He proceeded smartly into the kitchen.

"How was your, uh, your religious thing?" Varazda asked, when Leto had gone through into the sitting room.

Dami answered distractedly. "It was—The shrine is beautiful—Are you all right? You've been … Have you been … " He trailed off, paralyzed, as his instinct to be considerate warred with his instinct to be blunt.

"Crying?" Varazda suggested. "Mm. Not in a bad way, but—I might start again if I try to talk about it now. I'll tell you later." Tipping his head toward the sitting room, he said in Zashian, "This is about work."

Dami nodded curtly. "I'll make myself scarce."

"No, you can come hear what she has to say—I'd like you to. I'm not going to keep secrets from you." After a moment he revised, "Any more. I'm not going to keep secrets from you any more. Though to be fair this is less a secret and more something that I haven't wanted to be bothered to talk about."

"I see," said Dami. "Lead the way."

CHAPTER 15

"The other day," Leto said to Varazda, as she sat perched primly on the edge of a divan, "you said that you thought Lykanos Lykandros might be jealous of Themistokles."

"I did say that. You weren't in the room at the time."

"No, I was listening at the door," she said, as if he was being very stupid and she was being very forbearing. "The thing is, you're right. He's wild with jealousy."

"Really."

"Oh yes. Not just over Kallisto, but because of the sculpting, too. He used to be a sculptor, you know, but he gave it up—I guess he wasn't very good. But he'd do anything to be revenged on Themi."

"Interesting," said Varazda. It *was* interesting, but not in the way she presumably hoped. She was managing to tell him things he had already guessed in a way that made him not believe her. He wondered why that was. "Specifically, what might he do?"

"I don't know, but he's going to do it tonight at the Palace of Letters."

"How do you know that?"

"He told me so."

Varazda looked at her, and her cheeks flushed scarlet as she evidently realized what she had just confessed.

"Don't tell Kallisto," she snapped, a plea that sounded like an attempt at an order.

"Don't tell Kallisto … ?"

"All right. Look. He comes to me, not the other way around. He likes variety, you know? I have different ways of doing … *things* … " She took obvious pleasure in making Varazda uncomfortable with that. "And sometimes he likes that. So sometimes he tells me things, all right? And he told me that he's going to do something to Themistokles on the night of the dedication at the Palace of Letters. That's all I know."

"Why are you telling us, though?"

She looked at him as if she couldn't believe his stupidity. "So you can stop it?"

"You're fond of Themistokles, then?"

"Th—him?" She looked genuinely stumped for a moment. "*I'm* not fond of him, no. But Kallisto is, and he's her main client and everything. Of course I don't want him to get killed or whatever."

Varazda nodded. "Right."

"So," she said, gathering up her skirt, "that's all. I thought I ought to tell you."

There were various other questions Varazda thought he could have asked if he had believed any of this, but he had no interest in watching Leto tie herself into knots coming up with unconvincing answers.

"I see," he said instead. "Thank you. I will show you out."

He returned to the sitting room after closing the door behind her.

"That was odd," said Dami mildly.

"Quite odd, yes." Varazda ran a hand through his hair. He didn't want to think about this now. It seemed the least important thing in the world. He gathered himself together.

It wasn't the least important thing—it was his job, and he was proud of doing it. "There is some context which I should explain."

"Oh," said Dami quickly, "no. You don't need to."

"No, I do. It's related to things you already know, anyway. It's past time I filled you in on all of this."

He sat on the divan next to Dami.

"This has something to do with what happened in Laothalia?" Dami guessed.

Varazda nodded. "Do you know the outcome of the trials here?"

Dami looked at the ceiling. "Gelon was tried for murder, for killing Aristokles, and executed. Phaia was sentenced to Choros Rock for her part in it. Those were the only charges we heard about in Pheme. I assumed some of the others had been quietly exiled."

Varazda nodded again. "The Boukossians who had a part in the riot and burning the embassy were sent into exile without a public trial. Some ministers in the Basileon were upset about that, but there's a strong feeling we need to keep any of this from coming to the attention of the Zashian court."

"I can see how there would be. What about Helenos? He was the ringleader. Was he charged with anything?"

"No," said Varazda bitterly. "Helenos is Phemian. He couldn't be convincingly tied to the murder of Aristokles or to the riot in Boukos—he was obviously very careful there—so we had nothing to charge him with. He was going to be sent back to Pheme under guard to be charged in the business at Nione's villa—he and a few of the others—but someone paid off a clerk to lose a crucial letter, and they were released."

Dami drew a breath. "Damn. That's bad luck."

"The money to pay the clerk seems to have come, in a roundabout way, from Lykanos Lykandros."

185

"Kallisto's man. The one who likes to be choked while hearing about Themistokles?"

"That one. He of course denies having anything to do with it—not that he's been formally accused—and it's possible, plausible even, that the thing was planned by someone who works for him, and he really doesn't know anything about it. There's no obvious candidate, though, so I've been investigating Lykanos himself. I danced at his house and asked some discreet questions. He's not a die-hard anti-Zashian. He doesn't consort with philosophers. He seems pretty harmless. I was just coming to the conclusion that if he did pay to have Helenos escape, it wasn't to do with politics at all. Maybe he was doing a favour for Helenos's mother, who's an old flame of his. I don't know. And it really doesn't matter, if it was something like that. I mean it doesn't matter to the Basileon or to the Zashian embassy. Nione is owed reparations for what happened at her villa, and that shouldn't have been thwarted, but … " He made a hopeless gesture.

"I get it," said Dami. "Not really the mission objective. But now, something about all this has made you suspicious again?"

"I don't know," said Varazda with a frown. "I think it's just a coincidence that he's turned up in all of this, but it's given me a new perspective on him. I went to see Kallisto yesterday."

"Did you?"

"She's Zashian, you know."

"Is she really?"

"She is. I had to work that out on my own, though I suspect Ariston knows. I think they bonded over their shared history. I wanted to know if she'd seen any indication that Lykanos was anti-Zashian, and she hadn't. But she did give me an interesting piece of information about Themistokles. He's a progressive—favours the Zashian alliance, up to a point, thinks possibly slavery might be abolished, someday maybe."

"Hah. So … now we have this very thin story about Lykanos intending harm to Themistokles because he's jealous of him."

"It might all be nothing," said Varazda. "Lykanos just happened to do a favour for an anti-Zashian philosopher, and he just happens to have a personal grudge against a vaguely pro-Zashian sculptor with political aspirations."

"Or there could be a connection."

"A view that I incline to, honestly. I just wish I knew what Leto was trying to accomplish by coming here and telling us her story."

"Maybe *she* has a grudge against Lykanos herself."

"Oh, I hadn't thought of that. I was thinking of her as being on his side, because of the … you know, because they're … "

"Fucking," Dami supplied. "She's obviously a bit disloyal in general. I'd be surprised if she was on anyone's side but her own."

"Well," said Varazda, getting to his feet, "are you up for another walk? Because it looks like I'm on my way to Themistokles's studio to warn him, or—I don't know—hear his side of this story."

"Of course," said Dami, holding out a hand so Varazda could help him up. "I'll come. But—first, do you think you could tell me what happened before I got here that made you … er … "

"Oh, that made me cry." He'd almost forgotten that he had.

"Or at least," Dami hurried on, "tell me that it didn't have anything to do with last night."

"Last night? You mean … ? Holy angels, Dami, last night was so good. I loved every moment of it."

"Oh, that's—that's—"

"You are so good to me. Don't tell me you've been sitting here worrying that I have regrets about last night."

"I—I won't tell you that."

Varazda gave a slight whimper. "What happened this morning was that Yazata admitted—what I'd already begun to suspect—that he thought I was sleeping with you for work."

Dami reared back with a look of shock, putting his hand over his mouth. "He—what?" he said when he took it away. "Varazda, are you serious? He thought that you were—that you—"

"I've never had to do that, never been asked to do anything like that," Varazda assured him quickly.

"Yes. Yes, I remember." Dami sounded a little calmer. "You told me that."

"Yazata knows that too. But when I told him that you and I pretended to be a couple at Laothalia, he heard something different, and when I said you were coming to stay ... " Varazda shrugged, spreading his hands. "He knew I was still working on something connected with the events on Pheme."

"He thought I was *an assignment*." Dami looked sick. "Divine Terza, I'm sorry. I'm lucky he didn't try poisoning my labash. He must—he must trust you quite a lot, actually. If he was willing to accept that you knew what you were doing, to the extent that he did."

"Without asking me about it?" Varazda rolled his eyes. "I'm not sure I want that kind of trust." He looked down at his hands. "But yes. He does trust me. And he and Ariston were both worried about me. When I came back from Laothalia ... " He'd so profoundly wanted to avoid talking about this before, but he found that was no longer the case. "It was lucky, in a way, that I was injured. It gave me an excuse to cancel plans and go out as little as possible. I've hardly left the house in the last month, before you came. I couldn't sleep at first—I jumped at sudden sounds. Didn't dance at all for two weeks, which—imagine if you could go for two weeks without breathing, how you would feel by the end of it. And then imagine if the reason you hadn't been breathing was because you *just didn't feel like it*. That's what it's like."

Dami nodded, making what looked like a determined effort to tamp down an expression of anguish. "I was afraid you might have a hard time. I … I wish I had been there. But you had your family."

"I did. They were very good. Unruffled." Varazda smiled. At some point he had ended up in Dami's arms, in a loose but protective embrace. "They're very sweet when they want to be. And they've seen me like that before."

"Right. But as far as they knew, I was mixed up in what-ever had happened to you on Pheme, which meant I was not to be trusted. I did wonder if it might have been partly that. But I didn't want to ask. I thought you'd tell me if you wanted me to know."

Varazda leaned his forehead against Dami's, letting his eyes slip closed. He allowed himself a moment of feeling blissfully safe and not caring that he needed it. Then he straightened up, stepping out of Dami's arms.

"I can't go out wearing this," he said, displaying the unbelted white tunic. "I'll run upstairs and change."

Walking to Themistokles's studio to warn Ariston's master about some nebulous threat to his life was not the way Varazda would have preferred to spend Dami's last morning in Boukos. But they made it as pleasant as possible. Dami slung his arm around Varazda's waist, and Varazda returned the gesture and got used to accommodating the rhythm of Dami's uneven gait, swaying against him a little, and he could see in the little private smile that curved Dami's lips how much that meant to him. It was such a simple thing.

"I hope to be able to come back in a month," Dami said finally, the first of them to broach the subject. "If I would be welcome."

"You know you would."

He ducked his head in acknowledgement. "I might be able to stay longer then."

"Yes? Good."

Was it too soon to say, *Stay forever*? Yes, Varazda thought, it was too soon. Totalling up the days they had spent together, their acquaintance was still only two weeks old. Dami had only had one week to sample Varazda's life in Boukos. It had been an eventful week, too, hardly representative.

"I will do my best not to have any family crises arise next time," Varazda said.

"Oh, don't trouble yourself on my account."

"You are good in a crisis, it's true."

"So I've been told."

Themistokles was alone in his studio when they arrived. He came to the door with a chisel in his hand and a fine coating of white powder in his sandy hair. Varazda had often seen Ariston come home in the same state.

"Ah, hello! Pharastes, isn't it? You've just missed Tasos—I expect he's been telling you about the upcoming dedication? He's gone to the Palace of Art now to see to some last-minute preparations before tonight."

"Actually, we came to speak to you," said Varazda.

"Of course! Come in."

They had barely got through the doorway when Ariston came rushing through it on their heels.

"Themistokles, sir," he panted, "there's—what in Psobos's name are you two doing here?"

"More or less the same thing you were about to do, I

think," said Dami. "Warning Themistokles about the threat against him."

"What?" Themistokles stared at each of them in turn. "Threat?"

"Yes," said Ariston. "I've just heard about it from Leto."

"Kallisto's freedwoman?" said Themistokles. "But—what does she—"

Ariston leapt in. "One of Kallisto's other lovers—um, um, you know she has other lovers, right?"

"Yes, yes."

"One of them plans to attack you tonight at the dedication. They're going to sabotage the mooring of the frieze so that it falls on you when you're standing in front of it addressing the guests!"

Themistokles blinked at him in confusion for a moment. Dami and Varazda exchanged glances again.

"Who ... did you say ... is doing this?" Themistokles asked finally.

"It's Lykanos Lykandros, sir."

Themistokles gave a shouting laugh. "But that's preposterous! Lykanos and I are old friends. He was my first mentor, my first ... you know."

"He's jealous, sir, because of you and Kallisto."

"Pfft! He's not *jealous*—he was the one who introduced me to Kallisto in the first place, and gave me his blessing. Besides," Themistokles added, his expression becoming briefly pained, "he knows I'm giving her up. I told him about it just the other day."

Ariston shrugged hopelessly. "I don't know, sir. I'm just telling you what Leto said. I think we'd better go back to the Palace of Letters and check all the panels, and then set a strict watch, don't you think, Damiskos?"

Everyone looked at Dami. Themistokles said, "What?" again.

"I think that would be wise," said Dami carefully. "But I

do find it suspicious that Leto told a different story to you than she told to us."

"She what?" said Ariston.

"She came to the house earlier this morning," said Varazda. "Her story was that Lykanos was planning something at the dedication, but she didn't know what it was."

"She must have found out, after," Ariston said impatiently. "Then she came to find me."

"That may be it," Dami agreed.

"Or," said Themistokles, with a violence which startled Varazda, "she is making this whole thing up because she is a duplicitous slut who can't stand to see me happy."

There was a moment's silence. Then Varazda said, mildly, "How would that follow, if I may ask?"

"You mean why would she 'warn' me about a threat to my life, if she hates me? To ruin my moment of triumph, of course. My frieze is about to be unveiled in the Palace of Letters, I will announce my candidacy for councillor in the Basileon—it is going to be a important night for me, a great achievement. She can't stand to see that. I'm sure that's why she's doing this. Lykanos and I are friends."

Ariston's face twisted with worry. "I still think we should stand guard by the frieze, sir. Just to make sure."

"The Palace of Letters will be well guarded—the public watch will be there, I have been assured. And the guest list is set. You will be there, of course, Tasos, as my apprentice, but I want you to enjoy the evening—after all, your work has gone into this piece as well. You are due your share of the glory!" He put a firm hand on Ariston's shoulder, smiling reassuringly. "It will be all right. I'm grateful to you all for warning me, but I'm not worried."

CHAPTER 16

ARISTON BURST out the door into the street a moment after it had shut behind Varazda and Damiskos.

"What are we going to do?"

Dami and Varazda looked at one another. Varazda drew a deep breath.

"Well," he said, "I was invited to dance at the dedication party, but I turned them down. I can send a message and ask if I can be last-minute addition to the entertainment after all."

Ariston nodded. "Good, good. And Damiskos? We've got to have you there too, you'd be so useful. Perhaps you could sneak in through the—"

"Ariston," said Varazda warningly. "Nobody is sneaking in through anywhere, especially not Damiskos."

"I don't need to," Dami said easily. "I can come with Varazda."

"Oh, as his bodyguard?" Ariston suggested eagerly.

"As my accompanist," Varazda corrected him.

"That's what I was thinking," said Dami, smiling.

"All right, well, whatever," said Ariston. "The main thing is—"

"I think," Varazda interrupted him, "what you mean to say is, 'Thank you, Damiskos, for being willing to help me, especially on the last evening of your vacation.'"

"Wait, what? You mean—you're not going back to Pheme *tomorrow*?"

"I am, but ... "

"Holy God, Damiskos, you can't leave! It's not because of how we've—yeah, no, it is because how we've treated you, me and Yazata, isn't it? You know I'm sorry about that, don't you? I'd do anything to make it up to you. I'll talk to Yaza, too, I know he's treated you like shit. I think he was just a bit scared of you. Don't leave. I'd feel awful if you left."

"That's very kind of you," Dami cut across Ariston's babbling. "I do hope to come back soon."

"Oh." Ariston sagged with relief. "Oh, that's good! I thought you meant ... never mind. Anyway, I'm glad you're here to help out tonight, and *thank you*. Gods. I'm going to go straight to the Palace of Letters after I've finished my work here, and keep watch, but the sight-lines are bad because of all the scaffolding, so we'll definitely need all three of us patrolling. Find me when you arrive, all right?"

He ducked back inside Themistokles's house, leaving Dami and Varazda alone in the street.

"You think this is a fool's errand, don't you?" said Dami, looking at the closed door.

"Absolutely. But I'm not sure I buy Themistokles's explanation any more than Leto's."

Dami ran a hand along his jaw, his fingers making a little rasping sound on his stubble. "What's the Palace of Letters, anyway?"

"It's a library. It's quite old and was beginning to look a bit shabby, so a group of citizens commissioned a new frieze and some other things. This is their private party to celebrate the completion of the work."

"I see. I was imagining something a bit more spectacular,

from the way Themistokles talked about it. I didn't realize he was making this important announcement at a party in a library."

"Well, the people involved are some of the most consequential in the city, one way or another. It's a pretty reasonable place for him to announce his candidacy."

"Why did you turn down the invitation to dance?"

Varazda looked away. "I wanted to spend the evening with you."

Dami squeezed his arm. "Well, you will. So this thing about the frieze. You think it's a trap?"

"It think it is a trap. But I'm not sure for whom, or why."

"I suppose the only thing we can be sure of is that it's not a trap for *us*, so we might as well do what we can to help."

"That's what I was thinking," Varazda agreed. "Though I would have preferred to spend your last night here differently."

"Me too. Hey, I just thought of something. If Yazata has come round now, that leaves the goose as the only member of your family who doesn't like me."

"It does indeed. A good week's work."

They stopped at one of the wine shops where you could reliably find boys waiting to be sent on errands, and Varazda wrote out a message for the master of ceremonies, gave directions for its delivery, and asked for the answer to be brought to Saffron Alley.

They set off to walk home. Varazda scanned the street for a free chair for hire, but couldn't see one.

"I wish I didn't have to leave," Dami said. "I mean—" He cleared his throat. "I wish I could stay longer."

"So do I," said Varazda. He slipped an arm around Dami's waist again. From the other side of the street, he saw a couple of women turn to stare at them.

That had happened once or twice on their way to Themistokles's studio, too, now that he thought about it. It hadn't particularly registered, because Varazda was used to attracting a certain amount of attention. He thought about what Kallisto had said, or claimed that Ariston had said, about him being comfortable as himself. He wondered if that was true.

"Do you mind," he asked Dami, "that people are looking at us?"

"Eh? Are they?"

Varazda arched an eyebrow at him. "Really, First Spear. I thought you soldiers were ever alert to your surroundings."

"We're not on a battlefield. I don't know if you've noticed. But to your question—no, I don't mind being envied."

"You're very sweet."

"I don't know if it's that. To be honest, I just don't give a fuck. I've never had a lover I'd have been ashamed to kiss in the street. I don't now." He looked Varazda in the eye. "Want me to prove it?"

Varazda's hand flew to his mouth. "Oh, God," he said from behind it, "no, I don't. I—I'm sorry, but no."

Dami laughed that growly, pit-of-the-stomach laugh. "Let me know, any time you change your mind. And," he added more seriously, "if you don't, that's absolutely fine too. The street isn't my favourite place to kiss."

Varazda felt it was safe to take his hand away from his mouth. "Should I ask … what is?"

"Nah. I'd just have to say something dirty, and you'd start blushing again, and it would become a whole situation."

"Ah."

The message from the master of ceremonies arrived soon after Varazda and Dami made their leisurely way back to Saffron Alley. The master of ceremonies was delighted that Varazda would be available to dance after all, and reminded him that the party began at the twelfth hour and the theme of the entertainment was "The Goddesses of Letters."

"That's the other reason I turned them down the first time," Varazda admitted, subsiding onto the divan beside Dami after he had paid the messenger. "I'm always happy to dress up, but 'Goddesses of Letters?' What is that? Do they dance with swords?"

"Sure," said Dami comfortably. He had a cup of wine and one of Yazata's saffron buns, and had put his feet up. "You can be the goddess of epic. Or—" He sipped his wine with a mischievous expression. "—the goddess of Zashian—"

"That's blasphemous," Varazda cut him off primly. "There are no Zashian goddesses of anything."

"—sex manuals," Dami finished.

"That's blasphemous *and* in poor taste."

He allowed himself a moment more of relaxing next to Dami before he pushed himself up off the divan.

"I'll go change into a gown and we'll practice," he said. "Shall we?"

Dami looked up in surprise. "That—that sounds fun."

It was fun. Varazda danced with his hair down, in his pale blue gown, barefoot, with bracelets on his wrists that chimed when he moved, inventing a more feminine version of his family's ancestral dance that matched one of the Zashian tunes in Damiskos's repertoire. Dami sat to play on a chair in the corner of Varazda's practice room, and every time Varazda looked at him, he was smiling, either in concentration as he looked down at the lute while fingering a tricky passage, or glowing with delight as he watched Varazda dance.

When he had worked out a routine to his satisfaction, Varazda set down his swords, stretched, and shook back his hair. Dami sat with his forearms on his knees, cradling the lute and looking up at Varazda with a different expression now, an unsmiling intensity. Varazda stood for a moment with his hands clasped behind his head, mid-stretch. He remembered how it had gone after the last time they had been in his practice room together, when they sparred. Dami was thinking of it too, he could tell. Dami would never ask for anything—hadn't asked for anything last time, in fact. Varazda wondered if he would even say "yes" now, obvious as his desire was.

And it was obvious, in spite of the strategic way he was sitting. Varazda was surprised to realize how well he had come to be able to read Dami's moods.

He finished the stretch, bracelets chinking. "I haven't shown you the whole house," he said.

"Mm," said Dami, like someone startled out of sleep. "Haven't you?"

"No. There's an upstairs. My bedroom is up there."

"Oh yes."

"It has a bed in it."

"Mm." Dami laid the lute down carefully. "I'm not sure I'm in the mood for a bed."

"Oh. No?"

Dami got to his feet. "No. Does it have a wall?"

"A ... oh." Varazda's hand went to his throat. His loins seemed to have become molten.

"If it doesn't," said Dami, because he was Dami, "I'll understand."

"Yes," said Varazda with conviction, "it does."

If anyone in the house had stopped them between the door of Varazda's practice room and the stairs, he didn't know how he would have survived. But fortune was with them, and they got to the stairs and all the way up them uninterrupted. The door of Varazda's room stood open. They were reaching for each other as they went through it, and Varazda kicked it closed. Then they were in each other's arms, kissing as if their lives depended on it. It was some time before Varazda remembered to wriggle around and reach out to latch the door.

"The wall?" he gasped, tipping his head toward it.

He thought Dami might ask if he was sure this was what he wanted, but it must have been obvious that it was. Dami just looked into his eyes for a moment, and then, in the gentlest, most loving way imaginable, pinned him against the wall.

Varazda was liquid fire. Dami was everywhere, his hands and his mouth and his strong thigh between Varazda's legs, leading Varazda out to the very edge of what he could bear and holding him there in safety. He pulled aside the wide neck of Varazda's gown and did something halfway between kissing and biting Varazda's shoulder, while his hand moved firmly over Varazda's chest, cupping his pectoral muscle as if it were a soft breast. He gathered the skirt of the blue gown and slid it up Varazda's thighs.

If Varazda could have strung words together then, he would have apologized, because he'd realized that under the gown he was still wearing a man's undergarment, and for a moment he feared that might spoil Dami's pleasure.

It didn't seem to. Dami gave a warm chuckle as he pulled it off, and then he was kissing Varazda again as he freed his own erection. Then it was just skin on skin, the two of them rubbing against each other, the pleasure of it precarious and inelegant but so sweet in its reciprocity.

Dami pushed back, straightening his arms. Varazda made a pitiful sound like a dog denied a treat. There was a gleam in Dami's eye, and he wasn't sure what it meant. The blue gown slipped down again, caressing his oversensitive skin.

"Dami, please—I can't—"

"Yes, you can," said Dami, his voice warm and rough. "I

know you can, darling."

"Can what?"

"Wait."

"Unh?" Varazda whimpered. He pressed himself back against the wall as if Dami were still holding him there.

"If it doesn't feel good ... " Dami's breath was soft on Varazda's throat.

"Of course it doesn't feel good," Varazda wailed, writhing against the wall, not reaching for Dami. "You bastard. I'm in *agony*."

He could play this game. What was more, he loved it. He bit his lip, tensing with the effort of trying to keep himself on that precipice, but he knew he could do it, and he could make it look good.

Dami had stepped away to raid Varazda's dressing table for a bottle of oil. He paused for a moment with the bottle in his hand, unopened, looking at Varazda with an appreciative smile tugging at the corners of his lips. He looked intent, almost dangerous. Varazda stretched an arm over his head, arching his back against the wall.

And Dami was back, flipping Varazda like a doll so that he faced the wall, lifting the blue gown again, and slipping an oil-slick palm between Varazda's thighs. He moved against Varazda now with a controlled power, strong but gentle, supporting him from behind and caressing him in front. Varazda rolled his head back onto Dami's shoulder. And it wasn't truly happening, but Varazda felt as if his body was being entered, taking Dami in. It felt perfect.

He pressed his palms against the wall and fought the urge to reach down and grip Dami's hand—to still it, or speed it up, or take it away—he wasn't sure which he wanted, except somehow to feel in control. And at the same time, that was exactly what he did not want.

He managed to hang on, safe and surrendered to Dami's embrace, to Dami's whole body, for longer than he had thought possible. It probably wasn't very long. His climax was slow and spectacular, like a peal of thunder that went on and on. The aftermath, with Dami still between his legs, made him giddy with delight. He hadn't a hope now of continuing his game. He reached up with one hand to slide his fingers into Dami's hair, and gripped Dami's ass with the other. Dami made a startled noise, and a moment later his passion spent itself in a hot burst between Varazda's thighs.

They held each other against the wall for a moment, panting. Then Dami, pushing himself back slightly, looked down at Varazda's dress, as the fabric fell down between them again, and said in alarm, "Did I just ruin your dance costume?"

"Um … no? Was planning to wear something different. This was just to practice in."

Dami was looking into his eyes now with a different kind of concern. "You need to lie down," he said with decision. "Here."

"I need to lie down," Varazda admitted as he let himself be peeled off the wall and led the few steps to his bed.

He stretched out on his back and felt a little as if he was floating. It wasn't so much that he was physically tired as that the game he'd just played with Dami had taken something out of him, bared something, and he needed to float there for a minute and reassemble himself.

Dami lay down beside him, on his side, propped on his elbow. He laid his other hand on Varazda's stomach, in that way that he had of making the gesture itself a question, a seeking of permission. Varazda laced his fingers with Dami's, keeping him there.

"You did really well," said Dami, after they had lain like that for a little while.

Varazda opened his eyes. "Mm?"

"Well … you tried something new. It's not easy."

"Every time with you is something new."

"Good. That's how I want it to be."

"What do you mean by that?" Varazda thought he knew.

"I mean … I don't ever want you to feel like you're back in, well, in the past."

Varazda frowned slightly. He was still floating, anchored by Dami's hand on his belly, and frowning did not come very naturally. "That's not what I thought you meant."

"No?"

"You said, 'I like a lot of things.'"

"Yeah. It's true."

"I think," said Varazda slowly, "I think—but I'm not sure —when you say that, you might mean one thing, and I keep hearing another."

"Oh?" Dami wrinkled his brow.

Varazda drew a breath. "What it sounds like to me is, you're adventurous. You like variety. Novelty."

"No," said Dami quickly. "What I meant was, I'm easy to please."

"Right."

"You don't sound convinced. I can see how it might have sounded like something else to you. I'm sorry. I didn't think of that."

Varazda made an impatient noise. "You shouldn't have to watch your words like that with me."

Dami sat up now, and his hand left Varazda's stomach. The floating sensation went with it.

"You do with me," Dami said. "Terza's head. You're a master of it. I came off the ship walking with a cane, and you never once said anything about it. You never even looked like you were *thinking* of saying anything about it."

"I wasn't. It doesn't need an explanation, and I know you're self-conscious about your injury. Of course I wasn't going to say anything about it."

"Right. And I know you tie yourself into knots over whether you like sex enough, or too much, or, I don't know, both? I know that, and I should remember it when we talk about this stuff."

"It's not the same. Your injury is something that was done to you, but I ... " He stopped.

Dami was looking at him with wide eyes, as if he might be a moment away from saying, "Are you listening to yourself?"

He was listening to himself, and he'd realized what he had been about to say. *I'm just like this. This is my nature.*

I'm nobody's victim.

"I don't like thinking of myself that way," he forced out finally.

"No," said Dami, "of course not. Me neither."

And that was what finally broke through the ice of Varazda's pride. How could he hold himself to a standard to which he refused to hold Dami? It didn't matter that Dami's cataclysm was five years in the past, his own more than twenty years. What had been taken from him was a damn sight more than what Dami had lost.

"But I suppose ... "

"I think sometimes you have to," Dami finished for him. "Or you're too hard on yourself. We—I mean—both of us." He lay down next to Varazda again.

"You're better at that than I am," said Varazda.

"Better at feeling sorry for myself. Yes, I really am." He smiled wryly.

"I didn't mean that."

Dami touched Varazda's chest lightly. "I know. Sorry."

He stroked down Varazda's side to his stomach and rubbed in a small circle. He seemed to be nursing some embers back to life, low down in Varazda's belly.

"What were we talking about?" said Dami presently. "I think ... you were trying to tell me that you're worried that I'll get ... bored? Or that I'll want to do things in bed that you don't like?"

"I still don't see," said Varazda drowsily, "how 'I like a lot of things' can mean anything other than that."

"I really wish I had never said that. I'm not sure it's even true, any more. I like being with you. I like … exploring things with you, like we did today, but that's just a stage—I don't expect that to go on forever. We're finding out what you like, and it's … it's thrilling. I like—*love*—being the only man who's ever … " He smiled a little shyly down at Varazda.

"Made me climax?" The fire made a little leap, small flames licking up.

Dami stilled. "What. No. I didn't—*was* I?"

"Did I not say that at the time? No. Well, it's true. I knew that I *could*, I'd … um."

"Brought yourself off," Dami supplied, unembarrassed.

"Yes." That sounded like the right expression. "I have—I did—I *do*," honestly compelled him to choke out, "that, sometimes." The fire was raging.

"Well, good." Dami was giving him a rakish grin. "Do you think of me, ever?"

"Do I think about you. When I'm … ? Uh … "

"I'll take that as a 'yes.'"

Varazda bit his lip.

Dami gave him a little quirk of an eyebrow. "You'll have to show me some time."

"What? Why would you want to … " He thought about that, imagined Dami putting his strong, calloused hand on his own shaft and stroking, eyes closed, lips parted, his other hand perhaps moving over his belly … "Yes, well, that's an odd request, but, as you say, you like a lot of things."

"I'd like one thing in particular just now," Dami murmured. His eyes looked very dark.

Varazda drew up his knees, the ruined blue gown riding up, and let his thighs fall open. "Yes," he said. "Please."

CHAPTER 17

"What do you think?" Varazda asked, twirling to fan out the skirt of his embroidered gown.

"Divine Terza, that suits you!" Dami sat on the edge of the bed, grinning. He still wore his stained and crumpled tunic, and his usually disciplined curls were tousled. "I've always liked you in your finery. Even at Nione's, when you were dressed up to annoy the philosophers, I liked it."

Varazda beamed back at him. He sat down again at his dressing table to braid his hair, which he would take down again before the performance. He felt good: cherished and satisfied and at ease.

"Look, I have to ask," said Dami lightly, as Varazda was pinning up his braids. "The separate bedrooms. What's the story with that?"

"Oh." He'd noticed that it bothered Dami, but he hadn't really spent any time analyzing that. Perhaps Dami thought there was some sinister reason for it. "I couldn't really see it working any other way, honestly. I know you can climb stairs perfectly well, but it must take a toll on your knee to be doing it all the time. My bed isn't big enough for two—at least ... not big enough for two to sleep in—and then, you may not have noticed … " He pointed toward the little bed in the alcove. "Remi sleeps here."

Dami nodded. "I figured she probably did."

"So." Varazda shrugged apologetically. "That's why I put you in the room downstairs."

"Which you added to the house for my sake, and furnished and everything, and I can't tell you how touched I am by all that. I don't want to sound ungrateful. I'm not. I just wondered—of course it's none of my business … but no, you know, I think it is my business. Or at least … Look. I'm getting all tangled up in this—"

"I'd noticed."

Dami snorted. "I just wanted to know whether there's a particular reason you prefer me to sleep in another room. In case it was anything that we could talk about. Anything I could help with. If it's not, I understand, of course. And if you don't want to tell me, then don't."

Varazda considered that for a moment, trying to guess what it was that Dami was imagining. "It's really just Remi. She wakes up in the night sometimes."

"You wouldn't want to move her bed downstairs."

"What? To your room?" Now Varazda was incredulous. "You mean all three of us sleep in the same room?"

"Yeah. I don't want to deprive her of her father, but I'd like to sleep with you too. Just sleep, obviously—but there are lots of other parts of your house where we can, uh, explore the Gardens of Whatyoucall, as I suppose you'd say. It's not such a strange idea, is it—sharing a bedroom? People do it. Families. Not that—I didn't mean—"

"No, but you should have. Holy God. I've been so stupid. I want you to feel like family—that's exactly how I want you to feel. But I honestly thought you would be more comfortable in your own room when we couldn't … you know … if all we could do was sleep. I thought that I could

206

come down to see you, from time to time, and then go back to my own room … after."

Dami laughed. "Very Zashian—except you're the master of the house, you shouldn't have to come to my quarters. You should be able to summon me to yours. Don't you think?"

"What?" That was of course exactly how it was done in noble Zashian households with separate women's quarters. If Dami had been Varazda's concubine … The thought was too absurd to pursue. "Don't be ridiculous. That's not what I had in mind at all."

And it wasn't, he realized. What he'd had in mind, without realizing it, had been worse.

"It's what I used to do in Gudul," he said, after a long pause, looking away. "I lived in the women's quarters with the other eunuchs, and when a man … when a man wanted me in his bed, I would go to him. Then I'd come back. I didn't—" He looked up at Dami, whose expression of horror was just as he'd expected. "I didn't think. Let's find some other way of doing it."

"Immortal gods. Yes. Let's."

They arrived at the Palace of Letters in the late afternoon. Varazda wore his dark green, embroidered gown, his eyes painted to match, bracelets on his wrists. Dami had cleaned up and emerged with tidy hair and a fresh tunic, belted with a Zashian-style sash—his own, one that Varazda had not seen before. He had brought the lute from the music store. Varazda reminded himself he should really pay Gia for that lute, as they were clearly not going to give it back.

Ariston met them at the entrance to the library and immediately began talking.

"I think Leto got it wrong," he said. "I don't see how anyone could make the frieze fall on Themistokles at just the right moment. I've double- and triple-checked it. I think the plan is to sabotage the scaffolding, so that *he* falls."

"Hello, Ariston," said Varazda dryly. "Have you eaten?"

"What?"

"Dinner. Have you had any?" He produced a napkin containing a meat pie that Yazata had made for dinner. "Eat."

"No time," Ariston said, his mouth already full of pie. "Meh ev du divcus ftrategy."

Varazda brushed fragments of pastry off his gown. "Finish your pie and then we can 'discuss strategy.' And you can show us around. We'll go make ourselves known to the master of ceremonies in the meantime."

The master of ceremonies was a man named Heron whom Varazda knew slightly, an itinerant party-planner who served many of the great households of the city. He was delighted to see Varazda.

"Always a pleasure, Pharastes! And don't you look fetching in that gown?" His eyes widened at the sight of Dami.

"My accompanist, Damiskos."

"Wonderful! Please leave your things over here. I'm putting you on in pride of place, just before the meal."

"I'm flattered. What's the rest of the program?"

Heron ticked items off on his fingers. "I've got flautists for while the guests are still arriving, then some speeches, then Eudokia is going to sing, more speeches, and then I thought I'd put you on. Then dinner will be served, with the flautists playing again. After dinner they're going up to view the frescoes, and I'm told the sculptor, who's arriving late, wants to give another speech. I have the Glaphyra troupe for after dinner—I was going to put them on before, but when I found out you were coming, I thought you'd make a much more suitable centrepiece."

"I hope I don't disappoint," Varazda said in the tone of one who knew he wouldn't. "I thought we might take a look around before the guests arrive. My friend worked on parts of the frieze, and he wants to show off his artistry."

"Go ahead. I haven't had a chance to go up and look yet myself." He looked up at the scaffolding that effectively obscured the view from the floor of the room. "I tried my best with the decorations, but there's only so much one can do."

The scaffolding had been erected around all four sides of the library's main hall in order for the frieze to be installed around the top of the walls, and it had been left in place so that the guests could go up and look closely at the sculptures, which had been carved on the ground but painted in situ. Heron had decorated it with garlands and swaths of pink fabric. Under the frieze, the walls were lined with two levels of arcaded bookcases, one around the ground floor and one accessible from a narrow gallery above. The niches were filled with neatly piled and labelled scrolls.

Varazda could see Ariston already prowling around on the upper platform. He and Dami left their bundle of swords and lute where Heron had indicated, and climbed up the ladder.

"There you are!" Ariston exclaimed, as if he had not seen them a couple of minutes ago. "What should we do, Damiskos, do you think? I mean, how should we arrange our patrol?"

Dami looked like he was trying not to catch Varazda's eye as he scanned the wooden walkway that ran along the top of the scaffolding.

"Well," he said neutrally, "we've been told that the guests are coming up here immediately after dinner, which is after Varazda's performance. Do you think we could slip up during the meal and meet here?"

"Yes, yes," said Ariston eagerly. "We can check if anything's been sabotaged, and watch for anyone coming up."

"It's a shame we don't have a better view of the hall from here," Dami remarked, looking over the edge. "All those garlands and things block the sight-lines. Is there just the one ladder to come up?"

"No, there's three. The one for the guests to come up is around the front, near the door."

Dami nodded. "Well, you stick to Themistokles, and Varazda and I will follow you and keep our eyes open."

He turned and looked up at the wall. "These are impressive. Want to give us the tour?"

Ariston did want to, and it took his mind off the assassination plot for a little while to show Dami and Varazda around the perimeter of the library, explaining the subjects of the reliefs and giving exhaustive details of their production. He'd had a lot to do with the project, it seemed, and Varazda glowed with pride in him as he listened.

The frieze was beautiful, though viewing it up close was a little odd. The central carving of each panel showed a scene of culture and learning: gods and goddesses and mortals whose stories Varazda did not know, and Ariston did not explain clearly, playing musical instruments, poring over scrolls, writing on wax tablets, and sketching on walls. In between these scenes were decorative motifs, plants and animals real and legendary, repeated in a regular pattern with naturalistic variations in the Pseuchaian style. It was Dami who first noticed the significance of one of them.

"That's a lassa," he said, stopping in front of a brightly gilded figure in the frieze.

"I carved that," said Ariston proudly. "What'd you say it is?"

"A lassa," said Varazda. "A winged lion. It's an ancient symbol of kingship in Zash."

It was a magnificent piece, naturalistically worked in a way that was quite different from Zashian sculpture.

"It's a slightly odd thing to have in a Pseuchaian library," said Varazda.

"It is?" Ariston squeaked, dismayed. "I didn't know that! It wasn't my idea to put them in."

"Them?" Varazda repeated, looking along the frieze. The winged lions were indeed repeated at regular intervals. There were also pomegranates and stylized saffron crocuses. Varazda pointed to a cluster of these. "I suppose these weren't your idea either?"

"Well … " Ariston looked uncomfortable, as well as confused. "They were, sort of. I found that design on one of those little tables in your sitting room, and I sketched it and showed it to Themistokles, and he was the one who wanted to use it on the frieze. I thought it would look good, and, you know, you're always reminding me to embrace my origins and that, so … "

"I like it a great deal," said Varazda, touching Ariston's shoulder. "It was well thought of."

"Obviously," Ariston added stiffly, "I was mainly thinking about the volume of the shapes balancing the flow of the forms in the main panels, and the colour of the crocuses echoing the purple on the wings."

"Obviously," Varazda agreed.

They followed Ariston around the rest of the frieze, listening to his exhaustive explanation of how the marble panels were fastened to the walls, and descended by the ladder at the far end, leaving Ariston to check the knots of all the rope railings that had been secured for the safety of the party guests.

"Hard to believe it isn't a political statement," Dami remarked when they were on the ground again.

"The lassa and crocuses? Yes, that's what I was thinking. Mind you, I believe Ariston when he says he was mostly concerned with volume and whatnot, but I get the impression Themistokles is a different kind of character."

"We know he has political ambitions."

Varazda nodded. "Do you think he's really in danger?"

"Of falling to his death from the scaffolding? Maybe. It certainly wouldn't be hard to sabotage it so *somebody* would fall—though perhaps not with eagle-eyed Ariston on the job—but I'm not sure how you would make sure it was Themistokles who fell."

"True. I'm not sure why Leto told us it was the sculpture that was going to fall on him, either."

Dami scratched his stubble. "We've tried to warn him, Ariston has checked everything beforehand, and we're going to keep an eye on him all evening. I think we have it covered."

"I hope so," said Varazda.

The sound of flute music drew their attention to the performance area beyond the couches and tables. The doors had been opened and the first guests were beginning to arrive.

"Safflower," said Varazda suddenly.

Dami looked at him. "Yes?"

"Kallisto told me Lykanos has a lucrative business involving safflower. And he's in the spice trade. Safflower can be used to adulterate saffron."

"Hah. Is that … "

"Relevant? Yes, I think so. Adulterating saffron is a serious fraud in Zash—punishable by death."

Dami gave a low whistle.

"Well, so many things are. But most of the saffron you can buy in Boukos is adulterated, or so Yazata tells me. We get ours as a New Year's gift from the embassy, so I wouldn't know. But one of the things they're discussing in the Basileon is inspecting the saffron for sale in the markets to make sure it meets Zashian standards."

"Which, if you'd built your business selling adulterated saffron, would be bad news."

"Quite."

"That would give Lykanos a reason to want Zash out of Boukos. Also a reason to turn against Themistokles, do you think?"

"I suppose it depends how pro-Zashian Themistokles really is."

Dami cast his eyes up in the direction of the hidden frieze. "Maybe he just thought the winged lions and the crocuses looked good."

"Maybe," said Varazda.

After what they had learned of Themistokles's politics and what they had seen of the frieze, neither Varazda nor Damiskos was surprised to see the Zashian ambassador and his entourage arrive at the party.

The two of them were sitting on the floor in an alcove at the far end of the atrium from the door, knees and thighs gently touching on one side. It was a kind of moment that Varazda was used to: the entertainers waiting discreetly for their turn to perform, watching the guests come in, talking among themselves and ignoring the slaves who hovered around them. It was probably a strange experience for Dami. He had put out a hand to touch the skirt of Varazda's embroidered gown where it lay over his knee.

"I feel as if I'm having a tryst with a respectable Zashian girl," he whispered.

Varazda replied with a stifled laugh. A couple of the other entertainers waiting nearby gave them curious looks. *I don't mind being envied either*, Varazda thought, and that was a bit of a surprise.

"Oh, look," said Dami, pointing out into the atrium. "Is that who I think it is?"

Varazda looked, and saw Narosangha, with Babak, Shorab, and a couple of others in his retinue. He remained sitting in the alcove for a minute, watching the Zashians greet their hosts and the other guests. Some of them were conspicuous in their embroidered clothes and hats; some had adopted elements of Pseuchaian dress. All of them wore beards.

The first Zashian ambassador to Boukos, before Varazda's time, had been an embarrassing buffoon, who got himself kidnapped and nearly set off a war. There was a story at the embassy that he had paraded around the agora stark naked during the Psobion festival, but it was hard to know whether to credit that. He had been the king's cousin, though, so when it came time to establish a permanent embassy, the Zashian court felt that they could not insult the Boukossians by sending just anyone to head it.

Narosangha, the current ambassador, was a very distant relative of King Nahazra's mother, which satisfied that requirement, but he was also a superb diplomat, ideally suited to the job. Varazda liked him. Narosangha wasn't exactly his patron—the concept was unknown in Zash, and in any case the ambassador had never actually owned Varazda —but he treated all the freed slaves of the embassy rather the way a Boukossian nobleman might treat his clients.

"I should go say hello," said Varazda, reluctantly moving Dami's hand from his knee and gathering up his skirt. He paused. "Come. I'll introduce you."

Dami gave him a slightly wide-eyed look, as if he wanted to ask, "Are you sure?" But he got to his feet.

Babak saw them first, and waved to Varazda. He was one of the Zashians who had adopted local dress, along with much else. (His Boukossian mistress was an open secret at the embassy.) He wove through the tables with a grin on his face to tell Varazda in Pseuchaian that he looked "delectable" in his women's clothes. Varazda gave him the kind of look that a respectable Zashian girl would have given anyone who said such a thing to her, and Babak howled with laughter.

"Varazda!" said Shorab, coming up behind Babak. "We get to see you dance tonight? Excellent! Oh, but you're in what do they call it? Drag? So I guess you won't be using the swords tonight."

"Wait and see," said Varazda with a coy smile. "Babak, Shorab, this is Damiskos. My accompanist for the night. Dami, these are my friends Shorab and Babak of the Zashian embassy."

For a moment the two Zashian men looked at Dami with polite confusion. They recovered quickly to exchange greetings. Then Babak looked at Varazda and said, "Accompanist, eh? Is that what they're calling it now?"

Shorab gasped and shoved Babak in the shoulder, looking to Varazda with an apology obviously rising to his lips.

Varazda just shrugged. Babak shoved Shorab back.

"Well, uh, this is," Shorab stammered, "this is just—well, I'm happy for you both." He nodded encouragingly at Dami.

"You're a lucky dog," said Babak to Dami. "Is what he means to say. You know she's broken a few hearts around here over the years. Between you and me, we didn't think that ice was ever going to crack. Well done!"

Dami was giving Babak a tolerant look—not unfriendly, but not conspiratorial either—rather like the looks he had given Ariston when Ariston began exclaiming over women's legs and describing brothels on the Asteria.

"Is it public?" Shorab cut across whatever Babak was going to say next, gesturing between Varazda and Dami. "Can we tell people?"

"Honestly, Shorab," said Varazda, "do you really think I'd be confiding in Babak if it were a secret?"

"Hey!" Babak protested. "You didn't 'confide' anything, you close-mouthed bastard. I guessed! And it had better not be a secret, the way the two of you look at each other. Not that I blame you," he added to Dami. "If I didn't know what she's got under that gown, I'd fight you for her."

Dami folded his arms. "You wouldn't win."

At that point the ambassador himself appeared at Babak's elbow, and Shorab quickly assured him that they were both on their way to talk to the person he had sent them to talk to, and they melted away.

"Varazda," said the ambassador with a friendly nod. "God guard your coming and your going. I hope you are well?"

"Very well, Your Excellency. Your Excellency, may I present to you my friend Damiskos Temnon. Former First Spear of the Second Koryphos Legion of Pheme."

Narosangha gave Dami an openly intrigued look as he clasped his hands, Zashian-style.

"I am honoured," Dami said in Zashian.

"As am I," said the ambassador, "since I know at least a little about the Phemian army."

"Damiskos served on the Deshan Coast for several years and has travelled extensively in Zash. He speaks Zashian fluently."

"Indeed?" Narosangha was looking even more intrigued. "And you have retired from the military and settled in Boukos, then?"

"Yes," said Dami promptly.

"You must come share a cup with us at the embassy one day. You are here to see the new frieze?"

Dami smiled. "I'm here because Varazda needed an accompanist at the last moment, and I offered my services. But I have sneaked up to look at the frieze, and it's wonderful. Have you seen it yet, Your Excellency? There are elements of it that I think you may find very interesting."

"Hmm, I wonder why you say that!"

The ambassador went on talking to Dami like an equal, which pleased Varazda. He wasn't listening, though; he was thinking about how quickly Dami had said *yes* when Narosangha asked if he had settled in Boukos.

216

CHAPTER 18

THE COUCHES HAD FILLED with guests, Eudokia had sung, and someone from the Committee for the Promotion of Letters in Boukos had given a speech. Varazda stepped out of the alcove and walked demurely out into the performance area. His hair was loose down his back; Dami had unbraided it for him and combed it gently through with his fingers, making Varazda's scalp tingle.

Dami sat on a stool at the far side of the dance floor with his lute. He watched Varazda walking out, and there was such a smile in his eyes, as if he was right where he wanted to be.

Varazda glanced discreetly over the audience on their couches. He had already spotted a few familiar faces, besides the party from the embassy. Lykanos was there, reclining on a couch near the front of the room, looking more bored than anything. But as Varazda looked in his direction, Lykanos's eyes darted across the hall to the blonde girl who was sitting, with the utmost propriety, beside Shorab. It was Leto.

That was interesting. Varazda missed the expression on Lykanos's face as he looked at her, which he regretted, as it might have told him much. But he had no time now to study the audience. He had to dance, and even if this one still would not be solely for Dami, Varazda wanted it to be good.

The sword dance of the clan Kamun, vishmi kokoro, was a men's dance. There were women's sword dances in other regions of Zash, but Varazda had never learned any of them. What he danced now was a pure invention of his own. He had learned to dance like a woman at Gudul, because that was the sort of thing they had wanted there, and it was a skill that had served him well since. He also enjoyed it.

He walked to the middle of the dance floor with his swords held loosely at his sides, and then began with a flourish, because that was how Dami had told him epic poems were meant to begin, sweeping up his right arm and giving the sword a quick twist, stopping, holding it there, looking out at the audience. There were murmurs of appreciation.

He danced a scene of battle in a flow of feminine drapery, a goddess presiding over a field of death, but it was something else, too. It was a story of rising glory, of a career in the ascendant; and then, as the dance reached its most triumphant moment, there came the cataclysm. Varazda slumped, dropped the swords, wilted in a controlled fall to the floor. There were gasps from the audience, a little tentative applause—was it over? Did the story of the dance end in tragedy?

It didn't. He rose to his knees, then to his feet, without the swords, and raised his hands, crossing his wrists, in the opening pose of the village wedding dance that he had danced on the beach at Laothalia a month ago. He glanced at Dami, who nodded and began the tune he had played that night.

He ended the wedding dance to delighted applause, and curtsied graciously. A couple of the men, presumably thinking he was a woman, beckoned him imperiously to share their couches, but Varazda just smiled. He did accept a drink from the ambassador, and shrugged off some ribald comments from Babak. Shorab had a few warm words of praise for him, but was too busy making almost comically proper conversation with Leto to say much.

The food began to be brought out, which provided Varazda an opportunity to make his exit. He could have stayed, of course; plenty of guests, from Babak to the head of the Committee for the Promotion of Letters in Boukos, would have been happy to have him share their couches. But Dami had disappeared back into the performers' alcove, and Varazda had no desire to linger out here.

Leto glanced over as Varazda was getting up from Narosangha's couch.

"Is it 'he' or a 'she'?" she asked Shorab, quite audibly. "I've never been sure."

Shorab looked confused for a moment, then Varazda heard him say, "Oh. Oh, well, we always call them 'he,' you know, because—because, well, they used to be boys, so 'she' wouldn't be quite right, would it?"

Varazda walked away without reaction. It was the sort of thing that barely ruffled the surface of his calm these days, though in truth he would have expected a little better from Shorab, whom he considered a friend. But he thought about Dami hearing things like that, and somehow that hurt.

"I didn't know you were going to do the wedding dance at the end," said Dami. They sat eating together on a couch in the corner of the hall. Varazda's swords and Dami's lute had been stowed in the alcove with the other performers' things. "Didn't know you were going to flop on the floor like that, either."

"I hope I didn't alarm you?"

"No, I could tell you knew what you were doing." After a moment he said, "Was that dance… "

"Mm?"

"No, never mind. It was brilliant, and they loved it."

"They were a good audience. You're an absolute dream as an accompanist, you know that?"

"What? You're just saying that because you like me."

"I'm saying it because it's true. You watch me so attentively."

"Now that is because *I* like *you*." Dami grinned.

"We're a perfect team."

Dami's grin softened to something warm and intimate, but a little wistful. "Yeah. We are, aren't we."

Varazda leaned his forehead on Dami's shoulder, closing his eyes. Something nameless ached inside of him. *This isn't right*, he thought. Damiskos should be here as a guest, the equal of His Excellency Narosangha. A man from a good family, retired from a brilliant military career, shouldn't be posing as an accompanist for a eunuch dancer in women's clothes. He should have been commanding a person like Varazda, not staying in his house and doing favours for him.

Varazda felt Dami's lips lightly brush the top of his head. "It's warm in here," Dami said. "Want me to braid your hair up for you again?"

"Would you know how?" Varazda sat up.

"No, but I'd love to learn."

Ariston wove through the tables to present himself breathlessly in front of their couch.

"What is it?" Dami asked.

"Leto just spoke to me. She said she's seen Lykanos giving somebody orders, and pointing up at the frieze. He must be about to go sabotage the platform—or the panels—or whatever it is he's planning. We've got to get up there and catch him."

Varazda looked out over the couches with a frown. Lykanos was still eating and seemed deep in conversation with his neighbour. That proved nothing in particular. Leto was nowhere to be seen, and Shorab was gone too.

"Themistokles isn't here yet," Dami observed, reaching for his sandals.

"Heron said he would be late," said Varazda. "But to miss dinner altogether?"

"Do you think something's happened to him already?" Ariston fretted. "I thought he'd just been caught up at Kallisto's, but—"

"Kallisto's?" Dami repeated, on his feet now, sandals fastened. "What's he doing there?"

Varazda stood and stepped into his shoes.

"Saying goodbye to her," said Ariston. "He planned it this way—he has to cut ties before announcing he's standing for election, and he's getting engaged soon too. He thought it would be symbolic to break it off with her right before the dedication."

Varazda suppressed the urge to roll his eyes. Dami evidently didn't.

"I know, I know," said Ariston. "But she knows it's coming—it's not as if it's going to be a surprise."

The guests were still finishing their meal as the three of them climbed the least noticeable of the ladders up to the scaffolding and began making their way quietly around the room under the frieze. It was shadowy up here now; the guests would have to be accompanied by servants with torches in order to see the carvings properly, but it would make for a dramatic presentation. Varazda had to hold up the long skirt of his gown to pick his way carefully over the boards.

Ariston was poking into the cracks between panels of the frieze, and Dami was testing the ropes that bordered the scaffolding, when he stopped and put out a hand.

"What is it?" Ariston squeaked, just as Varazda felt the vibration of other footsteps on the boards of the scaffold.

There were three of them, and they were armed guards, in the green sashes and leather helmets of the public watch. The noise from the party below must have covered the sound of their ascent. They were not making any effort to move quietly now.

"You there!" one of them hailed Varazda and his companions. "Stop what you're doing!"

Varazda stepped forward, making a gently shushing gesture. "No need to create a scene, my friends. We were looking at the sculptures—Ariston here was explaining the work to us. But if you want us to get down, of course we'll get down."

The watch captain did not look placated. "Who are you?"

"Tashmat son of Rohaz," Ariston gabbled out. "Themistokles Glyptikos's apprentice—ask anyone!"

The watch captain jabbed a finger at Varazda. "Who are *you*?"

"I? Part of the entertainment. You didn't see me dance just now?" Varazda gave them an innocently disappointed look.

"Of course we didn't. We've been busy. Had a tip about some foreigners snooping around the new frieze. And lo and behold, here you are, right where they said you'd be. You'd better come with us."

"Come with you where?" Varazda asked, stalling.

One of the other watchmen spoke up. "Just down to the watch-house, if you don't mind. It's probably all a misunderstanding—"

"Don't try to talk to them," the captain interrupted. "It'll just give them the chance to twist you round their little fingers. That's what these dickless Sasians do, talk and talk until you don't know which way is up—they learn our language just so they can lie to us in it."

The remaining watchmen looked uncomfortable.

"They aren't foreigners," the third one ventured. "They're

the Chief's friends, Pharastes and whatsisname and, um." He looked at Damiskos.

The captain gave him a sour look. "Nevertheless."

"Who gave you the information about us?" said Varazda, with a sudden flash of uncomfortable intuition.

"You've no call—"

One of the insubordinate ones interrupted their leader. "Young girl, blonde—servant type, but pretty. She said her patron had sent her."

"Did she," said Varazda grimly.

"As I say, I'm sure it's all just—"

"Move!" barked the watch captain. "Now, all of you! No, not you." He waved his hand impatiently at Dami. "You're not a suspicious foreigner, are you?"

"Uh, but—" one of the junior watchmen started to object. "Hadn't we better—just to be safe … "

"What? Arrest a military veteran who was minding his own business?" the captain snapped.

"Much appreciated," said Dami. "As a matter of fact, I was questioning these two about their motives before you arrived."

"There you see?"

Dami fell back a couple of steps to allow the watchmen to surround Varazda and Ariston.

Their departure, with the watchmen marching them out the main doors of the Palace of Letters, caused a stir among the guests, and Varazda gritted his teeth angrily, thinking of the damage this was going to do to his carefully cultivated reputation. Narosangha and Babak looked like they were contemplating stopping the watchmen, but Varazda waved to them and rolled his eyes as if to say it was all a misunderstanding, not to worry.

"Do you think," Ariston whispered in Zashian, as they were descending the steps outside, "they were talking about Leto? The blonde servant type?"

Varazda nodded. "It sounded like her, didn't it?"

"But why?"

"I don't know," he admitted. Under his breath he added, "At least I hope I don't know."

At the watch-house, on the edge of the agora, they were escorted into a cell, and the watch captain took obvious pleasure in refusing to let Varazda send a message to Marzana. They sat on a straw mat on one of the benches that lined the room, their backs to the wall.

"This is insane," Ariston said, repeating a line he had used many times already on the way over. "What is going on? What is this about?"

Varazda pinched the bridge of his nose. His eyes felt itchy, and he wanted to scrub his hands over his face, but he was wearing too much makeup, with no prospect of being able to wash it off any time soon.

"Lykanos wants us out of the way, apparently," he said.

"So we can't stop him pushing Themistokles to his death!"

Varazda shook his head. "I don't think so. It was Leto who told us about the murder plot in the first place, then Leto who set us up to get arrested. If she's doing Lykanos's bidding, doing *both* those things doesn't make sense."

If she was doing Lykanos's bidding, both times. Varazda didn't say that.

"Unless," said Ariston, "unless Lykanos isn't planning to kill Themistokles at the party at all. Maybe he's planning to kill him on the way to the party."

"That's possible," said Varazda doubtfully. Something about that still did not quite make sense.

Ariston had got a look of terror on his face suddenly. "Oh God, oh God. What if he's going to kill Themistokles at

Kallisto's house and frame her for it? He could—uh, strangle Themistokles with one of Kallisto's scarves or—and I'm sure some people know about her—her thing that she does. She'd be suspected for sure!"

She would, that was a fact. "Shh, shh. Setting aside the fact that Lykanos is at the Palace of Letters right now, not in Temple Walk, why would he want to frame Kallisto for anything? Isn't he supposed to be jealous and want Themistokles out of the way so he can keep Kallisto for himself?"

"Oh. Oh, you're right."

Well, thought Varazda, *not really, because I don't think that is what Lykanos wants.* But he badly needed Ariston to be calm right now, and speculating about an imaginary murder plot was not going to help achieve that.

He hoped it was imaginary. He couldn't help remembering that Themistokles said he had told Lykanos he planned to break off his affair with Kallisto. It wasn't a stretch to think that he might have mentioned when and where he planned to do it.

Ariston pushed his hands into his hair, disarranging the sleek locks. "What are we going to do?"

"Right now, we have to wait for Damiskos to get us out of here."

Ariston looked surprised. "How's he going to do that?"

"By fetching Marzana and telling him what's happened. It's not as romantic as cutting his way through the guards and breaking down the door, but it's more practical."

Ariston managed a wan smile. "I'm sorry, you know."

"Hm? Sorry about what?"

He shrugged awkwardly. "That I was rude about Damiskos. I mean, he's a great guy—a *great* guy, I really like him—but, you know, I should have been nicer about your whole … thing, even before I knew that."

"Thanks."

"Shit. I really hurt your feelings, didn't I?"

"Ah. Well ... "

"Shit fuck. I'm so sorry, Varazda. Yazata was just worried about you, that was why he was being so weird, but I wasn't *worried*—immortal gods, I know you can take care of yourself, you take care of all of us. I just thought it was ... you know, why did you have to go and do something so *not normal*? Is what I thought."

"I understand."

"Yeah. But it's stupid. I want so hard to be normal, but nobody I really love is, so what's the point?" He made a frustrated noise. "That's not what I mean. I mean, you and Yazata, you just are who you are. And Yazata, well, he spends most of his time in the house, and just visits a few friends and lives quietly, but you? You go to public baths, you wear women's clothes and a nose-ring and dance Zashian dances at noblemen's houses. You're so much just *who you are*." He spread his hands hopelessly. "I don't know how to explain it better. But you're my family, you and Yazata and Remi, and if the only way I could really be normal was by pretending you're not, that's not something I want.

"And ... the other thing is ... if I really want to be normal, I should find a girl like Dia, from the bakery—not her, obviously, she's having Skyphos Bariades's kid, but somebody like her—and forget about Kallisto. Because the gods— God—knows *that's* not normal."

"I think," said Varazda slowly, "that maybe we should stop using the word 'normal,' because I'm no longer sure what it means—but falling in love with someone and wanting to be with them is pretty common. Even somebody older or younger—or the same age—or who has a strange job or comes from a different sort of family or any of that."

"Yeah, but ... I don't have an ambition to one day become one of Kallisto's lovers—clients—or replace Themistokles, or anything like that. I don't know what I want, but it's not that. I want to be her partner, somehow. I don't even know what that means. I just know, when I'm with her, I can be who I am, and it feels like we could make up our own rules and 'normal' isn't maybe even real.

"But the other thing is, being who I am means being Ariston, not Tash, and wearing Pseuchaian clothes, and—and calling myself a man. It means being, well, really different from you."

"I know that," said Varazda gently. "That doesn't bother me. If it doesn't bother you. I'm very happy for you to be yourself. I've never wanted you to be embarrassed by me or anything I do."

"Holy angels. I've been such a shit to you."

"No, Ari. Come on."

"I have, though. If I can ever make it up to you … "

They heard the door to the cells being opened, and they scrambled up to look out from their own cell to see Marzana striding down the passage. Dami, Varazda was surprised to see, was not with him.

"Marzana! God guard your coming and your going. We are so glad to see you!"

"I'm not sure that you should be," said Marzana sternly.

He arrived in front of the grille that separated their cell from the passage, and made no move to unlock it. He was carrying a bundle of canvas under one arm.

"What is it?" asked Varazda, feeling cold with apprehension. His first thought was that something had happened to Dami. He didn't speak it aloud.

"You were arrested on insubstantial grounds, and I would have had no hesitation in ordering your release. However, new evidence has come to light, and you are now being held on a charge of murder."

It was Ariston who spoke first. "Murder? Varazda? Are you joking?"

"Of course not," said Marzana. He unfolded the canvas surrounding his bundle, and held out the matched pair of

Varazda's bronze swords, the blades stained all down their length with blood.

"Who am I supposed to have killed?" Varazda managed to ask, through the increasingly difficult effort to breath, as the world closed steadily into a black tunnel around him.

"His name was Alkaios, but I would not have expected you to know that. He was one of my volunteer watchmen. He was nineteen and engaged to be married."

"Varazda wouldn't kill anybody like that!" Ariston cried. "Anyone—I mean—anyone at all! Have you gone insane? And when was he supposed to have had a chance to do it? He's been in here ever since your men arrested us."

Marzana looked at him levelly. "Alkaios was killed on the scaffolding at the Palace of Letters, where he had been patrolling throughout the evening. He was found there by his fellows shortly after they arrested you—on the same scaffolding."

"Ohh," said Ariston, nodding, "so you think we killed him just before that, during dinner, because he found us doing something up there—that makes sense. I mean—uh—"

"Marzana," Varazda said, holding onto the grille to stay upright. "You don't believe that I did this?"

"I don't want to. But one of my men has been killed, with your swords, and it has been brought home to me recently that I don't know you as well as I thought I did. I don't even know the nature of your work for the embassy."

"The embassy?" Ariston cut in again. "The 'nature of his work' is that he's a dancer, Marzana! What the fuck?"

"Be quiet," said Marzana commandingly, and Ariston clamped his mouth shut, which was something of a relief. Marzana rewrapped the stained swords. "You will have to stay the night here. In the morning, my men will investigate, and I will decide how to proceed." He paused a moment.

"I'm sorry, Varazda. Of course I don't think you're guilty. Just be patient, and this will all be sorted out."

Varazda swallowed hard and nodded. "The swords were —I'd left them, in a place where anyone might have picked them up. They were out of my sight all through dinner. Damiskos can confirm that. I suppose you've checked that the, that the wounds match the blades?"

Marzana nodded grimly. "They do."

"Yes. You'll—you'll figure it out, I'm sure."

Marzana looked at him for a moment. "I'm going to send someone to bring you some water. I will see you in the morning."

And he turned and strode out.

CHAPTER 19

VARAZDA SAT in a corner of the cell, holding the cup of water that the duty guard had brought him, and trying to stop his hands from shaking long enough to drink. Ariston was pacing back and forth—not that there was much "back" or "forth" in the small room.

"What are we going to do, what are we going to do?" he moaned.

"Ari," said Varazda finally, "is there … any possible way that you could calm down? It's just not—not all that helpful for both of us to lose our cool right now."

"Lose our cool? You're not losing your cool—you're just sitting there!"

"I'm not—I'm not doing terribly well. Actually."

Ariston stared at him for a moment. "Oh," he said finally. "Right."

He came over and sat on the floor beside Varazda, squeezed his shoulder, and then kept his hand there.

"Thanks," said Varazda. He took a sip of his water. "I'll tell you something, if you like." He felt it would help to talk. "It will seem funny, under the circumstances."

"Sure. What is it?"

"When Marzana said he doesn't know what I do for the embassy ... I don't work for the embassy."

"Yeah, I know."

"I work for the Basileon."

Ariston stared at him blankly. "You ... what?"

"I'm a confidential agent for the Basileon. I supply information on things that are going on in the city—mostly from the great houses where I dance, but I've had other assignments. That was what I went to Pheme for in the Month of Grapes."

"You're a spy."

"Mm."

"You're a *spy*. How long—how long have you been doing it?"

"Oh ... well, they approached me almost as soon as I was freed. So about seven years."

"Does Yazata know?"

Varazda nodded. "I told him a few years ago."

"But you didn't tell me."

Varazda looked at him affectionately. "I'm telling you now. It isn't the sort of thing one is supposed to advertise widely."

"Yeah, yeah." Ariston smiled wryly. "What about Damiskos, though? Does he know?"

"He found out at Laothalia in the summer. He knows."

"That's good. I mean, you've got to be honest with lovers, haven't you?"

"Um. That is my understanding."

Ariston laughed. "I'm learning so many new things about you, Varazda. I always thought you were like Yazata, you know, totally uninterested in sex or romance or anything—and then you suddenly bring home this soldier. And now it turns out you've been a spy almost the entire time I've known you. Is there anything else I'm going to find out?"

Varazda shook his head. "Nothing comes to mind."

After a minute Ariston said, "Why did you think I'd find that funny?"

"What? Oh, I ... don't suppose I seem very competent right now. Getting myself arrested and suspected by one of my close friends ... "

"It's all part of the job, though, isn't it?"

"No. No, this is not part of the job. I don't know why this happened."

"Oh." Ariston looked like he was trying very hard not to get up and start pacing again.

It wasn't quite morning, and Varazda was not quite asleep, with his head resting against the stone wall, when he heard voices from the atrium of the watch-house.

"I'm surprised. This would be considered a perfectly reasonable hour in the Phemian army."

"Does this look like the Phemian army to you?"

"No." A crisp and understated insult, delivered in Dami's usual grave style.

"Well, go on in," the duty guard grumbled. "I don't know who's in there—they just pay me to watch the place, they don't give me the details."

Varazda could almost see the curt nod that would have been given in response to this. He heard a key being turned in a lock, a door swinging open, and Dami coming down the passage. He pushed back his hair and rubbed one bleary eye with the heel of his hand, then he looked down and saw his palm smeared with black and green and remembered his makeup.

Dami stood in front of the grille, looking in. He didn't have his cane, but instead wore his sword, and the Zashian sash was gone. Varazda felt himself beginning to shiver again, and didn't know why. Ariston was sprawled on the straw mattress beside him, fast asleep and snoring. A couple of drunks who had been put in with them a few hours ago were similarly asleep on the other side of the cell.

"What is this Sasian woman doing in here?" Dami demanded of the guard.

"I told you, I've no idea." The guard came down the passage anyway to look in at Varazda. "Not bad-looking, if you like that type."

Dami shot him an extremely stern look. "Is it usual in Boukos for women and men to be held in the same cell?"

"Uh … no. Actually. I don't know what happened there. Want me to move her? I'll do that."

"No," said Dami. "I have orders from your commander to remove this prisoner and her slave." He withdrew a small scroll of paper from his belt. "I assume you would like to examine them?"

The guard looked at the scroll and snorted. "Yeah … I'm sure they're fine. Here, I'll open the door for you."

The guard fiddled with his keys, found the one he wanted, and turned it in the lock. Then Dami was coming into the cell, standing over Varazda, and speaking in Zashian.

"Are you all right?"

"Yes. Yes. I'm not hurt, or … Just having a … "

"Yeah. I'm going to get you out of here." He nudged Ariston with the toe of his boot. "Wake up!" he ordered in Pseuchaian.

Ariston jerked awake and sat up, staring around in confusion. "Wha … who … huh?" His eyes lighted on Dami.

"You. Get up," Dami barked, before Ariston could give him away with a shout of joyful recognition. "I'm taking you and your mistress out of here. Now move."

"Yes sir." Ariston scrambled to his feet. "My lady, let me help you up," he added, holding out his hands for Varazda.

They made it out the door of the watch-house into the agora, where lights twinkled in a few of the shops, and wagons rolled past, making night-time deliveries now that the streets were open to wheeled vehicles. Dami led them around a corner into the nearest dark street before he turned and took Varazda gently and protectively by the shoulders and said, "Tell me what happened."

"Someone murdered a watchman with Varazda's swords," Ariston supplied eagerly, "and Marzana isn't convinced it wasn't Varazda!"

"I know that," said Dami, still looking at Varazda. "I heard it from Chereia when I went looking for Marzana. But … what happened at the jail?" He asked the question very softly, addressing it only to Varazda.

Varazda realized what he meant. He stiffened and tried to stand up straight in Dami's grip. "Nothing. Nothing happened. Marzana showed me the swords with b … with blood on them, that's all." He shrugged off Dami's hands. "It was nothing."

"How did you manage to get an order from Marzana to release us?" Ariston wanted to know.

"I didn't." Dami looked away from Varazda finally.

"It was a bluff? Immortal gods, that takes balls!"

Dami gave him one of his stern looks. "I can assure you it doesn't."

Ariston gave a startled laugh. "Oh! I never thought about it that way. It's just an expression, isn't it?"

"Do you want to see what the paper is really?" Dami asked, holding it out to Varazda.

He took it and unrolled it. It was a prayer, or a charm, addressed to Dami's patron god, Terza, asking, in fairly graphic terms, that he grant the bearer stamina in bed.

"A friend got it for me when he heard I was coming to Boukos to visit my lover. It was the only piece of paper I had handy."

Varazda looked up and managed a weak, appreciative

smile. If Dami wanted to help him pull himself together, it was a good gambit.

"What is it?" Ariston was clamouring. "Let me see!"

Varazda tucked the scroll down the front of his gown. "It's mine now," he said.

"I look forward to the results," said Dami, without emphasis. "We shouldn't stand here in the street talking. I'm supposed to be escorting prisoners."

"What are we going to do?" Ariston wanted to know. "We have to find a way to clear Varazda's name!"

Dami hushed him and led the way further down the street. He stopped in front of the columned porch of the Temple of Hesperion, quiet and deserted at this time of night.

"Up here," he suggested, and glanced around the street before shepherding the two of them up the steps and into the colonnade.

There was a bench against the temple wall, where they sat. Varazda tried to wipe away his ruined eye makeup with the inside of one sleeve, but probably only made it worse.

"Darling," said Dami after a moment, "I'm sorry to have to ask this, but I think it likely to be important. When Marzana showed you the swords—where on the blade was there blood?"

The image rose up readily in Varazda's mind: his beloved bronze swords, their hilts chased with the patterns of his ancestors, the blades darkened with half-dried blood.

"All … down the length. Of both blades."

"Not just down one edge?"

"No … "

Dami let out a breath. "Divine Terza. That's what I was hoping you'd say."

Varazda nodded. "Because that's how it would look if they'd been used to stab someone—"

"—but you couldn't stab anyone with those swords. Exactly."

"Huh?" said Ariston.

"Marzana will figure that out," said Varazda. "The blades are just sharp enough to cut, but the points are dull on purpose. Everyone in my clan knew some story of a dancer who'd dropped a sharp sword on their foot or stabbed someone in the audience by accident."

"Marzana will figure it out," said Dami, "but he hasn't yet. I'd like to get a look at the body."

"Why?" Ariston grimaced.

"So we know what kind of weapon we're actually looking for."

"Oh."

"Would they have taken it to the Temple of Nepharos? Do you do that here?"

Varazda nodded. He had twice had occasion to visit the mortuary behind the temple of the Pseuchaian death god. It was where they took the bodies of people who had died in the city by violence or under mysterious circumstances.

"I'll go by myself," Dami assured both of them.

"I'd like to come," said Varazda slowly. "I feel … I should see the man's face."

Ariston made a small noise that was not quite a whimper, and then said, with an attempt at bravado, "I'll tag along too, if I may."

"You do realize," said Dami sternly, "that I may be able to bluff my way into the mortuary the way I did at the watch-house, but I can't bring just anyone in with me."

"Oh, come," said Varazda, shaking out his skirt briskly. "I'm a grieving widow, and Ariston, as we've already established, is my servant."

"What?" said Ariston. "Oh. Oh, right."

The man's face was white, his eyes closed; the blood staining his garments looked black in the shadowy vault of the mortuary. He was, as Marzana had said, very young, almost a boy. Varazda's hands clenched into fists at his sides.

"It's as we thought," said Dami in a low voice, as they stood with heads respectfully bowed by the side of the bier. "He was stabbed, not slashed. You can see most of the blood came from this wound on his left—this was what killed him. This wound on the other side hardly bled at all, because it was made after he was already dead, for the look of the thing. So that it would appear he had been stabbed with two swords." He bent to look closer at the body, then straightened up. "It's hard to see in this light, but the wounds are messy, because a larger, blunt weapon was forced into them —so we're looking for a smaller blade, maybe a dagger or a knife." He glanced sharply to one side. "Steady there, Ariston."

"I'm fine," murmured Ariston, and clutched Dami's shoulder for support.

They stole softly back out of the mortuary, Dami tipping the guard at the door, and out through the dark temple of Nepharos with its rows of skulls and black marble altars, and emerged on the street.

Ariston bent over and put his hands on his knees and took deep breaths for a minute.

"All right," he said heartily, straightening up, "what do we do now?"

Dami had put his arm around Varazda's shoulders, just a light, undemanding touch. Varazda was surprised to find how much it helped. Dami looked at him now.

"Now we want to take a look at the place where the young man's body was found," Dami said. "It will be morning by the time we get there, and we'll be able to look around, but we'd better do it quickly before Marzana's men get there too."

Varazda nodded.

"What—what would we be looking for at, um, at … " Ariston attempted.

"Whatever's there to be seen," said Dami.

"So we're going back to the Palace of Letters," said Varazda.

"Wait!" said Ariston suddenly. "What about Themistokles and Kallisto?"

Dami frowned. "What about them?"

"Are they all right? Did Lykanos try to kill Themistokles, or frame Kallisto, or, or—and why did he try to frame Varazda at the same time, and—"

"Whoa," said Dami forcefully. "Slow down. I don't know anything about what may have happened to Themistokles or Kallisto. As far as I know, they're not involved in this."

"But did Themistokles make it to the party? Oh, God! I should have been there. What will he say when he learns I was in jail when I was supposed to be assisting him at the unveiling?"

"Steady, Ariston," said Dami again.

Varazda's feet hurt by the time they arrived back at the Palace of Letters. He wished Dami had brought his cane but did not say so. The city was beginning to waken by this time, the sky lightening overhead as shopkeepers put up their awnings and the vehicles of the night rumbled out of the streets.

"I must look a wreck," Varazda remarked, running a hand through his hair.

Dami looked at him assessingly. "A beautiful wreck."

Ariston snorted.

The door to the Palace of Letters was open, and Heron the party-planner was inside, supervising the removal of his decorations.

"Oh, Pharastes! Immortal gods, what happened to you?"

Varazda wasn't sure whether the question was about where he had gone last night or why he looked in such a state this morning.

He settled for saying, "It was a long night."

Heron rolled his eyes. "For all of us! Were you still here when they found that poor boy stabbed?"

"No—we were gone by then. What happened?"

"Well, nobody knows. I didn't see it myself—the watch was keeping everyone away. It was one of their own, poor fellow. Oh ... oh, that's right." Heron's expression turned confused. "Someone said the watch was here to arrest you. That's not ... is it?"

"It was a misunderstanding," said Varazda quickly. "But it does explain my pathetic appearance this morning."

"How awful! Some people are still so quick to think ill of Sasians. I don't know how they have held onto their prejudice so long with everything the way it is. But you must be back for your things—you left some of your belongings behind last night. I remember seeing your lute," he told Dami.

"Thanks," said Varazda. "All right if we go in and fetch it?"

"Of course, go ahead. The watch has cleared out now."

Ariston nudged Varazda in the ribs. "Ask him whether Themistokles ever made it to the party."

"What's that?" said Heron, having overheard. "There was no party after they found the murdered boy. Themistokles was here, by then." He rolled his eyes. "And not too pleased to have the unveiling cut short. But the poor boy was lying dead up on the scaffolding—they couldn't very well step over him to go on their tour, could they?"

"Quite," said Varazda.

Dami's lute lay undisturbed in the corner where they had left it with Varazda's swords. Dami picked it up.

"So Themistokles made it here after all," said Ariston. "That means … what does that mean?"

"Fuck if I know," Dami muttered. "Ariston, do you think there's something important that you need to check up on the scaffolding just now? Something to do with the volume of shapes and the balance of the fiddly bits?"

"Huh? Oh! Uh, yeah. Sure. Themistokles wanted me to make sure the watch didn't damage the paint carrying the body out."

"Good," said Dami with a nod. "I'll come up with you. Varazda, you stay down here and have a look around the couches, if you can. You've mislaid something small—a bracelet, maybe—and it could be anywhere. You're looking for a knife or a dagger, with a blade about this long." He held out his hands half a foot apart.

"Got it," said Varazda.

Dami and Ariston climbed up to the scaffolding, and Varazda went back out into the dining area. Heron insisted on helping him look for his missing bracelet. Varazda said he remembered taking it off when he sat down with someone, and that it might have fallen between two couch cushions.

"Oh yes, I remember you were sitting over here with His Excellency the ambassador," said Heron, heading for the couches on the right side of the room.

"Was I?" Varazda hunted absently under pillows on the opposite side of the hall.

"Yes, I think this was the ambassador's couch—I remember one of the servers spilled wine on the floor just in front of it—or was it this one? Oh, gods! What's *this*?"

Varazda looked sharply up to see Heron with a cushion in one hand, and in the other, dangling between his thumb and forefinger, a slim, mother-of-pearl-handled knife, its blade dull and smeared.

And a moment later there was a shout from above on the scaffolding, and a splintering crash as one large, marble panel of the frieze broke the boards of the walkway, tearing away one of the guide-ropes, and plunged down to smash on the floor of the library hall.

It had happened so quickly that no one even screamed. The slaves who had been cleaning up stood frozen. No one had been near the falling marble, but that was sheer chance. It had landed in the middle of the stage where the entertainers had performed the night before.

"Holy angels!" came Ariston's wail from above. Varazda saw him teetering on the edge of the broken section of scaffolding, with Dami holding onto him. "Holy blessed Orante! Is anyone hurt?" he called down.

Heron swayed and folded forward, and the knife dropped from his fingers. Varazda just managed to catch him before he hit the floor.

CHAPTER 20

"ALL RIGHT," said Dami, scratching his stubble, which was beginning to look rather more like a beard than usual. "So the knife was an ordinary Pseuchaian knife that might have belonged to anyone, but it was hidden in the cushions of a couch where some member of the ambassador's party was sitting. As far as Heron can recall. And the frieze *was* sabotaged, but either not very effectively, or not with the express purpose of killing Themistokles."

"Did you do anything in particular to it, Ariston, before it fell?"

"Me? No! Oh, I see what you mean. No, I didn't even touch it. We were looking at the boards for traces of blood," he added importantly. "We hadn't found any."

"So," said Varazda, "the panel was sabotaged to fall *at some point*, not specifically to murder Themistokles, but rather—perhaps—to ruin an important moment in his career? Whether it killed a tumbler or a flautist, or just spoiled everyone's evening, wasn't important."

"It was Leto who told us that it was meant to kill Themistokles," said Dami.

"She may have thought it was," said Varazda. "Or she

may have been exaggerating the threat to make sure we went to the party ourselves rather than just warning people. Because it was also Leto who told the watch that there were suspicious foreigners meddling with the frieze."

"I want to go see Kallisto," said Ariston suddenly. "I'm worried about her."

"Finish your food," said Dami firmly. "And then we'll go straight to Temple Walk."

They were standing in the half-open market behind the Palace of Letters, eating steaming pastries and sharing a small bottle of surprisingly excellent Kastian red wine. Dami, finished with his pie, licked his fingers and slung an arm around Varazda's shoulders again. He plucked the bottle out of Varazda's hand and took a swig.

"Mm done," said Ariston, around his last, large bite of pastry. "Leff go."

They could tell something was wrong at Kallisto's house as soon as they approached the front door. It stood open, and muffled sounds of shouting came from inside. Dami passed the lute he was carrying to Ariston, and put his hand on the pommel of his sword.

As they hesitated on the doorstep, Lykanos burst out into the hall, hair standing on end, tunic and mantle rumpled. His eyes went wide at the sight of Damiskos, Varazda, and Ariston.

"Shield me, blessed Soukos," he croaked. "What do *you* want? No, no, I don't care—send for help! Call the watch!"

Ariston looked as if he was about to obey before he remembered that they were fugitives from justice.

"What has happened?" Dami asked commandingly, stepping inside the house to place a heavy hand on Lykanos's shoulder.

The merchant tried feebly to shrug him off. "I don't know!"

There was a crash from deeper within the house. The shouting voices were female, and Varazda recognized one as Kallisto's.

"If you've hurt her—" Ariston pushed his way past Varazda into the hallway, brandishing Dami's lute in front of Lykanos's face.

Lykanos reared back, but was held in place by Dami. "Hurt who, for the gods' love? They're in there, fighting like a pair of she-lions, and I'll be damned if I know what's going on. You—" he waved a hand at Varazda, "you're that jumped-up dancing-girl from the Sasian embassy, and you're Themi's apprentice, but who in the hells are *you*?" He gave Dami an aggrieved look.

"We ask the questions, not you!" Ariston barked. "What have you done to Themistokles? Did you or did you not try to kill him?"

Varazda felt this was wasting time. The noises from inside the house were sounding to him like a brawl. "I'm going inside," he muttered to Dami as he edged past. Dami nodded.

"I did not!" Lykanos was protesting. "Kill him? Blessed Orante, what do you take me for?"

"Be quiet," Dami ordered. "Both of you."

Varazda had reached the inner door from behind which the noise was coming. He edged it open warily and looked inside. A whip snaked through the air and snapped like a thunderclap. Involuntarily, Varazda jumped back.

The room beyond the door had lush red walls and a large couch surrounded by filmy curtains. Kneeling on the bed, naked and with the coverlet clutched to his chest, was Themistokles. Between him and the door were Leto and Kallisto.

The whip was in Leto's hand. Kallisto had a chain

wrapped around one fist and in the other hand a short leather scourge of a kind that Varazda hadn't seen since his childhood in Zash, and had never very much wanted to see then. His first thought, accompanied by a cold lurch in the pit of his stomach, was that he was witnessing a scene put on for Themistokles's benefit, and that Lykanos was overreacting in the same way Ariston had when he overheard Kallisto a week ago. He almost snapped the door shut at that. Then he saw that Kallisto was bleeding, and that Leto had a knife as well as the whip.

"You bitch, you Sasian bitch, I should have known!" She was in tears of fury. "They're right—you're like a plague on Boukos, you and your horrible beardy men. We have to drive you all out!"

"Leto, calm down." Kallisto was obviously struggling to keep her voice level. The blood was trickling from a long scratch on her arm. She did not have a scrap of clothing on. "I have never intended you any harm."

Leto slashed the air with the whip. She knew what she was doing with it. "You stole Lykanos from me!"

"You keep saying that, Leto, but it isn't true. I never accepted him as my principal client—if he told you I did, he was lying."

"Yes, you crazed slut!" Themistokles piped up from the bed. "She's—"

"Shut up!" both women roared at him. Themistokles clamped his mouth shut obediently.

Dami had come up behind Varazda, with Lykanos in an armlock and Ariston on the other side of him making menacing faces.

"I don't know what's going on," Lykanos was whimpering. "I swear by all the gods, I don't know—"

Kallisto looked toward the door, and she and Ariston stood frozen, staring at one another. It struck Varazda, in one of those moments of strange, slow clarity in the midst of a crisis, that she was what a goddess of battle would really look like: naked and bloodied and powerful, with her hair down around her shoulders and weapons in each hand.

And then Leto's whip was whistling through the air again, and Varazda dove into the room, dodging under the lash and spoiling her aim, so that on the return stroke she hit him—a dull thump cushioned by his embroidered gown— instead of Kallisto.

"Get out of here! Horrible thing!" she shrieked at him.

From the doorway Ariston was shouting too. "No! Varazda! Kallisto! Leto, stop!" He gave a grunt as someone— Dami—silenced him.

"Put that thing down before you break it." That was Dami too, presumably talking about the lute.

Varazda dodged the whip again, slid around to Leto's far side, and seized her whip hand at the wrist. He was stronger than she was, but not by a lot, and she had a knife. The blade caught in the embroidery of his gown, and he twisted, pulling her off balance. Dami caught her under the arms as the knife dropped, and she struggled and kicked as he pulled her away from Varazda.

Ariston was already at Kallisto's side, offering her a mantle to wrap around herself. Leto slumped in Dami's grip, defeated.

"You fucking men," she muttered petulantly.

Varazda picked up the knife from the floor and caught Dami's eye. Dami raised his eyebrows, wordlessly asking if Varazda was all right. Varazda nodded.

"Well!" said Themistokles, swinging his legs off the bed and standing, still holding the blanket. "That was exciting."

He was met by a wall of baleful glares. Only Lykanos, a little unsteadily, laughed.

Dami had let go of Leto, who was breathing heavily and glowering, but seemed otherwise to have calmed down.

Lykanos chose that moment to say, "I don't know what

all this was about, dear, but under the circumstances I must reiterate that it is over between us."

"I know that!" Leto spat. "It's because I slept with that nasty Sasian for you, isn't it?"

"What? No, of course—I don't know what you're talking about. I think I had better be—"

"Don't even think about it," said Ariston, and Dami moved toward the doorway to back him up.

"Don't even think about it," Leto echoed mockingly. "Tell them about your plan to 'get the Sasians out of Boukos,' Lyky darling. What a joke that was! You don't really care at all about that, do you?"

Lykanos held up his hands in a caricature of earnestness. "Look. I've nothing against Sasia or Sasians, in the grand scheme of things. It's just business. I'm in the spice business, and Sasian trade is not good for that business. That's all it is. So when I heard that some young firebrands were planning to stir up trouble to get the Sasians out of Boukos—well, it would be good for my business. So I helped them out. I gave them a little money. I introduced Leto to them because I thought she could help—she's very, you know … she can get men to tell her things."

"You should hear some of the things *he's* told me," Leto sneered.

"So you told her to join the group," said Varazda, "but then she became a true believer."

Lykanos waved a hand impatiently. "I didn't know that was going to happen. If you want the truth, I thought that was the last thing in the world that would happen, because I always thought she was all business, just like me."

"It didn't occur to you that I might think for myself, is what you mean."

"Probably," said Varazda, looking at Leto. "So then he got you to pursue an affair with a clerk from the embassy to get information for his 'firebrands'?"

She wrinkled her nose. "He paid me for that, but it wasn't his idea. It was mine."

"And what sort of things did Shorab tell you?"

"Well … " She looked away. "Secrets, you know. Things he shouldn't have. He's a stupid man."

"Did he tell you, for instance, about a Zashian diplomat visiting Boukos this past summer, carrying important military documents?"

"Yes, yes. He told me about that—he said he thought I'd be pleased to know Sasia and Boukos were 'drawing close together—just like you and me.'" She rolled her eyes. "Then my friends stole the silly things and took them away to Pheme to sell them, and then someone from the embassy… " She broke off and looked sharply at Varazda. "He told me about you, too. He didn't know exactly what you do, but he said you weren't what you seem—he said you're always around the embassy and probably up to something. It was you, wasn't it? On Pheme in the Month of Grapes. It was you, I know it. I was right to think we needed to get rid of you. Not," she added quickly, "that I had anything to do with that."

"Of course not," said Varazda. "And did Lykanos know that you had 'warned' us he meant to kill Themistokles at the Palace of Letters last night?"

"What?" Lykanos gave a sharp laugh. "She's got completely off the leash! I had nothing to do with that. Women! What can you—"

"No," said Dami, "no, you don't get to appeal to us for manly sympathy, you sack of shit. You bankrolled a riot that left three men dead, you helped the guilty parties escape justice, you introduced your girlfriend to a group of dangerous criminals, and—if I've got this part right—you also tried to spoil your ex-boyfriend's moment of triumph last night by making a piece of his frieze fall off the wall? You're culpable as fuck."

"Now look here!" Themistokles protested. "I told you Lykanos would never do such a thing!"

"Well, somebody did," said Varazda. "A whole panel fell off early this morning, when we were there searching for the knife that killed the watchman last night."

"What?" said Themistokles.

"Knife?" said Leto. "He wasn't killed with a knife—he was killed with your swords."

"What?" said Kallisto and Themistokles at the same time.

Varazda gave Leto a long look. She paled.

"He was killed," Varazda said slowly, "by your lover—the other one, Shorab—with a knife, but at your instigation. I wonder what story you told Shorab to get him to do it. That the young man had offered you some insult? Or maybe that he was a member of the anti-Zashian faction himself. Shorab lost a close friend in the riot. I can imagine he might have been willing to take the law into his own hands. And you know—" He shrugged. "We Zashians like to do that."

"Why would I have wanted Soh-rab"—Leto mispronounced his name carefully—"to kill some watchman who was doing nothing but guarding a stupid scaffold?"

"I think it was because you saw an opportunity. I'd left my swords unattended—all you had to do was slip up after your lover had done the messy part and plant them on the body. You had already set me up to be arrested, on your information and thanks to your warning to Ariston. When the frieze fell off the wall, of course, that would have proven I'd been 'up to something,' but how much better if I had actually killed a man. And if Shorab were caught instead—well, you wanted to be rid of him anyway."

"That is all utter nonsense," said Leto, but she was very pale by this time.

"I came here this morning to tell her it was over between us," Lykanos put in irrelevantly. "I knew she had something to do with that murder last night. I saw her hide a knife in her couch cushions, and there was a look of triumph on her face … " He shuddered. "I couldn't afford to keep up the association any longer. Besides, I knew Kallisto was about to lose her principal lover, and I thought it only right that I should finally step into that role. I tried to break it to Leto gently, of course."

"But Kallisto is *not* about to lose her principal lover," said Themistokles grandly. "What else do you imagine I'm doing here? You spoiled my moment of triumph as you desired, Lykanos—I had no idea you nurtured such jealousy, after all these years, honestly it's rather flattering. You may not have done it the way you intended, but by unleashing that little slut on my party, you ruined the unveiling of my finest work and the announcement of my candidacy for the Basileon. I'm sure I'll forgive you for it in time—I always do—but you're not getting Kallisto away from me, not now."

Varazda looked over at Kallisto. She stood wrapped in her sky-blue mantle, and Ariston was beside her, nestled against her side, in fact, with an arm around her. While everyone else had been making accusations and excuses, they had obviously been talking in low voices. They looked oddly perfect together, her with her broad shoulders and brown skin, him willowy and pale. She still held the chain, though it dragged on the ground now. She had to lean down to let Ariston whisper something in her ear. A slow smile spread across her face.

"That might be nice," she said aloud, in Zashian that sounded rusty with disuse. She looked up at the others in the room. "Themistokles," she said, "please put your clothes on and go home. I took you in last night because you were so clearly in distress, but it is over between us, as you mentioned last night. Lykanos, I never want to see you again in my life. Leto, I am sorry—if it were just the conflict between the two of us, I'd be happy to put it behind us, but it sounds as though you've murdered someone, more or less, so I'm afraid we will have to call the watch. I suppose her accomplice can be found at the Zashian embassy?"

"Actually," said Varazda, looking through the door into the hall, "he is coming in right now."

Shorab looked as white-faced as Leto, and froze when he saw Varazda.

"What are you doing here?"

Varazda stepped out into the hall. "I'm sorry about this, Shorab."

"What? Has something happened to Leto?"

"Sohrab!" came Leto's voice, raised in a wail, from inside the bedroom. "Darling! Help me! They're—unh!" She broke off with an obviously feigned grunt.

It wasn't obvious to Shorab. He charged past Varazda, knocking him back against the wall, and plunged into the room with his sword drawn.

Varazda started forward in time to see Shorab charge at Dami, who was restraining Leto again. Dami swung her around behind him and drew his sword in one motion, smooth as a dance step. His blade clanged against Shorab's.

"Let her go, and I've no quarrel with you," said Shorab, giving ground hastily.

"I'm afraid that's not true." Dami parried a wild swing from Shorab and closed in another step, switching his sword from one hand to the other so that he could keep Leto more effectively behind him.

"Sohrab, don't let them! I'm so scared!" Leto wailed.

It was not a big room, and there were now seven people in it, not counting Varazda in the doorway. What happened next was such chaos that Varazda could only reconstruct in hindsight who must have done what.

He backed out into the hallway because he could see that Dami was forcing Shorab toward the door, to get his dangerously uncontrolled sword out of the way of the other people in the room. But Lykanos chose that moment to dive for the doorway himself, and attempted to wriggle out behind Shorab. There was a clanging crunch as Lykanos stepped on the lute that Ariston had left on the floor, and he fell, hitting Shorab and toppling him backward into the hall. Dami arrived in the doorway, and Leto tried to push her way under his arm. He stopped her, and she gave a howl of protest. As he turned to push her back into the arms of Kallisto inside the room, Shorab hooked his foot behind Dami's knee, and Dami overbalanced and fell sideways into the hall, landing half on Lykanos, half on the floor, the broken lute giving out another crash. Dami's sword was knocked out of his hand and spun to a stop at Varazda's feet.

In a moment, Dami would have risen, but he was slowed by Lykanos thrashing under him, and the remains of the lute, and Shorab was already getting up to his knees, sword drawn back to stab.

He never finished the motion. Varazda had seized Dami's sword from the floor and swung it, in a low arc that he had practiced thousands of times in his family's dance, and a great spray of blood followed the motion, spattering across Kallisto's hallway, before Shorab's body swayed and collapsed backward onto the floor.

He remembered Marzana saying, "One strikes a killing blow knowing that it may kill, yet not *desiring* the other man's death." So this was what that was like. He wouldn't have killed Shorab under other circumstances. He had never even wished him ill. Yet he had swung the sword knowing, and not caring, that it might take Shorab's life.

Dami was wiping blood from his face and looking up to meet Varazda's eyes as he got to his feet. He looked at Varazda as if the other people in the house—Lykanos writhing on the floor, Leto now laughing hysterically in the doorway while Ariston shouted at her to shut up and Kallisto and Themistokles argued about something in the bedroom—

might not have been there at all. In a moment Varazda felt as if they weren't.

"Thank you," said Dami simply. He put a hand on Varazda's shoulder. "Are you all right?"

Varazda nodded slowly. He looked past Dami at Shorab's body on the floor. The sword-cut had caught him cleanly across the throat, which was where Varazda had aimed it, and he was very obviously dead. There was a lot of blood.

He felt surprisingly calm. "I will have to answer for that," he said.

"You have several very reliable witnesses," said Dami. "He was going to kill me, and you had no time to consider how to stop him in a non-lethal way."

Varazda nodded. "I am all right," he said.

CHAPTER 21

DAMI AND VARAZDA sat side-by-side on the divan in Varazda's sitting-room. Dami had his leg up and a warm compress on his knee—Yazata's idea, but Dami hadn't protested. He and Varazda were both freshly bathed and dressed in clean tunics. Yazata brought in a pot of tea on a tray with cups.

Remi breezed by from the yard, carrying Selene. "I'm going to play at Maia's, Papa!" she called. "I hope your hurt goes away soon, Dami!"

Varazda winced, but Dami laughed and called back, "Thank you."

"I'm going to go make lunch," said Yazata, pouring out two cups of tea. "Can I bring you anything else?" He smiled tentatively at Dami.

"No, thank you," said Dami, smiling back. "This is lovely."

"Is it really only lunch-time?" said Varazda.

Dami squinted out the open garden doors at the sky. "I suppose so. Not even noon."

It had only been a few hours since they left Kallisto's house. Ariston had gone for the watch, who had arrested Leto and taken everyone's statements about the death of Shorab. Varazda, as a freedman in the eyes of the law, with several respectable witnesses, was permitted to pay a bond and remain free pending trial. Kallisto had paid the bond for him, as well as insisting on giving him money for the ruined lute. Everyone in Saffron Alley had been beside themselves with relief when they returned.

Marzana arrived while they were still drinking their tea. He brought Varazda's swords, thoroughly cleaned and polished. He set them on the table beside the tea-tray.

"Join us," said Varazda, smiling. "Have some tea."

Marzana looked at him for a moment with pain in his eyes. "What can I do to seek your forgiveness?" he asked.

It was a formal Zashian thing, a question Varazda had never imagined being directed at himself. He tried to remember whether it was insulting to the petitioner to refuse. He thought it probably was.

"Sit and drink tea," he said finally.

Marzana sagged slightly. "If you insist."

Varazda reached for the teapot and filled a cup. Marzana sat stiffly on the divan and accepted the cup.

"I have spoken with His Excellency Narosangha," he said. "He was not entirely surprised to hear that Shorab was passing information to his Pseuchaian mistress."

"Was he not? Well, we knew something of the sort must have been happening, to explain how Helenos and his crew knew about the documents that they stole."

Marzana nodded. "That would be counted treason in Zash, punishable by death. His Excellency says that on account of that, he won't lay charges against you."

"He—really?" Varazda hadn't even considered that possibility. Dami gave his arm a squeeze.

"Yes," said Marzana, "so there will be no trial. I'm a little sorry that Alkaios's family won't get to see his murderer brought to trial, but only a little sorry." He sipped his tea.

"I'm much sorrier that I treated you so callously in the watch-house last night."

Varazda waved a hand. "No, no. You were angry, and you'd every right to be—one of your men had been killed. And you were right—I've been secretive."

"As you have to be when you're a spy."

"I—what?" said Varazda innocently. "I've no idea what you mean."

Marzana gave him a crooked smile. "As to the rest, I don't know that we can expect particularly good results from Leto's arrest. She'll lie, of course, and with Shorab dead, there's no one to testify to most of what she did—not that he would have been a terribly helpful witness, if alive. As for Lykanos … " He shrugged hopelessly. "I doubt we can charge him with anything. The best we can do may be fining him for selling adulterated saffron. But we will keep our eyes on him in future, of course." He glanced at Varazda. "As will you and your lot, I'm sure."

"I hope," said Varazda, "you weren't too hard on the guard who let Dami walk off with your prisoners last night. He wasn't doing his job very well, admittedly, but then Dami was extremely convincing."

Dami snorted and bumped his shoulder against Varazda's.

Marzana's expression had turned thoughtful. "I have tried to instill greater discipline in the public watch—it has been my principal aim since I took over the running of it. But it can be useful, sometimes, to have a few imbeciles whom one can deploy when one does *not* want a job done well."

"Marzana!" said Varazda archly. "How extremely Zashian of you."

When Marzana had gone, Ariston came in with a strangely tentative look on his face.

"I, uh. You're both all right?"

"We are," said Varazda. "The tea's a bit cold by now, but if you want some … "

"Oh, no, I don't think … Yazata's almost finished making lunch. I just wanted to ask you—tell you—um, it's about Kallisto. You know she's lost both her main clients—well, given them the push, really." A little grin crept across his face, then he became serious again. "And her freedwoman is in jail, and then that fellow Shorab being killed in her house—not that she blames you for that, Varazda, she says it was one of the most amazing things she's ever seen, how you cut him down, and it was—I'd no idea you could do things like that. I'm afraid I've been underestimating you for years, and … Uh. But that's not what I was going to ask you about. Tell you about.

"The thing is, I don't know if I'm going to stay on much longer as Themistokles's apprentice. I'd like to, in a way, because I'm learning a lot from him, and I know I've still got more to learn. And I knew there was a good chance he was a bit of a shit—and he is, even his politics aren't all that great, not radical or anything, you know. But as a sculptor, he is brilliant, so … But I think he may not want to keep me on anyway, once he finds out."

"Er," said Varazda. "Finds out what?"

"I've asked Kallisto to marry me."

There was a moment's profound silence, broken only by the sound of Selene honking in the street.

"Did she say yes?" asked Dami.

"No. Well, she said maybe, after we've, you know, been together for a little while."

"So you're together, then," Varazda prompted.

Ariston nodded, bouncing a little.

"That's a win," said Dami. "That's a definite win."

"Congratulations," said Varazda.

"I never imagined it would happen," Ariston went on. "I think I must have lost my mind for a moment when I asked her, but I—I know she likes me, and I thought maybe she was ready for a change, and it was the only thing I could think of—I can't offer to support her as her lover, I mean a client—I couldn't afford that, but if she sells her house—anyway, we've discussed it, and we think it will work."

"I see," said Varazda. "What you're saying is you want her to move in here."

"Uh." Ariston looked nervous again. "Yes. Is that … "

"Yes," said Varazda. "Of course."

"Just for the time being, while I finish my apprenticeship or look for work, or—I've already talked to Yazata about it, and he said it's all right with him if it's all right with you."

"Of course," said Varazda, smiling. "I'd be delighted to have her live with us. I like her very much."

"You do?" Ariston glowed. "You do! I'm so glad. I'm going to tell her right now. Yazata," he called as he spun in the doorway and bounded out into the kitchen, "I won't be staying for lunch after all!"

Varazda leaned his head back against the cushions of the divan. "Can I fall apart now?" he said, looking up at the ceiling.

Dami picked up Varazda's hand and kissed his knuckles lightly. "If that's what you need to do, do it."

Varazda considered that. "I'm not sure that it is, actually."

Dami still had hold of his hand. "No. Sometimes it isn't. Don't ever let anyone tell you that you're not strong, Varazda."

Varazda smiled up at the ceiling. "No? Why not?"

"Because you are. I don't know how you do it."

Varazda laughed. "Don't be silly."

After a moment, Dami cleared his throat and said, "That dance at the Palace of Letters. Was it … " He still couldn't finish the question.

"Sometimes," Varazda said, taking pity on him, "you can tell a story with the sword dance. And the story I had in mind was about someone who'd risen through his own merit, someone in the midst of a brilliant career, suddenly brought down by fate and almost destroyed."

"And then rescued," said Dami.

"Mm." Varazda tipped his head to one side. "I don't know about rescued, but … Loved. I imagined … that would help."

"I think it would amount to the same thing."

They were silent for a long time then, resting side-by-side on the divan. Dami put his head on Varazda's shoulder, and Varazda wondered if he was going to fall asleep. He had been up all night, after all. Varazda was just about to suggest that they should both go to bed when Dami looked up at him through his lashes.

"You know I'm not leaving, right?"

"What?"

"I'm not leaving tomorrow. I'll write to the Quartermaster's Office—I'm not sure what I'll tell them, but it doesn't matter. I've been 'unavoidably detained' or something." After a moment, because he was Dami, he added, "You don't mind, do you?"

JOIN THE CLUB

Join my *Fragments Club* list to get exclusive short stories and snippets!

Sign up at **ajdemas.com**

LIST OF PLACES

Saffron Alley is set in a fictional world loosely based on the cultures of the ancient Mediterranean. Here are some details about the places mentioned in the story.

Pseuchaia: A group of city-states, mostly on islands, with a common language and religion, usually in alliance with one another but not always.

Pheme: An island and a very large city on that island. Pheme is a republic and the most powerful city-state in the region. The city is located on the west coast of the island; the interior of the island is mountainous, and there are villages and seaside estates around the coast.

Boukos: A city on an island of the same name, a short sea-voyage to the northwest of the island of Pheme. For the last eight years, Boukos has had a trade agreement with the kingdom of Zash. A permanent Zashian embassy was established seven years ago. None of the other Pseuchaian states has an official alliance with Zash. The governing body of Boukos is called the Basileon.

Zash/Sasia: A sprawling kingdom on the mainland to the east of the islands of Pseuchaia. Their language, religion, and culture are very different from those of Pseuchaia (and also diverse within the kingdom). Zash is what they call their land; Pseuchaians find this difficult to pronounce and so call it Sasia.

Suna: The main seat of the king of Zash.

Deshan Coast: A politically volatile region in the west of Zash. Damiskos served with the Phemian army in this region, and this is also where Varazda is from.

Gudul: An obscure provincial palace and city in Zash. This is where Varazda lived when he was enslaved.

Laothalia: Nione Kukara's villa on the north coast of the island of Pheme. This is where the events of *Sword Dance* took place.

Kos: Another island city of Pseuchaia, famous for its arts and learning.

ACKNOWLEDGMENTS

Thanks to everyone who helped me bring this book to fruition: Alexandra Bolintineanu, my faithful First Reader; Victoria Goddard, for editorial help and botanical recommendations; and May Peterson, for additional editing. Special thanks and big virtual hugs to Vic Grey, who created the splendid cover art, and Mary Beth Decker, who wrote the cover copy. More thanks (and real hugs) to my husband, Mike, for continuing to support and encourage me. I'm so lucky. Heart eyes all around.

SOMETHING HUMAN

They met on a battlefield and saved each other's lives. It's not the way enemies-to-lovers usually works.

Adares comes from a civilization of democracy and indoor plumbing. Rus belongs to a tribe of tattooed, semi-nomadic horse-breeders. They meet in the aftermath of battle, when Rus saves Adares's life, and Adares returns the favour. As they shelter in an abandoned temple, a friendship neither of them could have imagined grows into a mutual attraction.

But Rus, whose people abhor love between men, is bound by an oath of celibacy, and Adares has a secret of his own that he cannot share. With their people poised for a long and bitter conflict, it seems too much to hope that these two men could turn their fleeting happiness into something lasting. Unless, of course, the relationship between them changes the course of their people's history altogether.

Something Human is a standalone m/m romance set in an imaginary ancient world, about two people bridging a cultural divide with the help of great sex, pedantic discussions about the gods, and bad jokes about standing stones.

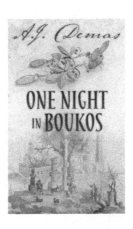

One Night in Boukos

On a night when the whole city is looking for love, two foreigners find it in the last place they expected.

The riotous Psobion festival is about to begin in the city of Boukos, and the ambassador from the straightlaced kingdom of Zash has gone missing. Ex-soldier Marzana, captain of the embassy guard, and the ambassador's secretary, the shrewd and urbane eunuch Bedar, are the only two who know.

Marzana still nurses the pain of an old heartbreak, and Bedar has too much on his plate to think of romance. Neither of them could imagine finding love in this strange, foreign city. But as they search desperately for their employer through the streets and taverns and brothels of Boukos, they find unexpected help from two of the locals: a beautiful widowed shopkeeper and a teenage prostitute.

Before the Zashians learn what became of their ambassador, they will have to deal with foreign bureaucracy, strange food, stranger local customs, and murderers. And they may lose their hearts in the process.

One Night in Boukos is a standalone romance featuring two couples, one m/f and one m/m.

CPSIA information can be obtained
at www.ICGtesting.com
Printed in the USA
LVHW031808101221
705865LV00010B/1172